The Prizefighter's Hart

Headstrong Harts, Book 4

by Emily Royal

DRAGONBLADE PUBLISHING, INC.

ARE YOU SIGNED UP FOR DRAGONBLADE'S BLOG?

You'll get the latest news and information on exclusive giveaways, exclusive excerpts, coming releases, sales, free books, cover reveals and more.

Check out our complete list of authors, too!

No spam, no junk. That's a promise!

Sign Up Here

www.dragonbladepublishing.com

Dearest Reader;

Thank you for your support of a small press. At Dragonblade Publishing, we strive to bring you the highest quality Historical Romance from the some of the best authors in the business. Without your support, there is no 'us', so we sincerely hope you adore these stories and find some new favorite authors along the way.

Happy Reading!

CEO, Dragonblade Publishing

Dedication

To Neil, whose understanding of the female psyche
was the inspiration for the hero in this novel

Additional Dragonblade books by Author Emily Royal

Headstrong Harts

What the Hart Wants, Book 1

Queen of my Hart, Book 2

Hidden Hart, Book 3

The Prizefighter's Hart, Book 4

London Libertines

Henry's Bride, Book 1

Hawthorne's Wife, Book 2

Roderick's Widow, Book 3

The Lyon's Den Connected World

A Lyon's Pride

Chapter One

WITH A BODY that looked like it had been carved out of marble, and an air of masculinity which set her pulse racing from halfway across the courtyard, he was, without doubt, the most perfect, primal male specimen she'd ever seen.

And he was exactly the sort of man who wouldn't look twice at a woman like her—what would a prizefighter in his prime, with the pick of beauties for his bed—want with a dried-up spinster?

He was tall—taller even than her brother.

And all muscle. A solid, immovable wall of muscle.

Blonde hair, too long to be respectable, brushed his shoulders, damp with sweat, and framed a face with strong features—a high forehead, chiseled jaw, and a nose that bore a slight kink in the center.

But the most arresting feature was his eyes. An intense, clear green—capable of striking fear into the heart of the stoutest opponent.

Most battles were won or lost before they began, and to this man, the battle was won the moment he stepped into the arena. He was a natural-born warrior, like the conquerors of old who brought opponents to their knees with a single glance.

The Mighty Oak they called him. And tonight, he was the favorite to win the bout at the Queen's Head.

He strode toward the ring—crudely marked on the ground—amid the cheers of the crowd.

To Thea, he was Hercules—a demi-god who wrestled with Death and conquered Titans.

Heat bloomed in her cheeks and threaded through her body, where a faint pulse throbbed deep within. She knew what would happen next, for she'd seen it before.

He unlaced his shirt—slowly. The atmosphere among the crowd thickened with anticipation. She could swear she heard gasps of desire from the watching women.

Then he pulled his shirt off, revealing his torso, and the crowd sighed. He crumpled the garment into a ball and tossed it into the air. Eager hands thrust out from the crowd, accompanied by shrieks and the sound of a scuffle. Then he flexed his body, his chest muscles rippling in the light of the setting sun, and lifted his arms to the sky as the crowd erupted into a cheer.

The sound of clinking metal echoed across the courtyard as money exchanged hands. Fortunes would be won or lost this evening—on the strength of his fists.

"All hail, the Mighty Oak!"

He nodded, acknowledging the adoration.

If Thea closed her eyes, she could imagine herself in the crowd at the Colosseum. Maybe she would have been Caesar's wife or a Roman noblewoman, cheering the gladiator she patronized.

But she was neither. She was a phantom, hiding in the shadows, watching him from afar—unobserved, ashamed. And such fanciful notions usually earned her a lash from her brother's tongue.

If Dexter knew she was here, he'd be furious. But why shouldn't she indulge in a little fun? By day, she was the spinster aunt—too old to make a respectable union that didn't smack of desperation. And, in Dexter's eyes, nobody in the Hart family was permitted to tarnish his reputation by appearing desperate.

She uncurled her hand to reveal indents in her palm where she'd dug her fingernails into the flesh. But the physical pain couldn't offset the pain in her heart. Why shouldn't she indulge in a little passion? She'd only ever wanted one thing in life, yet, of all her siblings, she was the one who seemed doomed never to have it.

And that was a family—a home, and children of her own.

Nobody expected her to have feelings. Passion was for the young—and not for her. Thea's place in life was by the side of whichever of her siblings had need of her.

But at night, when Dexter wasn't watching…

At night, she could indulge in a little pleasure, even if that pleasure was merely a product of her imagination. At night she dreamed of a mighty warrior—and what he was capable of doing with that big, muscular body of his.

What he was capable of doing to *her*.

His opponent entered the ring. A big brute of a man with a shaven head—but even from a distance, Thea saw the defeat in his eyes. Nevertheless, he raised his arms, pumping his fists in the air.

A small cheer erupted from his supporters, but he was no match for the beast who dominated the courtyard. If he were lucky, he might last the first round.

A third man entered the ring and held his hand up, brandishing a white cloth, to signal that the fight was about to begin. Tension crackled in the air, and Thea held her breath and shrank back into the shadows, even though she already stood apart from the crowd.

A cry rang out, and the cloth fluttered to the ground. The two gladiators raised their fists and circled each other trampling the cloth underfoot. Even from a distance, Thea noticed the tension in the other man's stance, a sharp contrast to the easy, arrogant gait of the Mighty Oak, who prowled the ring as a panther might patrol the perimeter of his territory.

And it *was* his territory—his kingdom. Not only did he own the inn where the fight took place, but he owned the man who dared challenge him. And he owned the crowd—every last man and woman.

Including her.

A small groan escaped her lips as the sinful little devil in her mind whispered of all the wicked things he could do to her body. Then he glanced in her direction, and she caught her breath.

She was too far away—but for a moment, it was as if he'd looked right inside her and understood her need.

Foolish woman!

Was this what she'd been reduced to? A desperate woman wanting the attentions of a man—something she was constantly being told was now beyond her? She could just imagine Dexter's words.

Dorothea, your place is with your family. Isn't it time you acted like a grown woman and not a schoolgirl made giddy by her first crush?

She bit her lip to stem the tears of shame.

If the Mighty Oak knew of her obsession, he'd laugh at her. They'd *all* laugh. Dorothea Hart—the spinster aunt, with girlish fancies beyond her circumstance.

His opponent rushed toward him with a roar. The Mighty Oak parried the blow, and their fists clashed with a slap of flesh. He dodged to one side, and Thea marveled at how such a large man could appear so light on his feet. His opponent gave a growl of frustration and charged again. This time he was ready, and he leaned forward, meeting him with full force as they crashed to the ground.

The crowd erupted, whoops of glee echoing round the courtyard. The two fighters rolled in the dirt, sending clouds of dust into the evening air. Then they parted, and Mighty Oak sprang to his feet, fists at the ready.

"Mighty Oak! Mighty Oak!" The crowd chanted as more coins exchanged hands. Baying for blood, they screamed at him to finish his opponent. But he stepped back, waiting for the other man to rise to his feet.

A beast—and a gentleman.

They circled each other for another minute, then his opponent rushed toward him, swinging his arm with the need of a man who knew the game was lost. And it didn't take long for the Mighty Oak to secure his victory. With an almost graceful movement, as if engaged in a dance, he swung his fist upward and caught his opponent in the chin.

Without a sound, the other man crumpled to the ground.

A cheer rose up, and the Mighty Oak turned and saluted the crowd. He wiped his chest, smearing dust and sweat across his skin. Then he strode toward the water trough at the edge of the courtyard, his leg muscles rippling in his tight breeches, and splashed handfuls of water onto his chest. The water beaded on his skin and ran in rivulets across his body, following the contours of his muscles. He strutted like a lion who'd bested his rival in a fight for domination over the pack.

And a lion he was. Female voices cried out his name. Which of them would be warming his bed tonight? Or would he take them all?

A woman rushed toward him with his shirt in her hand—she must be the lucky female who'd caught it earlier. Was that how he chose his conquests? How might he react if Thea caught his shirt next time?

The woman draped her arms round his chest as if she owned him, and a stab of jealousy pierced Thea's heart. He grasped her buttocks amid lewd remarks from the crowd. Then he pushed her away and strode toward the inn. Undeterred, the woman followed, and they disappeared inside.

With their hero gone, the crowd dispersed—some scattered into the night, the rest followed him into the inn. There would be drinking aplenty tonight.

She ought to go home, but she couldn't. She had to get a final glimpse of him.

It wasn't long before her wish was granted. A familiar silhouette appeared at an upper window where he stood, as if looking out.

Did he know she watched him—dreamed of him?

Then a second silhouette joined the first and shattered her dream. The two silhouettes merged into one, and Thea's eyes stung with tears as she imagined them locked in a passionate embrace.

He drew the curtain, shutting out the night so that she was, once more, an outsider looking in.

She wrapped her cloak around herself and set off for home.

She might never have the life she yearned for, but nobody could stop her from dreaming.

Chapter Two

GRIFFIN DREW BACK the curtain and watched the cloaked figure disappear into the dusk.

It was the figure of a woman. And she'd been waiting in the distance, even before the crowd had gathered. Another admirer, most likely—a bored wife wanting to escape the drudgery of her marriage and seek a little variety between her legs.

He'd had enough experience of bored wives to know that they spread their legs for any man if it gave them gratification.

A pair of arms wrapped round him.

"Isn't the Mighty Oak going to claim his reward?" a voice purred.

Damn the doxy! He'd fought off Billy Bates, but now needed to defend himself against a desperate, lust-fueled female.

She caressed his chest, moving lower until she reached his waistband. Then, with a little sigh, she slipped her hand into his breeches.

"My," she purred, "The oak has a thick, strong trunk."

Did she really think he'd not heard *that* one before?

He turned to face her. Blonde, buxom, breasts spilling out of the top of her gown.

And her scent—cheap perfume meant to allure, but it only inspired nausea. She rubbed her body against his like a cat in heat.

Then he caught another odor.

Alcohol. The last thing he wanted to bed was a drunken whore.

She squeezed his manhood, barely disguising her frown of disappointment when he didn't react. Any other woman, and he'd be buried inside her by now—but the smell of ale and spirits turned his stomach.

He closed his eyes, but the image remained—a painted face, lips pouting, a moist pink tongue sweeping along the seam of her mouth in a calculated attempt to seduce. And he'd fallen for it.

Every bloody time.

Louisa.

What trouble she'd caused—all because he'd been too free with his cock and with his heart.

If only he could erase her memory from his mind. But it would remain with him until the day he died. She was immortal because she lived on in another.

He pushed the doxy aside and moved toward the door where his coat was hanging and pulled out a handful of coins. Her eyes widened, greed glittering in their expression.

"Open your hand," he growled.

She did so, and he tipped five shillings onto her palm. She curled her fingers round her bounty.

"There's much I can do for five shillings," she said.

"I'm sure there is," he replied, "but I only want one thing from you."

"I know." She unlaced her bodice until her breasts spilled out, exposing her creamy flesh and the dark, pink nipples. But he was in no mood for a drunken wench. He'd had enough of that for a lifetime.

"I want you to cover yourself up and go."

Her smile disappeared for a moment, making her face quite ugly. "Am I not good enough for the Mighty Oak?"

"If you're concerned about your reputation as a whore, I'm happy to tell the world that you fucked me, and I loved every minute of it."

Her smile returned. "From behind?"

He shrugged. "If you like."

"For five shillings, I'll say you were like a bull."

"Very well." He gave her a dismissive wave. "Now, get out."

"Don't I get a kiss?"

"No."

"Very well," she said. "I'll find another man to satisfy me."

Her words darkened his mood even more. An attempt to incite jealousy was the foulest act a woman could undertake. He'd learned long ago that such women were not to be trusted—whether they were a whore attempting to secure a higher price...

...or a wife who bedded her way through his friends.

"Get out before I crush that pretty neck of yours," he growled. "And if you want my advice, steer clear of the gin. A man might as well fist himself for all the pleasures a drunken slut can give him."

"I can always tell them you were unable to perform."

"Tell and be damned," he said. "Do you think I care what a two-penny whore thinks?"

"You'll never know what you missed."

He let out a bark of laughter. "I only need ask half the men in the bar downstairs—I daresay you'll be spreading for them within five minutes of leaving this chamber."

She gave a snort of exasperation, then exited the chamber, slamming the door. Not long after, he heard her voice, coaxing, as she propositioned a customer—most likely one of the merchants staying in the guest rooms.

Griffin removed his breeches, peeling off the layer of the Mighty Oak until he stood in nothing but his skin. His manhood stood proud, eager for release, and he took it in his hand and stroked.

Then he removed his hand, ashamed. He wasn't some lad of fifteen, fisting himself in secret. He was a man who could have any woman he chose.

But he was also a man with responsibilities. And tonight, now he'd had his release in the arena, he needed to resume them.

He reached into the wardrobe and pulled out a suit—an unfathomable array of polished boots, stockings, breeches, shirt, cravat, and waistcoat. Damned expensive—he'd commissioned it from a tailor on Savile Row so that he might not disgrace himself at tomorrow night's dinner party. Though, why his banker—what was his name, Sir Dexter Hart?—insisted on inviting him, he couldn't fathom. But it was an entry, of sorts, into society. And he wasn't in a position to be choosy over invitations.

Lord only knew in which order these bloody things had to be put on. But they were a necessary evil if those peacocks of London society were even to acknowledge his presence, let alone accept him. It was most likely a futile endeavor, but it had to be done.

For her.

For Rowena.

And, at that moment, even though she loathed him, Rowena was the only person in the world he loved—or would ever love. He wanted so much more for her than to share her mother's fate. He'd grown up in the gutter, fighting his way—literally—to a fortune, and he wanted Rowena to enjoy the life he could only ever have dreamed of as a boy.

A life of acceptance into society.

But it would take more than his wealth to achieve that. Rowena needed to learn the benefits of respect, self-restraint, and decorum. And however God-fearing Mrs. Ellis might be, the woman had failed. Rowe needed the guidance of a woman who understood London society, not the widow of a country parson.

In short, she needed a proper chaperone. A few discreet inquiries tomorrow might bear fruit. Sir Dexter was bound to have a wide acquaintance, and he might help Griffin find the solution to his problems.

Preferably in the form of the plainest, primmest, most sexless woman in all of London.

Chapter Three

"WHERE THE DEVIL have you been, Dorothea?"

Thea sighed. Just her luck—the moment she crept in through the back door, her brother happened to be in the kitchen.

He moved toward her, his body seeming to fill the space in the room—a tactic he used on employees to intimidate them. But it wouldn't work on her, no matter how much he considered her a subordinate.

Not when she'd seen a man to whom her brother couldn't compare, even if he was a knight of the realm.

How would he fare against the Mighty Oak?

"Have you nothing better to do than follow me around, Dexter?" she asked.

"It's past nine o'clock."

"That doesn't answer my question." She shed her cloak, approached the fireplace, and inspected the contents of the pot suspended over the dying embers.

"You missed dinner," Dexter said.

"I can cook my own supper," she retorted.

"It's not the done thing, Dorothea, and you know it."

Dorothea? He only used full names when cross or when admonishing his children.

But this wasn't the time to fight, and she didn't want him knowing where she'd been. If she kept her cool, he'd eventually tire of bullying her and retire, and tomorrow it would be forgotten. A night in his wife's arms always soothed his temper.

"Why don't you go to bed?" she suggested. "You shouldn't keep Meggie waiting."

His expression softened, as it always did, at the mention of his wife.

"Meggie's with the children," he said. "*You* were supposed to tend to them tonight. You'd promised to read them a story."

"I'll apologize to them tomorrow."

"You're their aunt, for heaven's sake!" he snapped.

"And you're their father!" she cried, unable to keep her temper. "I love my nieces and nephews, but am I not permitted a life of my own?"

"Not if it means parading around, unchaperoned, at night," he growled. "We've our reputation to think of."

"And with *that*, you've lost the right to speak to me," she said. "Your knighthood has gone to your head. Must I address you as Sir Dexter now?"

"Don't be a fool."

"Leave me alone, Dex," she said. "I'm tired."

"Where were you, Dorothea?"

"Why persist when I shan't tell you?"

"Because you came in by the back door as if you had something to hide," he said. "I don't know what's happened to you lately. You've always been so mindful of decorum. But this past fortnight..." He hesitated. "Do you have a lover?"

She let out a snort.

If only that were true! But the only lover was the Herculean warrior who visited her dreams. If Dexter knew about him, he'd laugh at her foolishness.

His expression darkened. "Well? Do you?"

"Of course not," she retorted. "You've said, countless times, I'm too old to attract a man."

He flinched. Having engaged his efforts to find a titled spouse for their younger sister, and then for himself, Dexter had passed Thea by, declaring her the least favorable prospect for securing a titled match. And now she was the only unmarried sibling, he considered her too old for marriage. For, as he said on countless occasions, to himself, to her—and, most likely to anyone who cared to listen at Whites—Dorothea Hart was far too old to secure a respectable marriage without appearing desperate.

"Go and see the children," he said, his voice softening. "You know now much they love you."

Curse him! He knew how to erode her defenses. She abandoned the pot, retrieved her cloak, and made her way to the door. He caught her sleeve as she passed.

"Don't forget tomorrow night," he said. "I don't want you running off when we have guests. I'm depending on you."

"Meggie's an excellent hostess," she replied.

"You know how uncomfortable she is with large parties," he said, "especially strangers. You're much better at talking to them."

"Wooing your clients and their wives, you mean?"

He frowned.

"I'll not let you down," she continued. "Not when I've spent the past two days in this very kitchen with Mrs. Green."

"I know." He smiled. "I've tasted the shortbread."

He'd always had a weakness for shortbread—ever since they were children.

"Is there any left?" she asked. "Mrs. Green won't be pleased if we need to make a new batch for your guests because you've eaten them all."

"Mrs. Green's already admonished me," he said. "I assure you, there's plenty left for tomorrow."

"Good," she replied. "I wouldn't want to have to make more, though I would if Meggie asked me to."

"You're a great help to Meggie," he said. "She loves you."

He averted his gaze, as he always did when voicing emotion. A shrewd businessman he may be, capable of dominating a board-room—but when it came to matters of the heart, he stumbled like a child and avoided the issue. He only ever showed true affection toward his wife, the once-timid creature he'd married unwillingly but who'd captured his soul.

"I love..." he hesitated. "I'm fond of you also, Thea. I don't want you doing anything to jeopardize your happiness."

Before she could respond, he gave her arm a gentle squeeze, then turned away.

"If you go now, the children will still be awake," he said, the gruffness in his voice not completely disguising his feelings. "They've been waiting up for you. Apparently, you were going to read a story about an ogre who finds love with a gentle maiden."

His lips twitched into a smile. "Which sounds like the story of how their mama and papa met."

"You're not an ogre, Dex," she said.

He patted her arm. "You've not lost your diplomacy, Thea."

She exited the kitchen, leaving her brother with these thoughts— and, doubtless, the opportunity to steal another slice of shortbread.

She wanted to hate her brother, but she couldn't. He'd worked hard to elevate them from poverty, and, in his own way, he thought he was doing what was best for her. He gave her a respectable existence, living in his home, tending to his children—a place in society where she could be treated with respect as the sister of the prominent banker and knight Sir Dexter Hart. In time, she'd become a chaperone for her nieces. But for now, she had to settle with being the prim, spinster aunt, who helped run the home and played the hostess when he entertained his business associates.

And next week, he'd planned a party to celebrate her birthday.

But what woman wanted to be reminded that she was turning thirty—that she was destined to be a spinster and would never find love?

Chapter Four

"OH, THE TABLE looks lovely—well done!" Thea's sister-in-law gestured toward the dining table set for twenty, a stack of place-cards in her hand.

"Most of this was down to you, Meggie," Thea said. "And I must applaud your penmanship—those cards are excellent."

"My handwriting is poor compared to yours," Meggie said. "I still haven't mastered the letter 'f.'" She held a card up. "This man—Griffin—whoever he is—will struggle to decipher his name."

"He'll have more to concern himself with than his place card," Thea said. "You've placed the unfortunate man next to Mrs. Lewis."

"Have I done wrong?" Concern flickered across Meggie's expression.

Thea laughed. "No, Meggie—any man would be unfortunate to sit next to *her*. I see you've done her husband a service by placing him at the opposite end."

"Why must husbands and wives be split at dinner parties?"

"Because most husbands and wives prefer to spend the evening with others," Thea replied. "Imagine if a domestic argument were to spill over to a dinner party! Of course, you and Dexter are so blissfully happy together, you cannot conceive the notion of marital discord."

"I'd rather remain by Dexter's side," Meggie said. "The thought of having to talk to strangers still sends shivers down my spine."

"Why would it do that?" Thea asked.

Meggie's smile disappeared, and the familiar expression of inadequacy appeared in her eyes. "I never know whether they'll accept me, given my lineage."

"Nonsense!" Thea said. "It may be a flaw of a patriarchy, as Delilah would say, but when a woman marries, she assumes her husband's status."

Meggie laughed. "So a woman in society is respected, as long as she's married? I should be thankful Dexter was tricked into marrying me before I grew too old…" She gasped. "Forgive me. I meant no offense."

"It's not your fault I'm too old for marriage," Thea said.

"Nonsense!" Meggie replied, her voice a little too bright. "It's merely a case of finding the right man. A wider acquaintance can only be to your benefit. I'm sure that's why Dexter insisted you join the party tonight."

Thea snorted. "He wants me to tend to the children so that you might play the hostess."

"I'm sure that's not true, though Billy and Lillian do love you as if you were their mother."

Thea bit her lip to stem the pain, but the tears forming in her eyes spilled onto her cheeks.

A small hand slipped into hers and squeezed it.

"Forgive me," Meggie said. "You hide your need well."

"My need?"

"Your need for a child. Believe it or not, I understand it."

"You do?"

Meggie nodded. "It's like there's an enormous void in your heart, and you ache with the need to fill it. But nothing will do. So you learn to live with the pain."

Thea blinked, and a tear rolled down her cheek. "How can you understand?"

"I spent eight years grieving for Billy," Meggie said, "thinking he'd died and resigning myself to never having another child. When Dexter brought my lost son home to me—only then did I realize how broken I'd been. Sometimes you only understand the pain you suffer when it has eased."

She squeezed Thea's hand. "I'd do anything in the world to ease *your* pain."

Thea sighed. "I had always imagined I'd have a boy and a girl, just like you have," she said. "I'd even been foolish enough to give them names. Marcus—for the boy. And Helena for the girl." She shook her head. "I thought I'd pushed such fanciful notions to the back of my mind. But lately…"

"Lately, the need has returned?"

Thea crossed the dining room floor, making a show of inspecting the table decorations, but her sister-in-law was not to be deterred.

"Does it have something to do with your evening excursions?" Meggie asked. "Dexter said something about you venturing out—and we missed you at dinner last night."

"Does my brother seek to control me?" Thea asked.

"He worries about you. He thinks you're unhappy here with us."

"I'm happy enough," Thea said, "but sometimes I wonder whether my life would have taken a different turn had I been younger when we first came to London. Sometimes I wish I were not the sensible, dependable, respectable spinster aunt." She sighed. "Sometimes I want to just *live*—if even for a little while. Is that so bad?"

Meggie took her hand.

"My dear sister—you need new acquaintances to lift your spirits. Perhaps you'll find one among tonight's set of stuffy merchants all vying to do business with Dexter."

"That's unlikely."

"Then I'll make it my mission," Meggie said. "It's time the family stopped using you to help them—and helped *you* instead."

She pulled Thea into an embrace. Most unladylike, but despite Meggie now holding the title of Lady Hart, she would never lose her affectionate side.

And if Thea could not have a family of her own, she had a sister-in-law who loved her. Perhaps the secret of true happiness was not in wishing for more but in being content with what she had.

※※※《《

GRIFFIN WRINKLED HIS nose in distaste as he surveyed the room.

Bloody hell—did the men of society think their ridiculous attire gave them the appearance of masculinity?

The other guests were strutting peacocks. One man even wore a pink waistcoat—pink! He'd be ripped to shreds if he entered the Queen's Head—or the White Hart—dressed like that.

Pink Waistcoat had looked down his nose at Griffin, looking pointedly at his fingernails, which, no matter how hard Griffin scrubbed, still bore traces of dirt.

Mrs. Pink Waistcoat was even worse. She'd wrinkled her pretty little nose in a sneer, but as soon as she thought Griffin wasn't watching, she'd ogled him, the all-too-familiar lust in her expression. Pink Waistcoat clearly lacked any male prowess. His wife might despise Griffin's origins—but deep down, every woman, even the prim ones, yearned to spread her legs for a real man.

Their host approached him. Though Griffin topped him by a few inches, Sir Dexter possessed an air of dominance—arising from a sharp intelligence and strength of will rather than physical strength. The man filled out his suit well enough, his muscles toned rather than powerful—like a racehorse bred to stay the distance. He was evidently a man who took pride in his body and looked after it. Perhaps he exercised nightly by riding his wife.

"Mr. Oake, I presume."

Mouth set in a stern line, brow furrowed into a frown, clear blue eyes focused on him—Sir Dexter was not a man to cross.

Griffin took the proffered hand. Long, lean fingers curled round his in a gesture of dominance. He responded by squeezing back, and Hart increased the pressure again. Any moment the man would drop his trousers and insist they compare the size of their cocks.

At length, Hart released his hold.

"Welcome," he said. "My partner, Mr. Peyton, spoke highly of you."

"I suspect he spoke even more highly of the size of my account," Griffin replied. "Do you invite all your new accounts to dinner, or just those with the largest funds?"

"You seem a dangerously frank man, Mr. Oake."

"I speak as I find," Griffin said. "I'm not in the business of pleasing others."

"Quite," came the reply. "From what I hear, you're in the business of flattening them with your fists."

"Only those who deserve to be flattened," Griffin said. "There's more honesty in a man who uses his fists—rather than his wits—to best his opponents."

The corners of Hart's mouth twitched, and a faint sparkle gleamed in his eyes, then the frown reappeared.

Bloody hell—he was, most certainly, *not* a man to play cards against. But Griffin didn't need the man to like him—just take care of his money.

"Ah, Peyton!" Hart exclaimed, relief in his tone. "I have you to thank for persuading Mr. Oake to join us this evening."

A man approached them with a smile, and Griffin recognized the blonde-haired man who'd discussed his account at the offices of the Hart Bank last week.

"I'm so glad you could come, Mr. Oake," he said. "Sir Dexter considers his bank a family business and prefers to adopt the personal approach when meeting new clients."

"If you'll excuse me," Sir Dexter said, "I see Lord and Lady Cholmondeley have arrived."

Hardly the *personal approach*—the man couldn't wait to get away from him.

"I'm glad you chose to bank with us," Peyton said. "Our loan rates are very competitive."

"And profitable for you, I suppose," Griffin replied. "I've no interest in taking out a loan. I'd rather pay for something when I have the funds. I dislike the notion of being in debt to another."

"Businessmen have speculated for years."

"I'm content with what I have," Griffin said. "I'll leave the speculation to you. Isn't that the purpose of a bank? To persuade businessmen to invest their savings so that you might do a little prospecting yourself, on the back of another's wealth?"

"You understand much of investment," Peyton said, "considering…" he colored and looked away.

"Considering I'm a knucklehead?"

Peyton had the grace to blush, but before he could respond, he was interrupted by a soft, feminine voice.

"Mr. Peyton, you seem discomposed."

A woman appeared at Peyton's side. With her slight frame—soft brown hair styled in a simple fashion, loose curls framing a delicately-featured face—she looked a little out of place in a society party.

"Your interruption is timed to perfection," Peyton said. "You've prevented me from committing a grave insult. May I introduce Mr. Oake?" He turned to Griffin. "Our hostess, Lady Hart."

Lady Hart?

Was this soft-voiced little thing Sir Dexter's wife? Griffin couldn't imagine a more diverse match, other than, perhaps, one between a mouse and a lion.

He made no move, and a look of hurt flickered across her eyes.

The more he stared, he noticed the slight tremor in her body. Almost indistinguishable—but a lifetime of observing human behavior—all the better to pummel them in the ring—taught him to recognize apprehension.

And fear.

He held out his hand, palm upward, and she took it. Then he clicked his heels together and bowed, brushing his lips against the skin of her hand.

He wasn't going to let Sir Dexter, Mr. Peyton—or Mr. bloody Pink Waistcoat—think he lacked manners.

"A pleasure, Lady Hart," he said. "I was so glad to receive your invitation. Forgive me, you were not what I was expecting."

The look of hurt returned, and Peyton visibly stiffened.

"What were you expecting, Mr. Oake?" she asked.

"Someone distinctly less appealing," he replied. "From what I've seen of the people in London so far, the men strut around like peacocks, and the woman turn their noses up at anyone without a title. You seem friendly enough, which is just as well, for I wasn't looking forward to this evening at all."

Her mouth curved into a smile—and he understood the attraction. Warm brown eyes, like liquid chocolate, shone with kindness.

"I'm so pleased to hear you say that, Mr. Oake!" she said, laughing. Then she leaned forward and lowered her voice. "I confess, I wasn't anticipating a pleasurable evening myself, either. I struggle to warm to strangers."

"Then I hope that after tonight, Lady Hart, you'll no longer consider me a stranger."

Out of the corner of his eye, he spotted Sir Dexter moving about, his attention fixed firmly on his wife. There was possession in his gaze—as to be expected—but something else.

Protectiveness.

Sir Dexter might be a businessman, but the tender look he bestowed on his wife belied his stern demeanor. They exchanged a smile, Hart raised his eyebrows, and she inclined her head in a slight nod. Then he glanced at Griffin and scowled.

So—Sir Dexter loved his wife, to the point of jealousy. And from the expression in her eyes, she loved him back.

Lucky bastard. A well-pleasured, faithful wife was a rarity indeed. No wonder Hart glared at him. If she belonged to Griffin, he'd keep her under lock and key and pummel any man he caught sniffing round her.

He released her hand and placed his own hand behind his back, in the manner he'd seen gentleman adopt. A signal to Hart that he had no designs on his wife.

But Lady Hart didn't look the type of woman to respond to the advances of another man. How different from Louisa—who was willing to spread for as many men as possible.

Sir Dexter approached them and stood beside his wife, touching her arm affectionately. "I see you've met my newest client," he said.

She rolled her eyes. "Is that my prompt to tell him how fortunate he is to bank with you, Dexter?"

"I wouldn't dream of telling you what to say," he replied. "But I regret I must curtail your discussion with Oake. We've several new arrivals who've yet to be graced by your presence."

Good Lord—had the man turned into a milksop? Were it not for the fact that their love for each other was evidently very real and very deep, Griffin might have retched at such sweetness. But in Lady Hart, it seemed just right.

She was a perfect little thing. Perhaps she might be the one to assist him in finding a chaperone for Rowena.

"Where's Dorothea?" Sir Dexter asked. Lady Hart shook her head. "I've no idea. Perhaps she's with the children."

"That's all I need," he huffed. "The most *reliable* member of the household playing truant when guests need looking after."

He'd said *reliable* as if it were an insult.

Who the devil was Dorothea? A nursemaid?

"Dexter!" Lady Hart admonished, a flash of anger in her eyes. Whoever this Dorothea was, she had a champion.

"At least my *brother* knows his duty," Hart continued, "even if my sister doesn't."

Ah—a sister. How strange that Hart referred to her as a member of the household—almost as if he thought her a servant. Perhaps there was something wrong with her.

Sir Dexter gestured toward a man at the far end of the room. He stood, alone, silhouetted against the window, his features obscured in shadow. "Devon, come and meet the bank's newest account."

The man hesitated, then moved into the light.

Griffin stifled a gasp.

His face was a mess—the left side looked like it had been ripped in two. A jagged scar ran from just below the eye to the corner of his mouth. Griffin had sustained many blows to the face over the years—but nothing compared to what this man must have endured.

He approached Griffin, a look of challenge in his eyes. No doubt he'd had to face ridicule, revulsion, and—the worst of all emotions—pity.

"Mr. Oake, allow me to introduce my younger brother," Sir Dexter said. "Major Devon Hart."

"*Major* Hart?" Griffin asked. "What regiment are you in?"

"The Thirteenth. But I'm no longer in the militia."

Griffin gestured toward the scar. "Were you injured in battle? That doesn't look like the mark of a sword."

"You're offended?"

"Merely curious," Griffin replied. "My apologies. I trust *you're* not offended by my curiosity." He raised his hands, displaying the callouses and scars on his knuckles. "My weapons are my fists, which administer as much damage as a blade."

"Actually, it was a gin bottle," the major said.

"That must have hurt," Griffin said. "The militia must be in a sorry state if their soldiers have to resort to gin bottles. I trust you gave as good as you got."

"After a fashion."

"I prefer to get close to my opponent," Griffin said, "to look him in the eye—feel every blow."

Recognition dawned on the major's face. "Griffin Oake!" he exclaimed. "I should have known—you're the Mighty Oak, aren't you?"

"My reputation precedes me."

"For good reason." The major turned to his brother. "You never said your newest client was famous, Dex."

Sir Dexter looked none the wiser, and his brother nudged him. "I must have told you about the Mighty Oak—the man who flattens his opponents at the first blow."

You've seen me fight?" Griffin asked.

"You won me two guineas." The major's grin broadened, showing even white teeth. "It should have been twenty, but I couldn't get better odds. I've never seen a man felled so quickly." He turned to his brother. "It was marvelous, Dex—ten years ago, but I remember as if it were yesterday. You rarely see a fighter who combined skill and brute strength—most rely on one or the other—but this fellow here possessed both qualities." He resumed his attention on Griffin, eagerness in his eyes. "Do you still fight?"

"On occasion," Griffin said. "I was at the Queen's Head last night."

"I'm sorry I missed it. The proprietor must have appreciated the trade—you'd have attracted a crowd."

"*I'm* the proprietor."

"You own an inn?"

Griffin smiled. "I own several, hence my association with Sir Dexter."

The major rolled his eyes. "*Sir Dexter*—I'll never get used to that."

25

He winked at Griffin. "Mind you continue calling him 'Sir,' or he'll foreclose on your loans. As for me, I can call him Dex, for I'm no longer beholden to him—though I prefer to call him an arse."

A giggle to the left indicated that Lady Hart was within earshot. Sir Dexter, however, made no move to admonish his brother. He merely rolled his eyes, took his wife's arm, then excused himself to go and speak to Pink Waistcoat.

"Who the devil's that?" Griffin asked.

"The man with the flamboyant taste in waistcoats?" Major Hart laughed. "He's a silk merchant—Mr. Lewis. Shall I introduce you?"

"That explains a lot," Griffin said. "And no, thank you."

The major laughed. "I hear his wife insists upon him wearing it. According to Dex, he has a waistcoat to match every one of her gowns, as well as her lapdog's coats. It's an extraordinary sight when they're in Hyde Park together. I believe he considers it a form of advertising."

"Advertising what?" Griffin asked. "His business, or the fact that he's ruled by his wife?"

"Whatever he is, I believe Dex intends to make a pretty penny out of him. Bankers don't lend money out of kindness. Don't let the sumptuousness of tonight's dinner fool you. The clients Dex woos will pay him back a thousandfold in interest."

"I'm investing rather than borrowing," Griffin said. "I don't intend to take risks when I know what it's like to have nothing. My fighting days are over, save the occasional bout. At six and thirty, I must make way for the next generation. And I've been more fortunate than most."

"A pity," the major said. "I'd have liked to see you fight again."

"I could show you if you like," Griffin said. "Tach you a few techniques?"

The major's face lit up into a smile. "Rest assured, Mr. Oake, I'll hold you to that. My wife wouldn't object to your marking *my* face if we indulged in a bout."

"Is she here tonight?" Griffin asked.

"Sadly not. She's nearing her confinement." The major smiled, and his expression took on that familiar faraway look.

The look of the besotted.

Hell's teeth! Was he to be surrounded by an array of happy couples? The entire Hart family seemed to be blessed with fruitful and blissful unions.

Why did Griffin have to be so damned unlucky as to have wed himself to a harlot?

Chapter Five

S WEET LORD, IT was *him*!

He must be a figment of her imagination—made vivid by her desires.

Last night he'd visited her dreams again—bodies locked in a passionate embrace, crying each other's names... She'd woken, flushed and hot—even Dex noticed and had asked, during breakfast, if she was coming down with a chill.

Her brother was right—she was coming down with something. An affliction—a shameful, girlish affliction.

Lovesickness.

Thea blinked and shook her head. But when she opened her eyes again, he was still there—as large as life—talking to Dexter and Meggie.

She fought the urge to return to the nursery.

At that moment, Devon approached him, and Thea waited for the inevitable reaction to her younger brother's disfigurement. But, instead, she saw her brother greeted warmly by a stranger, who shook his hand, smiled, and looked him straight in the eyes.

Not only was he the epitome of virility and masculinity, he was capable of looking beyond Devon's scar, to the man inside.

Why did he have to be so perfect?

Why did her heart flutter at the mere sight of him?

As she watched, Devon grew more at ease. When the two men threw back their heads with laughter, her heart was lost.

Thea stepped into the room, and Meggie announced dinner was served, then led the way into the dining room on Dexter's arm.

Devon appeared at Thea's elbow. "I believe I'm your dinner companion tonight, sister," he said.

"You seem in good spirits, brother."

"Why shouldn't I be?" he replied. "I've a beautiful wife at home, about to furnish me with my second child, and I have my beloved sister for company tonight. Shall we?"

She took her brother's elbow and let him lead her into dinner.

MEGGIE HAD OUTDONE herself tonight. The meal was excellent, and none of the guests had reason to complain—not even Mrs. Lewis.

Thea had reason to curse Mrs. Lewis. Not only was she sat beside—*him*—but for most of the time, she obscured him from view. Each time the woman leaned forward, giving a clear sight of him, Thea stole a glimpse. He didn't eat with ease—she observed his hands as they curled round the handles of the cutlery and watched him lift a wineglass to his lips, licking her own lips as her gaze slid across the curve of his mouth.

What the devil was a prizefighter doing at Dexter's party? Had he unexpectedly inherited a title? Or a fortune? His jacket was tailored to fit his frame—the mark of the best establishments in Savile Row. And his necktie and waistcoat, though not made from the flamboyant silks favored by men such as Mr. Lewis, were clearly cut from the finest material.

But he looked uncomfortable. He had money—but didn't know what to do with it.

At that moment, Mrs. Lewis leaned to one side to call across to her husband and brought the object of Thea's obsession into full view.

"Thea?"

She turned to see Devon staring at her.

"What is it?" she snapped.

"What do you think?"

"About what?"

He rolled his eyes. "I've already asked you three times—what you think of the sorbet?"

"Oh—it's pleasant enough."

He glanced across the table. "You seem preoccupied. Has one of our guests discomposed you?"

"I was merely wondering…" she hesitated.

"Ah! I knew it. Do continue."

"I-I happened to notice you were getting on very well with that man over there." She lowered her voice. "The one next to Mrs. Lewis."

"Mr. Oake?" Devon picked up his glass. "He was famous in his day, you know."

"What for?"

"Can't you guess? You only have to look at him. He's a prizefighter. He made his name—and a fortune, I'll wager—fighting in the inns around Sussex. But he really came into prominence when he won a major fight in London, about ten years ago, which I was fortunate enough to witness firsthand."

"Does he fight now?" she asked.

"Not so much. He owns a number of inns around the country, including one in London. All bought with his winnings, can you credit that? Just think how many men he'd have to have felled. But you only have to look at him to realize the futility of resisting a body like that."

"Indeed…" she breathed.

"Why, sister dearest, I believe you're blushing!" he laughed. "Has the Mighty Oak captured your interest?"

"Keep your voice down!" she hissed.

"He's a fine choice. Shall I wish you joy?"

Why must he tease her? Thea loved seeing her brother's playful attitude return after years of bitterness—but not at her expense.

"He liked *you* well enough," she replied. "Not many can look you in the eyes without flinching."

"You give as good as you get," he said. "Have I touched a nerve?"

The object of Thea's interest ceased talking to Mrs. Lewis and was looking straight at her.

She shrank back. "Devon, that's enough," she whispered.

"Don't tell me you've turned into a virginal maiden getting her first flush of passion?" Devon chuckled. "I didn't have you down for a late developer—a *very* late developer, to have fanciful flutterings at your age!"

"Devon—please!" she cried. The company grew silent.

"Dorothea, what's the matter?" Dexter's voice boomed from the top end of the table.

"Nothing," she said, fixing her gaze on her plate, painfully aware that a pair of green eyes were trained on her. "Our brother likes to tease."

Meggie spoke up. "I fear that since Devon left the army, he's been looking for someone to fight with. Of course, the dining room is no place for a sword—and while his sword may have been honed to sharpness, he's yet to wield his tongue with any degree of expertise."

A ripple of laughter threaded through the company. Thea smiled at Meggie, acknowledging her sister-in-law's intervention with a nod.

Thank you.

The conversation resumed. She reached for her glass, and a hand caught her sleeve.

"Forgive me," Devon said. "Evidently, I'm still unused to polite society that I know not how to tease without causing offense. I didn't mean to hurt you, Thea. I, of all people, should know what it's like to be ridiculed for one's appearance."

"You insulted my age, not my appearance," Thea said, tartly, "unless you also find fault with how I look."

"Of course not. You're a handsome woman—any man worth his salt would notice that."

He released her sleeve. "Why don't I invite Mr. Oake to your birthday party next week? To make up for being an arse."

"Wouldn't it seem odd?" she asked. "A small party for friends when you barely know him?"

"Nonsense!" Devon said. "The quality of a friendship doesn't always depend on the duration of the acquaintance. He's promised to teach me the rudiments of pugilism, and I consider that the mark of a friend. I'd like to know him better—and what better circumstance to further a friendship than a family party?"

"He won't come."

"Then there's no harm in asking."

Thea sighed. There was no stopping Devon when he was determined. And at least, if he were the one to issue the invitation, *she'd* be spared the pain of witnessing Mr. Oake's rejection.

Chapter Six

THE DINNER CONCLUDED, the ladies retired to the drawing room, while the men remained in the dining room.

As Lady Hart led the procession of silk gowns and coiffured figures out of the room, Griffin's gaze fell on the woman who'd been sitting next to Major Hart. She wasn't present when he'd arrived that evening but appeared after dinner was announced.

She'd seemed uninteresting at first—hair scraped into a style which looked as if it had been designed to be as unflattering as possible, her gown free of any adornment. But the more he observed her during the meal, he caught glimpses of character—a flash of intelligence in her eyes. At first, he'd have said they were a dull gray, but on closer observation, they were, in fact, a pale shade of blue. The dark rims around the irises gave them a somewhat unsettling expression.

More than once, he'd caught her watching him, though her gaze shifted as soon as he looked at her.

She must be the other sister—the elusive Dorothea.

The air thickened with cigar smoke.

Griffin couldn't stand the stuff, and he refused Sir Dexter's offer of one. When a footman approached with the brandy decanter, he shook his head.

"Try it," a voice said. Mr. Peyton slipped into the seat next to Griffin and gestured toward the decanter. "That's Hart's finest. You'll not taste the like again."

"I prefer to keep a clear head."

"Not an easy feat when the air's blue." Peyton waved his hand, dissipating the smoke emanating from Mr. Lewis's cigar. "I can't abide the insistence on gentlemen separating themselves from the ladies."

"I'd have thought a room full of women an unappealing prospect," Griffin said.

"Not when you've spent the whole day in a boardroom full of men. There's a particular delight to be had in listening to female inanities about the latest fashions or hearing a song at the pianoforte."

"Who was the woman sitting beside Major Hart?" Griffin asked. "She seemed discomposed during dessert."

"Miss Hart? Yes, most unlike her. She's Sir Dexter's sister. She keeps house for him and Lady Hart and tends to their children.

"She sounds more like a servant than a family member."

"She had a house of her own for a time," Peyton said, "but she moved back after Lady Hart had her youngest child."

"Why?"

"I suppose she was lonely. The children adore her, and, with the exception of William, she's helped bring every one of her nieces and nephews into the world. She appears to have no ambition outside keeping house and looking after other people's children."

"Not much of a life for a woman of her station."

"But perfect for a spinster aunt," Peyton said. "She's nearing *thirty*."

The man might as well have said she was six feet under.

"It must be hard for her," Peyton continued. "She was the lady of the house until Sir Dexter married. And now, she's confined to a restricted circle and will remain so until the day she dies."

Yes—she might as well be in her grave.

Unless…

A spinster aunt, nearing thirty, with no ambition outside looking after the children of another.

She sounded like the answer to his problems. A respectable, dependable woman who was clearly underappreciated by her own family.

And perhaps he was the answer to *her* problems. The poor creature might appreciate a little adventure.

If chaperoning Rowena could be considered an adventure.

Sir Dexter rose, and the men followed suit and headed toward the drawing room. Good—it would give Griffin a chance to observe her more closely.

≫≫≫⋘⋘⋘

A FIRE CRACKLED in the drawing room, which was alive with activity and conversation. As the men distributed themselves among the women, the noise abated, and Lady Hart cleared her throat.

"Time for a little music," she said. "Lady Cholmondeley, would you be so kind?"

A tall, elegantly dressed woman with iron-gray hair approached the pianoforte.

"Dorothea? Might you oblige us with a song?" Lady Hart asked.

The lone figure sitting beside the fireplace stirred and glanced around the room. Her cheeks flushed pink—perhaps due to the heat from the fire. As her gaze settled on Griffin, the bloom on her cheeks deepened.

"Perhaps another time," she said. "My throat's a little sore."

Lady Hart approached her and whispered encouragement, but she shook her head.

"Leave her be, Meggie, if she's unwilling," Major Hart interjected.

At that moment, the door burst open, and two children ran into the room—a young boy, followed by a toddler.

"Mama! Lily's taken my nightshirt again!"

"William!" Sir Dexter roared. "How many times have I told you…"

"Leave him alone, Dexter. I'll deal with it," Miss Hart interrupted, speaking with an authority that belied her painfully shy air of before. She strode toward the children.

"Billy, dear," she said, "remember what we discussed?"

"Not to disturb Mama and Papa when they're entertaining."

"Quite so. And why must you not disturb them?"

"Because I wouldn't like it if they interrupted *me* when I'm with my friends."

"And what else?"

"That obedience is how I show Papa I'm capable of becoming a man." The boy bowed toward Sir Dexter and his wife. "Forgive me, Papa, Mama," he said.

"Aunty Thea!" the toddler wailed. Miss Hart scooped the child into her arms.

"There, now!" she soothed. "Shall I read you a story?" The little girl nodded, then relaxed her head on her aunt's shoulders. "Before then," Miss Hart continued, "I wonder if you might assist me in a search for your brother's nightshirt." She glanced at the boy. "Billy might be able to shed some light as to why you might have procured it. A lady shouldn't steal her brother's clothes, but neither should a gentleman provoke her into doing it."

She approached the door, but the boy remained where he was and glanced about the room. His eyes widened as his gaze fell on Griffin.

"Come along, young man," Miss Hart chided. Obediently, he trotted after her.

"Perhaps I should…" Lady Hart began, but Sir Dexter interrupted her.

"Thea has it under control," he said. "You know how she likes to be useful."

Lady Hart frowned but resumed her seat, and Lady Cholmondeley began to play a pleasant but dull air.

Or perhaps it was dull because Griffin was disappointed at missing out on the prospect of hearing Miss Hart sing. Given the passion simmering beneath her veneer of dullness, he suspected her voice might be the only way she could express her feelings.

"We'll not see her again," Mr. Peyton said.

Griffin tore his gaze from the door. "The children seem rather a handful."

Peyton laughed. "They are. Miss Hart is more than capable of handling them. Some adults have the ability to communicate with children as if they have a sixth sense in knowing precisely what to say. I wonder how she does it."

"Through strict discipline, I imagine."

"I've never heard a cross word from her. Miss Hart possesses the perfect blend of authority and compassion—at least where children are concerned.

"She seems a remarkable woman," Griffin said, "and somewhat undervalued—though I'd prefer you didn't tell Sir Dexter that."

"Don't tell my brother what?"

Shit.

Major Hart stood before him.

"I hadn't noticed you approach," Griffin said.

"I'm known for being light on my feet. It's useful when I want to effect an ambush." Major Hart glanced across toward Sir Dexter. "You're right, of course, Mr. Oake."

"In what respect?"

"My sister is both remarkable and undervalued. Two qualities which, if found together in the same person, make for a particularly tragic combination."

"You pity her?" Griffin asked.

"I want more for her. I wonder…" he hesitated, "…if you don't think it too forward, would you oblige us by accepting an invitation to a party next week?"

"A party?"

"Just a small gathering for family and friends. You strike me as the kind of man who'd prefer a less formal setting."

Mr. Peyton laughed. "Is Mr. Oake supposed to be honored that you see him as a friend, Hart, or insulted that you consider him unsuited to formal occasions?"

"I meant no offense," Hart said. "It's a party to celebrate my sister's birthday."

"Lady Hart?"

"No, Dorothea."

Griffin shook his head. "I'm sure your sister would object to a stranger invading her party."

"She'll not object."

"Why don't you tell him the real reason you're asking him?" Mr. Peyton laughed. "Mr. Oake, I believe Hart wishes to engage in a bout with you before you return to the country."

"You're not staying in London?" Hart asked.

Griffin shook his head. "I'm anxious to return to my daughter in Sussex."

The major's eyes widened. "You have a *daughter*? I'd no idea you were..." He broke off and glanced toward the door through which Miss Hart had left. "Is she alone in Sussex, or perhaps your wife...?"

Griffin shivered at the memory of Louisa. Two pairs of eyes watched him with curiosity.

He glanced at the clock. "Forgive me. I must be going."

"I trust I've not offended you by asking about your wife," Major Hart said.

"No, I'm just tired," Griffin said. "I'm unused to the late hour of London parties, but I look forward to seeing you next week."

The major hesitated, then nodded. "Tuesday, seven o'clock. I'll ask my sister to issue an invitation."

"And, if your sister does not object, I can show you how to throw a good punch."

"He can do that already," Mr. Peyton said. "Major Hart once had the most fearsome reputation for fighting on the streets."

"Then we have much to talk about," Griffin said.

"I suppose we do."

Griffin bowed, and the two men reciprocated, then he approached Sir Dexter to take his leave.

As he exited the building, he wondered what had come over Major Hart. At first, the man seemed eager to further their acquaintance, but as soon as he'd mentioned Rowena, his enthusiasm had waned. Perhaps he'd been offended by Griffin's abrupt tone when he'd mentioned his wife—but Louisa was not a subject he wanted to discuss.

⟫⟪

WITH THE CHILDREN at peace once more, Thea smoothed her hairstyle, then hurried back to the drawing room.

The strains of music reached her ears as Lady Cholmondeley made a gallant effort to play a Mozart sonata. Pleasant enough to an untrained ear, but Thea detected a number of mistakes, particularly in the passages where the left hand took on the melody.

Emboldened by having dealt with the children, she was now determined to sing—to show the company she was more than a glorified nursemaid.

With a little brandy to steady her nerves, she might even sing the Italian love song she'd practiced. The words would convey the feelings of her heart—the beauty being that hardly anyone in the room, save Devon and Meggie, understood the language.

She could sing it for him—*to* him—even if he was unaware.

She pushed open the door and surveyed the room.

He wasn't there.

"Thea!" Devon approached her, hands outstretched. "I didn't think you'd return. I know how demanding Lillian can be."

"I didn't want to shirk my responsibilities here." She glanced around the room again.

"He's gone," Devon said, lowering his voice. "I invited him to your party."

A spark of hope ignited within her. She'd see him again. Next time she'd summon the courage to speak to him.

"I'm sorry," Devon continued.

"What for?" she asked. "You did well."

"He's married—with a daughter."

The spark died. What a fool she'd been! Of course he'd be married—a man of his obvious virility.

"I know you were attracted to him," Devon said, "but attraction isn't enough when it comes to a union." He gestured to his scarred face. "I'm glad of it, otherwise I'd never have found a woman willing to marry me!"

She turned away, blinking back the tears.

"Forgive me, Thea," Devon said, "I didn't mean to make light of your feelings. But if you're too afraid to *talk* to a man, let alone sing before him, then that's not love. It's infatuation—obsession—and it's not healthy."

Devon was right. She hadn't been in love—she was a childish fool.

Next week was her thirtieth birthday party. Time to grow up and accept life as it was.

BY THE TIME Griffin had returned to the Queen's Head, he'd decided that the prim Miss Hart was just the woman to turn Rowe into a lady. Undervalued by her family—that's what Major Hart said, almost as if he was pleading on her behalf.

The main parlor was empty—the patrons having either gone home or retired to their rooms—save for the manager, who hailed Griffin as he entered.

"What can I get for you, Mr. Oake?"

"Information on the Harts," Griffin said. "Do you know anything about them?"

"A little—my cousin's under-gardener at Sir Dexter's house. But I'm not one for gossip."

"Quite," Griffin said. "But I'd like to know if Sir Dexter's an honest man."

"There's none fairer, so my cousin says. Sir Dexter made his fortune from nothing, much like you, Mr. Oake. And he's weathered scandal with his sisters—but I don't know if I should say."

"I shan't tell."

"His younger sister got herself in the family way—though she married a duke, in the end. You don't see her in London anymore. They live in Scotland."

That part was true. Sir Dexter had mentioned a brother-in-law who was a duke who owned a distillery in the Highlands. He'd suggested Griffin buy a few casks of the stuff—but who in the Queen's Head, or even the White Hart, would drink whisky when gin was to be had at a quarter of the price?

"And his other sister?" Griffin asked.

"I'd heard in the Nag's Head that his older sister had a child from an illicit union, but it was hushed up. It happened before they arrived in London. My Millicent knows more. Would you like me to ask her?"

"No—best not spread gossip," Griffin said. But the more he heard about Miss Hart, the more she intrigued him. Her dull exterior disguised a passionate woman. Did it also disguise a fallen woman?

In which case, she was likely to be grateful for any offer which removed her from being beholden to a family that viewed her as a disgrace. It wouldn't take much to persuade her to leave.

And persuade her he would—next week, at her party. Few women her age would be given the chance of a new life. She'd be a simpleton not to take it.

Chapter Seven

THEA STOOD IN the hallway, greeting the guests. They paid her every courtesy, but she saw the pity in their eyes.

Tonight marked her thirtieth birthday.

A widow in her thirties was always to be respected, for she'd weathered marriage and bereavement and, most likely, had the comfort of her children. And she had the experience to advise young ladies.

But a spinster was universally known to be undesirableand fated to live out her days being a burden to others.

She looked up as another guest arrived.

Oh no...

Her humiliation was complete. The object of her futile infatuation strode toward her.

She curled her mouth into the bland smile of the spinster aunt and held out her hand.

"Mr. Oake, I believe," she said. "I'm glad you've come."

Her hand was swallowed up in a huge paw, and thick, strong fingers enclosed it in a firm grip. She looked up, and her heart jolted.

From a distance, he'd been an impressive man, but at close quarters, he was a god. His whole body vibrated with power.

"Miss Hart," he said, his deep voice reverberating in her chest. "We meet at last."

Heat spread throughout her body, then settled in her stomach, forming an uncomfortable but thrilling ache. Her voice caught in her throat, and she responded with a nod and swallowed.

Devon came to her aid.

"Oake!" he cried. "I didn't think you'd come."

"I leave for Sussex the day after tomorrow."

He fixed his gaze on Thea. For a moment, they stared at each other, and the noise around her seemed to fade until she could only hear her own breathing.

His mouth twitched into a smile, and she lowered her gaze to his lips.

What pleasures could be had from a mouth such as his?

"Dorothea, darling!" A familiar voice broke the spell, and she looked around to see Anne Pelham rushing toward her. The giant stepped aside to make room and, with a rush of silk, Anne drew Thea into an embrace.

"We've been so looking forward to seeing you tonight," Anne said, "haven't we, Harold?" The man beside her nodded and smiled. "Of course, my love," he said. Then he glanced at the giant.

"Ah, Mr. Oake," he said. "I hadn't known you were a family friend. I'd been hoping to meet you again after Mr. Peyton introduced us. I believe we may be able to enter into an arrangement for our mutual benefit."

"No business talk tonight, Harold," Anne chided, tapping her husband's arm with her fan. "We're here for Thea, not for your profits."

He looked suitability chastised, and the pair of them moved into the drawing room, followed by Mr. Oake.

"That's the last of the guests," Meggie said, appearing at Thea's elbow. "Shall we wait until they're settled in the drawing room, then make a grand entrance together? It's *your* night, after all."

Dear Meggie! She meant well, but sometimes she didn't realize that the world was not always kind, even within the little circle of people

Thea called friends. Their well-meaning words of kindness gave rise to more hurt than a direct insult could ever achieve.

But tonight was not the time for ingratitude. Her family loved her, and that was all that mattered. And if it was the only kind of love she could hope to experience, then it was better than nothing.

>>>><<<<

THERE WAS NO doubt about it—he was watching her.

Every time Thea looked up, she saw his green eyes trained on her. Even when he was talking to Devon, his gaze flicked over in her direction.

Why did he make her body melt and her knees weak?

"He's rather impressive, isn't he?" Meggie had arrived at her side again.

"Who?"

"The man you've been staring at half the night!"

"Hush!" Thea hissed.

"Nobody can hear us. And you cannot deny it—you've gone as red as Mr. Pelham's burgundy wine. Why don't you go and speak to him?"

"I can't do that."

"Devon's with him," Meggie said. "Go and talk to Devon, and the rest will happen naturally. It's plain to see that you like Mr. Oake."

"He wouldn't be interested in someone like me," Thea said.

"You give yourself too little credit," Meggie replied. "You're intelligent and a good conversationalist."

"I'm sure Dexter would object if he saw me trotting after a married man."

"What makes you think he's married?"

"He has a daughter!"

"He's a widower," Meggie said. "He lost his wife over ten years ago, I believe, and has not remarried."

"Poor man," Thea said, fighting her guilt at the little nugget of hope.

Meggie offered Thea her glass. "Here—a little wine to fuel your courage."

What did she have to lose? Thea drained the glass, then handed it back to Meggie.

"Hurry," Meggie said. "They're moving toward the terrace. But don't appear too eager. You don't want him thinking you're desperate."

Why not? Given that she'd turned thirty, the whole room would view any attempt to speak with a man as an act of desperation. But she had no wish to dampen Meggie's enthusiasm.

As Thea approached the two men, they stopped in the doorway leading to the terrace. Devon bowed and wandered off toward the Pelhams, and Mr. Oake continued outside.

Curse it! Thea looked about her. She'd been striding in such a purposeful manner that the party would think it odd if she veered off. Emboldened by the wine, she followed him outside.

He stood on the terrace, looking out at the garden, his face in profile. The light of the evening sun highlighted his strong nose and full lips. He filled his suit out to perfection, and her gaze followed the contours of his broad, muscular frame. Then he lifted his hand and ran his fingers through his hair, the act sending a bolt of need through her. What might it be like to feel his hands through her hair—or on her skin?

Her courage wavered, and she took a step back.

"Don't leave on my account," he said, his voice a deep rumble. He turned to face her, and his eyes glittered in the sunlight, which cast a warm, pink glow across his face.

Why did he have to be so beautiful?

"Why don't you join me?" he asked. "Or do you prefer to be inside with the others?"

"Oh, no!" she exclaimed. He frowned.

"I mean…" she hesitated, "I prefer to be out here."

"Shall *I* go inside?"

"Please stay!"

He raised his eyebrows at her outburst, and she tore her gaze from him and looked out across the garden.

At length, he drew near. She swallowed and kept her gaze focused on the armillary sphere in the center of the garden.

"Your brother has a…" he hesitated, "…a very pleasant-looking garden. His gardener is to be commended."

His voice wavered as if he wanted to say something else. Was he nervous?

"I tend to the garden," Thea said. He turned to her, surprise in his expression.

"Not all of it, of course," she continued. "The gardener works under my direction."

"It's very…" He waved his hand toward it as if searching for a word.

"Pleasant," she prompted. "I believe that was the adjective. You're too kind. Most people think it out of fashion, but I dislike formal gardens."

"You do?"

"I see little point forcing Mother Nature to bend to the will of aesthetics."

"Forgive me…*aesthetics*?"

"Trees and shrubs grow in accordance to how Nature wishes them to," she continued. "While some degree of discipline is necessary in order to appreciate its form, a tree which is overly forced into a shape a man considers to be *pleasing* will not bend. It will break."

"So what do you do, Miss Hart, when faced with a particularly obstinate tree?"

He was making fun of her.

"I seek to enhance its natural form."

"Like you would a child?"

"You understand!" she cried. "It's *exactly* like a child. I wonder if parents should be made to tend to a garden before they consider raising a family. Most parents spend the first part of their marriage eager for children, then when those children arrive, they palm them off onto nursemaids and governesses."

"Perhaps the care of a child requires more than an understanding of gardens," he said.

"Such as?"

"Natural ability."

Whether it was the wine, or the heat from the evening sun—but a delicious warmth had begun to envelop her, fueled by the spark in his eyes.

"Miss Hart," he said, "Forgive my forwardness. I must ask you something but have no wish to cause offense."

"You wish to ask me something?"

He nodded. "I'm not sure if I should ask Sir Dexter, as the head of your family…"

"I'm my own person, Mr. Oake," she said. "My brother doesn't own me."

"Then I'll ask *you*."

Her heart skittered as he moved closer. The scent of wood and smoke thickened in the air, along with another scent—not the expensive colognes that gentlemen adorned themselves with to make themselves appealing to the female sex, but something else—the primal scent of man—of work, toil, and sweat.

Her palms grew slick, and her breath caught. She closed her eyes, recalling the image of him at the water trough—dipping his head into the water, then flicking it back, sending beads of water flying behind him—his hands, those big, brutish hands, wiping his chest, following the contours of the muscles…

He lifted his hand and ran his forefinger along his lip, tracing the outline of his mouth, then he moved his hand toward her.

Driven by raw need, and emboldened by the wine, she took his hand. His eyes widened, and she curled her fingers around his hand and stroked the back of it with his thumb.

"What are you doing, Miss Hart?" he whispered, raising his eyebrows.

"I…" her voice caught in her throat as she gazed into his beautiful eyes.

Their inquiring expression changed into one of surprise, then finally mirth.

"Miss Hart—do you think I want to *seduce* you?"

An uncomfortable heat bloomed in her cheeks. She tried to withdraw her hand, but he held it firm.

"Good grief, woman!" he laughed. "I have enough women eager to spread for me without having to seek one out—and I wouldn't want to rut a woman like you!"

Stunned into silence, she could do nothing but stare back, shame and anger coursing through her.

"I'm looking for someone to teach my daughter how to behave," he said. "I'm not in search of a doxy."

"I'm no doxy!" she snapped.

He let out a laugh—a bellow, which seemed to echo round the garden.

"Then you thought I wanted to *court* you?" He shook his head. "I'm not a man to waste his time in such a pointless activity. I'll never understand women of your class. You interpret a smile as an offer of matrimony, which is not a state I intend to shackle myself to again. I couldn't imagine anything worse!"

She withdrew her hand and, with full force, slapped him across the cheek. Though her palm stung, it made a satisfying crack.

He jerked back, rubbing his cheek.

"How dare you!" she cried. "You're nothing but a crude, uncouth..." She gestured toward him.

He caught her wrist and pulled her hard against him.

"You get the first blow for free, woman," he said, "but be prepared to pay the price if you strike me again."

"What price?"

He crushed his mouth against hers, and her body tightened at the determined, confident gesture of a man who knew how to claim a woman.

Then he slipped his tongue inside her mouth—sweeping through as if he wanted to devour every inch of her. At first, she felt his arrogance, as if he were proving a point, then he slowed the rhythm. Despite his huge frame, his kiss was tender—as if he treasured her.

She clung to him, savoring his domination. Tentatively, she touched his tongue with hers. He rumbled his approval, and she curled her tongue round his as if they were engaging in a slow dance of seduction. A low whimper escaped her lips—a whimper of needs unmet, as if her body understood and yearned for the pleasures she'd been denied all her life.

His hands claimed her body. One hand grasped her hair, tipping her head back as he deepened the kiss, while the other...

Dear Lord! His other hand clasped her derriere. Then he squeezed, and her body fizzed with need.

Muffled laughter came from inside the house, and she broke free. What the devil was she doing, acting like a harlot for a man who saw her as nothing—and had proudly declared as much?

What was she thinking? This man had addled her senses, and she needed to get away. But not inside—to a room full of happy couples.

"Miss Hart..." he began, but she held up her hand.

"No!" she cried. "You've insulted me enough, sir. Leave me be."

"But, I..."

She turned and ran across the terrace toward the stairs leading to the main garden. He might be a brute, but with his big, lumbering gait, he'd never be able to outrun her.

She descended the steps, two at a time.

"Miss Hart!" he cried. "Wait, please. I'm sorry!"

She glanced back and turned her ankle. Her feet lost their purchase, and she tumbled down the steps and landed on her back on the lawn. She tried to move but let out a cry at a sharp pain in her ankle.

She lay back, mortified, wanting the ground to swallow her up.

A tall frame appeared at the top of the steps. "Miss Hart? Are you all right?"

"What the devil does it look like!" she cried. "Go back inside and leave me be. You've done enough damage to my dignity."

She'd made a fool of herself, letting her attraction be known, and he'd rejected her.

And now, she lay at his feet, her hair in a mess, and her skirts around her waist.

Things couldn't get any worse.

"I can't leave you there," he said, crossing his arms, "though you're a delectable enough sight."

How dare he!

Her eyes stung with tears, and she willed him to leave her alone, but he descended the stairs until he stood beside her crumpled, disheveled form. He crouched beside her and offered his hand.

"Forgive me, Miss Hart," he said, his voice unexpectedly gentle. "I've behaved appallingly—my lack of upbringing, I'm afraid. Perhaps now you understand why I'm in need of a gentlewoman to educate my daughter, for I've no wish for her to turn out like her father."

"I'm not taking your hand," she said.

"I'll do nothing untoward, I promise."

"How can I trust you?" she cried. "I'm sure a beast such as yourself prefers your women to—what was it, spread?—for you out of doors."

"At least let me help you up, Miss Hart," he said. "You've injured your ankle and, rest assured, I have no wish to rut you in your brother's garden."

"I should bloody well hope not!" a voice roared. "What the devil do you think you're doing with my sister?"

Dexter stood on the top of the steps, silhouetted against the light from the drawing room.

Dorothea had been wrong. Things *could* get worse—a lot worse.

And they just had.

⤛⤜

THIS WAS BAD. Very bad.

Even Griffin, with his limited understanding of society, knew that it wasn't the done thing to be caught in his host's garden, with the man's sister spread-eagled at his feet, as if they'd just been engaging in a coupling.

"Did you hear me, Oake? I said, what are you doing with my sister!"

A small party gathered beside Sir Dexter.

"Dex?" Griffin recognized Major Hart's voice. "Good Lord—Thea! What are you doing?"

"I'd have thought that was bloody obvious," Sir Dexter growled.

A smaller form joined them.

Shit—that's all Griffin needed—the gentle Lady Hart witnessing Miss Hart's humiliation at his hands.

He shifted position to shield Miss Hart from view. But they'd already seen her. Without waiting for permission, he grasped her hand and pulled her upright. She squealed in pain, lost her footing, and fell against him, and he caught her in his arms.

"Dorothea!" Sir Dexter roared.

Her body trembled, and Griffin's gut twisted with guilt. He'd insulted her, laughed at her, and now—on top of humiliating her in private, he'd publicly compromised her.

"I demand you make reparation, Mr. Oake," Sir Dexter said, his voice dangerously low. Griffin didn't know which was worse—the man's anger or the icy control he displayed now.

"Reparation?"

"You've compromised my sister, Mr. Oake. You must therefore choose."

"Choose?"

"Either meet me at dawn and settle the matter or restore my sister's honor."

"Dexter, there's no need for that," Miss Hart pleaded. "We're among friends—nobody need know what happened tonight."

"Be quiet!" Sir Dexter snapped. "It doesn't matter whether it was just me, a few friends, or the whole of bloody London—you've been caught with your skirts about your waist like a common whore!"

She flinched, and Griffin placed a protective arm around her.

"There's no need to insult your sister, Sir Dexter," Griffin said. "I think..."

"It's plain to see, Mr. Oake, that you struggle with the act of *thinking*," Sir Dexter said coldly. "Do you view women like my sister as easy prey?"

Miss Hart had no need of Griffin to humiliate her. Her brother was doing an excellent job of that on his own.

"I had no designs on your sister," Griffin said, "at least not in the manner you refer to. I wanted to engage her as a companion for my daughter."

"It's true, Dex," Miss Hart said. "He told me..."

"Dorothea, I told *you* not to speak!" Sir Dexter approached the top of the steps and folded his arms. "Mr. Oake, am I to believe that you considered employing my sister as a *servant*? I should shoot you, here and now!"

"Steady on, Dex!" Major Hart interrupted. "I'm sure we can settle this amicably."

"That's for Oake to decide," Sir Dexter said, his voice laced with threat, "and I expect you to be my second, Devon. I'll not have our family name laughed at because of our sister's indiscretions."

"Oh, for heaven's sake!" Major Hart cried. "Is that all you care about—the family name? Thea's not a commodity to be traded in one of your business deals."

"I'm afraid that's exactly what she is now, and she only has herself to blame. If she cannot behave properly, then I must decide what's best for her." Sir Dexter began to descend the steps.

"No!" Miss Hart cried. She freed herself from Griffin's grip and limped up the stairs. Sir Dexter caught her arm.

"Leave me alone!" she cried. "Haven't you insulted me enough? It was an accident—and I wish it had never happened!"

"So do I," Sir Dexter said. "No man wants his sister to behave like a slut the day she turns thirty!"

"Dexter!" Lady Hart cried. "Release Thea, and let me take her inside." Her voice seemed to calm her husband as if he were unable to raise his voice to her, no matter how much he shouted at everyone else.

"Meggie, my love…"

"You may settle your differences with Mr. Oake in any manner you choose," she interrupted, "but this is no place for Thea. She's distressed, and, however deplorably *this man…*" she looked at Griffin, her lip curled into a sneer, "…has behaved, *her* welfare should be utmost in your mind. Let me take her inside."

Sir Dexter released her, and Lady Hart took her hand.

"Come along, Thea, dear," she said. "We'll send the guests away, then make you some hot chocolate."

Miss Hart looked close to tears, but she nodded, took Lady Hart's arm, and let herself be led back inside.

Major Hart joined his brother. A formidable pair they were. A man on his own could only do so much against the world. A faithful friend or loyal brother who had his back gave him invincibility. But Griffin knew, to his cost, that even the best of friends couldn't be trusted. Particularly when there was a woman involved.

"So, Mr. Oake," Sir Dexter said. "I believe the time has come to discuss business."

"Is the garden the proper place to broker a deal?" Griffin asked.

"You should have thought of that before you ruined my sister," Sir Dexter said. "Setting aside the insult regarding your offer of employment, I presume you intended to pay my sister for taking care of your daughter?"

Griffin nodded. "I was—and still am—prepared to pay handsomely."

"Then the commodity you require is still for sale, Mr. Oake. Though I trust you'll not object if we draw up a contract to prevent either party from changing their mind."

"As you wish."

"I believe we have a deal," Sir Dexter said. "It only remains to settle on a price."

"A price?"

"Of course. But, unlike most business deals, I'm afraid the price is nonnegotiable. Rather than paying in coin, I require your hand in marriage."

"My *what*?"

"Come, come," Sir Dexter tutted, "surely even a man of *your* background must understand the consequences of your behavior. My sister's reputation is ruined. And though her prospects for matrimony are severely diminished due to her age, she still—until tonight—had her respectability. The only satisfactory outcome which doesn't end with your lying in Hyde Park with a bullet in your head at dawn is marriage to my sister. I know it—and so does she."

Which, presumably, explained why she'd bolted inside.

"Forgive me, Sir Dexter," Griffin said, "but though you may be able to persuade me to agree to this, I doubt you'd want to place a gun to your sister's head."

"My sister will do what I tell her—she knows her duty. I only seek satisfaction from *you* tonight."

Bloody hell—he'd come here tonight in search of a companion for Rowena and was now under threat of matrimony.

But would it be that bad? Miss Hart was loyal and dependable—and he'd chosen her for Rowe because she was good with children. If she could keep house for him as well, then perhaps the notion of marriage wasn't so unpalatable—particularly as there'd be no need to pay her a wage.

As for *her*—he'd be a damned sight kinder to her than her brother. And she needn't worry about him bothering her in bed, either. Those days were gone, however much he'd relished holding her in his arms.

However soft her lips had been…

Or those little noises she'd made, those mewls of pleasure which had sent a fireball into his groin…

"I'm waiting, Mr. Oake."

Hell—he was standing at the foot of the stairs, having compromised Miss Hart, with her brother threatening a duel and a cockstand straining against his breeches. No wonder they thought him a savage.

He shifted position to hide his erection.

"Sir Dexter," he said, "if you wish it, I'll marry your sister."

"Good," came the reply. "I'll have the marriage contract drafted, then make arrangements to have the banns read."

"Shouldn't you secure a special license?" Major Hart asked. "What if he bolts?"

Shame pricked at Griffin's conscience. He'd hoped to call Major Hart a friend—and the man didn't trust him.

But had he given him any reason to?

"I'll not have Thea's reputation tarnished by the need for haste,"

Sir Dexter said. "We'll do this properly." He turned to Griffin. "Mr. Oake, I'm sure you need to make arrangements in Sussex to receive my sister, in which case, you have my permission to leave town. But if you don't return at the appointed date, I shall hunt you down and tear you apart."

"Understood."

Sir Dexter held out his hand.

"What's this?" Griffin asked. "Brotherly affection?"

"It's a *gentleman's* way of sealing the deal."

Griffin took the proffered hand, then returned inside, flanked on either side by the brothers as if he were under guard.

As courtships went, it wasn't the most romantic. But his first marriage taught him that romance only led to betrayal.

And death.

Chapter Eight

THEA BREATHED A sigh of relief as she entered the breakfast room. Her brother wasn't there.

When she'd woken up, she thought last night had been a dream— a humiliating dream. But as she climbed out of bed, the pain in her ankle was a sharp reminder that everything that happened was real.

To think she'd been foolish enough to believe he'd wanted to court her!

As she'd spent the past thirty years learning—dreams were far from reality.

At least they were for her.

The clock struck seven, and the footman standing by the buffet straightened his stance as she spooned eggs onto her plate. As soon as she took her seat at the center of the table, he approached, brandishing a pot of tea, and poured her a cup. Two-thirds full, to enable her to top it up with cold water.

Just as she liked. Every morning—exactly the same.

"Thank you, Charles."

She reached for the jug of water, then hesitated.

Was she that predictable? Safe, reliable—and every conceivable word that was a synonym for deadly dull?

Well today, she'd be different. Pushing the jug aside, she picked up the sugar bowl, then dropped two spoonfuls into her tea. The footman's eyes widened, but he made no comment. Then she took a sip.

Disgusting! Perhaps she should have tried brandy instead. It would give her courage to face whatever admonishments her brother intended to throw at her. She couldn't disappoint him any more than she had already, so she might as well enjoy herself.

But she needed to clear her head. The cocoa Meggie brought to her chamber last night had the familiar bitter aftertaste of laudanum. Meggie must have laced the drink to calm Thea's nerves—and to ensure she escaped Dex's wrath by virtue of being unconscious.

The door opened to reveal her brother.

The moment she'd dreaded had arrived.

"Good morning, Dexter," she said, keeping her voice even.

He gestured to Charles, who scuttled over with the tea, while he took his place at the head of the table. Then, with a flick of his hand, he dismissed the footman and leveled his blue gaze at Thea.

"It remains to be seen whether it's a good morning, Dorothea."

"What do you mean? Are we expecting rain, perhaps?"

"You know perfectly well what I mean," he said. "After your little spectacle last night, you're ruined. Be thankful I've been able to repair the damage and persuade Mr. Oake to marry you."

Marry her? She tempered the small pulse of longing.

"Why should I be forced to marry just to suit you?"

"Don't you care about your reputation—the impact ruination would have on your life?"

"I fail to see how my life will change," she said. "I'm already an object of ridicule and pity—the dependable spinster aunt, beholden to her family—Dorothea the Dull. A reputation as a fallen woman can't be any worse. At least they'll no longer think me dull. You should be grateful."

"Grateful!" he exclaimed. "I could lose accounts over this! Some of the older families took a great deal of persuasion to bank with me—

families who value respectability."

"And their idea of respect outweighs my wish to be happy? Am I to be the sacrificial lamb on the altar of your profits?"

"Don't be so melodramatic," he said. "It's a sad fact—but a fact nonetheless—that a lady's reputation will impact on her family. I'm thinking of *all* of us—the people I love most in the world, Meggie, the children, you..."

He broke off and looked away. When he spoke again, the undercurrent of emotion had gone, evident only in the slight shake of his hand as he picked up his teacup.

"Mr. Oake isn't what I would have wanted for you, Thea, but he's not a bad man. Your life with him will be little different to the life you lead now."

"Really?"

He smiled, a glimmer of shame in his eyes. "You'll be subject to the whims of one adult, not two," he said, "and you'll be mistress of your own home. Wouldn't you like that? Rather than believe you're a burden?"

Tears stung behind her eyes. "You think me a burden?"

"Of course not," he said, "but I'm not your brother for nothing. The Hart pride may be more prevalent in me, but you have a little of it yourself. If you marry, you'll be free."

"I'll never be free," she said. "Marriage is merely an exchange of ownership."

"Why do you have to be so stubborn?" he asked, his voice rising. "You think you'll get a better offer? At your age?"

"Dexter!" a voice cried.

Meggie stood in the doorway.

Dexter rose to his feet. "Meggie, my love, I was just saying..."

"I heard," Meggie said. "Mr. Oake may be a brute, but he has nothing on you! I suggest you go and take your breakfast elsewhere—your study, perhaps."

"My dear…"

She held her hand up to silence him. "Better still, why not take an early morning stroll before you leave for the bank?" She placed a hand on his arm and spoke more softly. Almost at once, the tension in his body disappeared.

"Remember what we said about the difference between belligerence and tenacity, Dexter, dear?"

Thea couldn't help but smile to herself. Meggie spoke to Dexter as if he were her ten-year-old son, not her husband.

At length, he sighed.

"Forgive me, Dorothea," he said. "It takes my wife to point out my poor behavior. I'll leave you in her care, where you'll be better looked after than by your bad-tempered old brother."

"I thought *I* was the old one," Thea said.

"I'm just bad-tempered then," he replied, his mouth curling into a smile.

"I'll not challenge you for *that* label, brother."

He nodded, then dropped a kiss on Meggie's cheek and exited the room. Meggie helped herself to eggs, then, defying tradition, ignored the place setting at her end of the table and took the seat opposite Thea.

"How are you this morning?"

"My head's clear if that's your concern," Thea replied.

Meggie blushed. "I did what I thought was best. You weren't in a fit state to do anything other than sleep."

"I'm sure Dexter had a lot to say last night."

"He said very little," Meggie replied. "In fact, he spent a good deal of the evening *listening*."

She gave Thea a sidelong glance, then ate a forkful of eggs.

"You astonish me, Meggie," Thea said. "How you've managed to control Dexter, I cannot imagine."

A slow smile curled on Meggie's face. "Love does that to a man."

"I struggle to believe Dexter capable of such an emotion."

"He expresses it differently depending on the person," Meggie said. "For example, where *you're* concerned, he does it by insisting Mr. Oake does right by you."

Perhaps it was best that Thea had dropped half the sugarbowl in her tea. The sweet taste offset the bitterness of her shame. Last night, she'd behaved like a lovesick adolescent.

"Do you like him?" Meggie asked.

"Dexter?"

Meggie laughed. "You know full well who I mean. Mr. Oake."

Thea sighed. "There's no denying that I find him—attractive. But that's no reason to marry the man."

"Ah," Meggie said. "Is the head of Sensible Dorothea warring with the heart of Passionate Thea?"

"Perhaps."

"Dexter thinks highly of him," Meggie said. Then she grinned. "Well, he did, until he caught him last night! Mr. Oake took little persuasion to do the right thing by you—I think he likes you also."

"That's not what he said last night," Thea said, shame warming her cheeks at the memory of his laughter.

"Pshah!" Meggie snorted. "Take no notice of what a man *says*. Instead, look at what he *does*."

"Mr. Oake has done nothing."

"That's not what you said last night." Meggie sipped her tea. "Of course, the laudanum affected your lucidity, but you said something about a kiss?"

She leaned forward. "A kiss which transported you to a world you had never experienced?"

Thea felt her cheeks flaming. The addictive dangers of laudanum were well known—but nobody had warned her that the drug would loosen her tongue and reveal her innermost feelings.

"I don't know what came over me," she said, "when he—when he kissed me. It was…" she hesitated, then lowered her voice to a whisper, "…it was *wonderful.*"

"Then you *do* like him!" Meggie said.

"He was kind to Devon," Thea said. "Few men can look at Dev in the face, on a second, or even a third meeting."

"If you are to yield your freedom to a husband," Meggie said, "who better than a man who's already proven himself to be beyond the vanities of society—as well as being an excellent kisser? But, if you don't want to marry him, you shouldn't be forced."

"But Dexter insists…"

"Dexter wants you to understand the consequences of refusing Mr. Oake," Meggie said. "I want you to understand the consequences of accepting him if you are to make an informed decision."

"And if it were you?" Thea asked.

"Dexter and I met for the first time on the day of our wedding," Meggie said, "and neither of us wanted the match. Love can find a home in the most unlikely of places. And, unlike me, you wouldn't be relinquishing all your independence."

"I don't understand."

"Dexter's love often manifests itself in decisions involving money. He employed his negotiation skills to great effect last night with the marriage contract."

"Dex made it abundantly clear last night that he viewed me as a commodity," Thea said.

"You know that's not true," Meggie replied, "but you must admit that where it comes to the distasteful act of negotiating the terms of a marriage contract, an older brother with a reputation for ferocity has its advantages. Mr. Oake has agreed to relinquishing control over half your dowry."

"I didn't realize that was negotiable."

"Everything's negotiable when *both* parties are eager for the transaction to proceed."

Footsteps approached outside, and Meggie clicked her tongue in annoyance.

"I told Dexter to leave us in peace!" She rose and approached the window, then her frown morphed into a smile.

"The man himself! Come and see."

Mr. Oake stood on the pavement, staring at the house.

"Why doesn't he come in?" Thea whispered.

"He's summoning courage," Meggie said. "Maybe he thinks Dexter awaits him with a sword. But I can see he comes a-courting, so his head is safe."

He was dressed in an elegant suit, the deep green jacket accentuating the color of his eyes. His hair shone in the sunlight, with golden highlights, as if he glowed from within. In his hands, he held a posy of flowers, the delicate blooms only serving to emphasize his huge hands.

He was like a bear—a giant bear.

A very *male* bear.

The posy was a mixture of flowers and grasses. Not the elegant blooms to be found in hothouses—they'd been snatched from the park or hedgerow—or perhaps even stolen from a nearby garden. Thea could swear she spotted one of Lady Stainton's roses—their distinctive yellow color was not to be found everywhere in London.

He smoothed the blooms, then lifted the posy to his face as if to check their scent. A smile crept across his lips, and he nodded as if in approval. The care with which he tended to them made her heart twitch with hope. Was he capable of tenderness? Perhaps, even love?

The memory of his kiss—and her body's instinctive but scandalous reaction—warmed her blood. The sharp tingling sensation in her breasts had been an unexpected—shameful, yet pleasurable sensation. As she watched him, that sensation fizzled deep inside her body, just out of reach.

He's magnificent...

"You like what you see?" Meggie whispered.

Sweet Lord! Had she just said that out loud?

He disappeared from view, and a few minutes later, the footman entered the breakfast room, brandishing a card.

"Mr. Oake for Miss Hart," he said. "I took the liberty of placing him in the morning room."

"Then I'll leave you," Meggie said.

Thea caught her hand. "Don't go—I'll need a chaperone."

Meggie laughed. "My dear sister, I doubt the meeting he seeks is one where a chaperone is needed."

"But…"

"If you cannot attend him alone, Thea, he's not the man for you."

Meggie was right, as usual. Thea needed to face him and conquer the attraction which rendered her body weak in his presence.

But, deep inside, a wicked thrill coursed through her at the prospect of seeing him again.

Her body and her heart yearned for him. Now, she only needed to persuade her head.

⸎⸎⸎

THE DOOR OPENED, and Miss Hart entered. She focused her gaze on Griffin with a boldness that belied her trembling frame.

He rose to his feet and bowed.

He found himself nervous—as if he were a young buck courting a girl under the watchful eye of her disapproving parents.

In essence, that's exactly what he was doing. Her brother had made it abundantly clear that he'd slice Griffin's balls off and serve them to Lady Hart's pug if Griffin did anything to upset his sister.

So the bastard had a heart, though he hid it well.

She sat beside the window, then gestured to a chair at the opposite end of the room.

"Please sit, Mr. Oake."

He held out the flowers, and she arched a dark brow and stared at them.

Was this another faux pas? A lady was supposed to appreciate flowers from a suitor. At least, that's what Major Hart had whispered to Griffin last night.

Perhaps they weren't to her taste. They were, after all, the spoils of theft—mostly from a nearby park, but the prettiest blooms had been procured from a neighboring garden, snatched on impulse as he'd approached the Harts' townhouse, an act which had earned him two scratches to his palm. Perhaps Mother Nature recognized the need to protect roses with thorns. Much as Miss Hart was protected by her brother.

He glanced at the blooms—the uneven stems, crushed under his ungainly hands, petals ragged and browning at the edges.

Maybe Miss Hart would prefer something from a hothouse, wrapped up in a ribbon. Something which confirmed to…what was the word?

Aesthetics.

He glanced across the room.

She was still trembling! The poor woman most likely envisaged a life living in the dirt, in some hovel. In that respect, at least, he could allay her concerns.

"You must know why I'm here," he said, his apprehension rendering his voice overly rough.

She narrowed her eyes, then nodded.

"My offer still stands," he continued. "I want someone to turn my daughter into a lady, and while I hadn't intended to marry again, a wife is better suited to that role than a governess."

She cocked her head to one side but said nothing.

"I won't require you to live with me," he blurted. "I understand if you find the prospect distasteful."

Her eyes widened, and she set her mouth into a firm line. Had he unwittingly insulted her? Again?

"Of course, I'd require you to be near in order for you to instruct the child, but I can find you a home nearby."

She continued to stare at him, her expression unreadable. Was he making progress? The least she could do was give him an indication before he made a complete donkey of himself.

"Miss Hart?" he prompted.

She shook her head. "No."

"You're rejecting my offer?"

"As it stands, yes," she said. "If I must proceed with this marriage, then I wish to live as a wife in your home, and not..." she bit her lip, then continued, "...and not as a spinster aunt tucked away out of sight."

"Then when we marry..." he began, but she lifted her hand to silence him.

"I haven't agreed yet," she said. "I take it that your sole reason, other than my brother's threats, is the need to turn your daughter into a lady. How old is she?"

"Fourteen."

"And she needs a little polish? Tuition on how to behave in society?"

"In truth, she needs a damned sight more than that," he said. "I don't know what to do with her. Her governess says she's too wild to handle. I thought about sending her away to school, but what if that makes her worse? What if it's too late? She needs instruction, discipline. But most of all, she needs..."

He broke off, fingering the posy of flowers, then flinched when a thorn pricked his thumb.

She needed a mother.

His little Rowe needed the love that only a mother could give—a love she'd been denied her whole life. The once bright, vibrant little girl had turned into a resentful young woman. Acts of kindness she exploited and acts of discipline she rebelled against. But worse of all, she loathed him—and he didn't know what to do about it. She needed someone to love her—but she had nobody to love.

"Mr. Oake? Is something wrong?"

He blinked, and moisture stung his eyes. Then he looked down and saw that he was crushing the bouquet with his hands.

His huge, uncouth, dirty hands.

"What chance does my daughter have in life," he whispered, "with *me* as her father?"

WERE THERE TEARS in his eyes?

Mr. Oake clutched the posy, the delicate stems crushing in his hands. Cracked and calloused, they were not the hands of a gentleman. Thea rose to her feet, and he followed suit. Then she crossed the floor and sat next to him.

"Are those flowers for me?" she asked. "I can put them in a vase."

He shrugged his shoulders. "They're not much."

"Nevertheless, if you picked them for me, I'd like to have them. Or do you forget what I said last night?"

"I remember *everything* you said last night."

Her cheeks warmed. "I meant what I'd said about the garden— that I prefer natural beauty to artifice." She nodded toward the bouquet. "They're very pretty—and I never thought Lady Stainton appreciated her roses enough to deserve them."

Now it was his turn to blush.

She placed her hand over his, running her fingertips over the calloused knuckles, reddened skin, and cracked fingernails. "Are your hands not terribly sore?"

"I've never considered it."

"I have a liniment which would ease the discomfort," she said.

"My sister-in-law gave it to me."

"Lady Hart?"

"No—my brother Devon's wife, Lady Atalanta. She made it up for my hands. It's particularly useful in the winter when my hands get overly dry, especially on laundry day."

"Laundry day?" he asked. "Does your brother make you do the housework?"

"I *choose* to do it, Mr. Oake."

"I'd have thought you'd..." he trailed off and averted his gaze.

"You thought I'd spend my time ordering others about while not lifting a finger?"

"Isn't that what housekeepers do?"

She let out a laugh. "You know nothing about running a home if that's what you think. I'll have much to teach *you*, as well as your daughter—if I accept your proposal."

He placed his hand over hers and brushed his thumb against the back of her skin. A gentle, delicate gesture, but her skin tightened in response. She met his gaze, and a secret thrill pulsed within her as his eyes darkened with the same need she'd seen last night, just before he'd kissed her.

Would he kiss her on their wedding night? Before he made her his? She closed her eyes, recalling the dreams she'd had—dreams where he'd taken her in his arms, and they'd cried together in ecstasy...

Then he withdrew his hand and stood.

"You needn't fear that I'll force myself onto you, Miss Hart," he said. "I'm not looking for love. I will, of course, abide by my vows as I expect you to abide by yours, but as to the more—intimate—matters associated with marriage, I promise I'll leave you be."

"Then, you won't..." Thea's voice trailed off as a flame of embarrassment engulfed her.

"No."

"But don't you..." she hesitated, "...I mean, you're a man, and..."

She gestured toward him, unwilling to say the words.

"A man has needs," he said, "but those needs can be curtailed."

"What of a woman's needs?" she asked, making her voice bolder than she felt.

His expression hardened. "Do you have a lover, Miss Hart?"

"Of course not!" she exclaimed.

"Good. Then we can add a vow of celibacy."

"Why not enter the priesthood?" she snapped.

"I'd make a poor priest."

"You could always confess your sins and give yourself absolution."

"What of *your* sins, Miss Hart?"

She looked away. Did he know she lusted after him? She'd felt nothing but lust from the moment she'd seen him, striding across that courtyard—shirtless, muscles rippling as he flexed his arms to demonstrate his raw, male power…

Lust was a sin. And she was sinning this very moment—imagining all the things he could do to her with his body.

His hard, very *male*, body.

"Perhaps it's best if neither of us mention our sins again," she said.

"I agree," he replied. "We're both of an age where we understand that the first flush of love is an illusion. It would be best if neither of us asks about the other's…sins."

He handed her the bouquet. "If you're prepared to accept me on those terms, I'll do everything I can to ensure you have no cause to regret your decision."

Hardly the most romantic of proposals. But what could she expect?

"Then, I accept," she said.

He lifted her hand to his lips, then dropped it almost instantly. Hiding her hurt, she moved her hand behind her back.

"Once I've finalized the details of the marriage contract with your brother, I must return to Sussex," he said. "I trust you'll forgive me for not calling again. I see no need for a public courtship."

"You don't?"

"The matter's settled, isn't it? And I must make sure your new home is ready for when you take up your position."

Her position?

Did he view her as a servant?

"I'll return for the wedding," he said. Then he bowed and took his leave as if he couldn't wait to be free of her.

Almost as soon as he'd gone, Meggie appeared at the top of the stairs. She descended, then took Thea's hands.

"Am I to congratulate you?"

"We're betrothed, if that's what you mean," Thea said.

Meggie drew Thea into her arms and kissed her. "He'll make you very happy. I *know* it."

"He doesn't want me."

"Of course he does!" Meggie exclaimed. "Dexter told me he needed little persuasion."

"No, I mean, he doesn't *want* me. He made it clear he's not marrying for love."

"There's still hope," Meggie said. "Love takes time. When your brother and I married, we didn't even know each other. But we worked together to overcome the difficulties of our situation, and love blossomed."

"Do you think I can find love in a marriage where my prospective husband has declared he'll never love me?"

Meggie smiled. "Love will come when it's least expected. Trust me—in a few months, you'll look back on today and wonder at your pessimism."

Perhaps Meggie was right, but a voice inside Thea's mind whispered that she was about to take the first step on the path to heartbreak.

Chapter Nine

THE WEDDING BANQUET was a subdued affair—if "banquet" was the word for half a dozen guests, but Griffin's new bride had insisted on a quiet event.

He led her toward a footman brandishing a tray of glasses.

"Champagne?"

She shook her head. "No, thank you."

She'd spoken the vows in the same monotone, as if reciting a laundry list. Had marriage turned her into a soulless statue? Perhaps he should put it to the test.

"Good," he said. "There's nothing worse than having a drunkard for a wife."

He caught the sharp intake of breath and immediately regretted his words.

"Forgive me," he whispered. "I'm finding today somewhat trying."

"And I'm not?"

"I'm sorry," he said, "I only meant—I'm unused to being the center of attention."

"What about when you're beating an opponent to a pulp in a tavern courtyard?"

Ah—the passionate spirit was there—though she concealed it well.

"I'm afraid, my dear, that I'm in my element in a dirty courtyard." He squeezed her hand. "Perhaps now, you understand why this marriage is very much to my advantage."

She gave him a quick, tight smile, then her gaze wandered over the rest of the room. Her smile broadened, and she withdrew her hand and crossed the floor toward Lady Hart, who stood next to Major Hart and Sir Dexter.

Four Harts together—a family to be reckoned with.

They would be Griffin's staunchest allies, provided he treated his wife properly.

If not, they'd be formidable foes.

He joined his wife as she embraced her younger brother.

"I believe I'll miss *you* the most, Devon," she said.

"Because you love me the best?"

"Good Lord, no!" She laughed. "I know Meggie will write, but you're such a poor correspondent, I'll hear little of you after I'm gone."

After I'm gone.

She made it sound like she was about to die. Was marriage to him so distasteful?

He placed a hand on her shoulder, meant to be reassuring. "You may visit your family as often as you please, Dorothea."

Her name felt unusual on his tongue, and it was only the second time he'd uttered it—the first being when he'd recited the vows not half an hour earlier.

"I'll write, Thea," Major Hart said.

"You mean Atalanta will," she said. "And Sebastian, of course."

A spike of jealousy needled at Griffin.

"Who the devil's Sebastian?" he asked.

"My three-year-old son," Major Hart said, casting a sidelong glance at him. "Thea's his favorite person in the whole world."

"I'm not," she said, blushing.

"You give yourself too little credit, Thea." The major turned to Griffin. "Did you know that, save for Meggie's Billy, Thea has brought every one of her nieces and nephews into the world, including my little Francine, last week?"

"Is that true?" Griffin asked.

"She so good with children, aren't you, Thea?" Hart continued, "you could almost be mistaken for their mama."

Griffin felt her stiffen against him, and he took her hand.

"Perhaps we should have a word with the parson before we leave, my dear."

He led her across the room. Though she avoided his gaze, he caught a glimpse of tears.

"Did you really bring all those children into the world?" he asked.

She nodded. "In most cases, I gave assistance, but little Francine arrived early, so I had to deliver her myself."

A note of pride laced her voice, which replaced the earlier sorrow.

"And her mother?"

"Atalanta? She's doing well. She nurses the baby herself..." She colored and turned her head away. "Forgive me, it's not something I should speak of."

Did he detect a deep longing in her voice?

He took her hand. Her fingers were delicate against his, and he felt like a great, uncouth oaf beside her.

"Why didn't you bring your daughter today?" she asked.

"Rowena?" he asked. "Did you *want* her here?"

"She gained a mother today."

"I suppose she did," he said.

"Are you ashamed of her? Or..." her breath caught, "...of me?"

"Forgive me," he said. "I hadn't considered it."

"Why not?" she asked. "Is it because I'm not really her mother? Did her mother..."

"Don't speak of her mother!" he snapped. The murmur of the guests stopped, and he strode across the floor to Sir Dexter.

"It's time we left," he said. "I wish to reach Sussex before dark, and

I'm sure you wouldn't want your sister to travel when it's unsafe."

"She has you to protect her," Sir Dexter said, his voice dangerously quiet. "At least, I trust she does."

Griffin shook hands with the vicar, then the party exited the house and approached the waiting carriage.

Lady Hart embraced Griffin's wife.

"Look after yourself, darling Thea," she said. She glanced at Griffin. "Write to me as soon as you've settled. I'll be anxious to know you're being taken good care of."

Sir Dexter took Griffin's hand and tightened his grip. Griffin smiled inwardly at the man's attempt to assert his dominance. He could crush the man's hand with a single squeeze, but out of respect, he merely nodded. Sir Dexter had other means of crushing his adversaries.

He ushered his bride into the carriage, and they set off. She leaned out of the window until the townhouse was out of sight. Then she settled back into her seat and stared straight ahead.

"We should reach Sandiford before nightfall," he said.

"Will your daughter be waiting for us?" she asked. "Rowena, isn't it?"

"Yes."

"Does she favor you?" she asked, her voice betraying her unease. "Or, perhaps her mother?"

"I thought I'd said her mother is not a subject I wish to discuss."

"But we're alone now."

"Nevertheless, I forbid it," he said. "You made a promise to obey me, and my order was not to speak of my late wife."

Her eyes flashed. "Your *order*?"

"My apologies—I meant my request."

"I'm not your employee."

"No," he replied, "you're my wife."

"I'd rather be your employee," she said.

"What on earth for?"

She crossed her arms, like a schoolteacher attempting to explain a simple principle to a particularly aggrieving child.

He squirmed in his seat. Why did she always make him feel guilty and bad-mannered?

"An employee has rights," she said. "He's paid a wage, and the duties he must perform are set out clearly before him. Should he find his position dissatisfying, he's at liberty to seek another position without approbation. In fact, he's often lauded for trying to better himself. As for a wife…"

She fixed him with her stare, and he found himself blushing.

"A wife has no rights," she said. "She has no wage nor is she permitted to seek respite should her position become untenable. On the rare occasion that she frees herself from her position, she's vilified for failing to commit to the sacred vows she uttered. In short—a wife is akin to an indentured servant—though in my case, I'm being transported to Sussex, rather than the Americas."

He stared at her. In their entire acquaintance, which consisted of two parties, one brief interview, and the wedding ceremony, she'd not spoken more than the occasional sentence. From where had that impassioned speech come?

He'd thought Rowena a handful, but it seemed that his wife was a worse hellion than his daughter. "What the devil have I gotten myself into?"

She blinked at him.

"Forgive me," he said. "I'm unused to polite society. I forget to guard my speech."

"I see no problem in being frank," she replied.

"It's just that Rowena is a handful—I'm afraid she's inherited her mother's temper."

"That's hardly fair if *you* can speak of my predecessor, yet I'm forbidden," she said. "I'd like to think that our marriage—which is more of a business contract than a true match—is a union of equals."

"Equals?"

"Yes, equals," she replied. "For example, you have access to half my dowry, but the rest is mine to spend as I choose."

"You saw the contract?" He couldn't hide his astonishment, and her lip curled into a smile.

"I'm entitled to, Mr. Oake," she said, "given that I'm the goods being transferred."

He took her hand. "Might you address me by my name?" he asked. "Mr. Oake seems overly formal given our new status."

"Very well—Griffin."

His name sounded good on her lips.

Too good. What might it sound like if she moaned it in ecstasy, while she spread for him?

But that wasn't why he'd married her—he had no wish to tread that path again.

He reached beneath his seat and pulled out a blanket. "Here, get some rest."

She took it, wordlessly, and covered herself as if she wished to shield herself from him as well as the cold. Then she closed her eyes, and before long, her body relaxed. She had fallen asleep.

Hardly the best start to the rest of his life.

Chapter Ten

THEA JOLTED AWAKE as a hand touched her shoulder, dissipating the delicious dream of being claimed by Griffin.

Where was she?

She didn't recognize her surroundings, and a wave of panic rippled through her.

"Dorothea?"

Deep, and rumbling, it was the voice from her dreams.

The voice of the man who was now her husband.

"Forgive me for waking you," he said. "We've arrived."

"Already?"

He smiled. "You slept almost the entire journey." He opened the carriage door, then hesitated. "I'm sorry—do you go out first, or do I?"

"*You're* supposed to," she said. "Then if I trip, you can break my fall—and it spares the indignity of you seeing me climb out from behind."

"That's a pity."

Her cheeks flamed as his gaze wandered up and down her body.

Then he climbed through the door, took her hand, and helped her out.

"Welcome to your home."

A lawn stretched before her, flanked by trees and bisected by a path that led to a large, red-bricked manor house.

"Sandiford Manor," he said, pride in his tone. "It was built during the reign of Henry the Eighth, in recognition of the military services of Henry Sharke, the first Lord Gillingham."

"He's not *your* ancestor, is he?" she exclaimed, then flushed and lowered her gaze. "Forgive me, I meant no offense."

He let out a laugh. "I've heard far worse from the current Lord Gillingham. His father lost most of his fortune speculating in the South Seas, and he lost the rest five years ago as a result of gambling antes—one of which was staked on a fight I won. He backed the loser and sold Sandiford Manor to clear his debts."

"To you?"

He nodded. "Lord and Lady Gillingham live on the outskirts of the village."

"I rather wonder at their remaining here after losing their home," she said. "I don't think *I* could."

He let out a laugh. "I paid handsomely for Sandiford Manor, but once Gillingham's debts were cleared, they had little left. They enjoy a life of consequence in Sandiford at little expense compared to London."

"Will we be receiving them?" she asked.

"I bloody well hope not," he said, and she flinched at his profanity. "They have their own circle of admirers and sycophants—and are never seen at the White Hart, where I spend most of my time. You'll see them at church, and that's it. Unless you wish to be received by the only titled family in the village?"

"I'd rather not," she said.

"Mr. Oake, sir!" a voice cried out in a soft country accent, and a young man appeared from the side of the building, dressed in plain trousers with a rough linen shirt.

He bowed to Thea. "Welcome home, Mr. Oake—Mrs. Oake."

Griffin looked about him. "Where is she, Will?"

"Mrs. Ellis can't find her."

"Very well," he sighed. "I'll hunt her down."

"Ned's waiting for you at the White Hart, sir."

"I'll go there directly, Griffin said. "I'm sorry, Dorothea. I'd told my daughter to make sure she was here to greet us—insufferable child!"

He led her along the path until they reached the line of trees, where he stopped.

"Rowe?"

Thea looked about her, but there was no sign of anyone. Then she looked up.

A pair of legs dangled from the nearest tree.

"Rowena Oake!" he growled.

A face appeared, like a wild wood nymph—unkempt dark hair with eyes to match.

The tree shook, then the nymph landed on the gravel path.

It was a young girl, dressed in a white muslin gown, streaked with what looked like grass stains. Her hair was a cascade of messy curls which tumbled over her shoulders. She was a beauty—but she either didn't know how pretty she was, or she was doing everything in her power to hide it. A smear of mud adorned her face, and her eyes flashed with defiance.

"Why weren't you here to greet us?" Griffin demanded.

"I'm here now, aren't I?" the girl said, her voice sulky.

"You know what I mean, Rowena. I expected you to greet your new mother like a lady, not like some urchin halfway up a tree!"

"Devil take you!" the girl cried. He stiffened and fisted his hands. "I should thrash you for that, you insufferable…"

"Leave her be," Thea said.

"What's it to you?" the girl sneered.

He stepped forward, his body vibrating with anger. "Damn it, Rowena, I've got a good mind…"

Thea placed a hand on his arm. Fear replaced the defiance in the girl's eyes as she shrank back.

"Why don't you go and see the man who's waiting for you—Ned, is it?" Thea suggested. "I'll take care of things here."

"Are you certain?"

"It's why you married me, isn't it? I might as well start now."

"Very well," he said. "I'll be back before supper. Will, take care of the mistress."

"Of course, sir."

As if relieved to rid himself of both his wife and his daughter, he turned and set off for the village.

"If you'll follow me, ma'am, I'll show you the house," Will said.

"Very well, lead the way," Thea replied. She offered her arm to the girl. "Rowena, will you accompany me?"

"You're not my mama," the girl replied, "and you never will be."

Ignoring the stab of hurt, Thea smiled. "That's a relief," she said. "I've no wish to mother a wildcat."

She turned toward the house. Shortly after, footsteps followed as the girl kept pace with her.

"Why did you marry Papa?" she asked. "Was it for his money? He's very rich."

"No, it wasn't," Thea said. "I have money of my own. Your papa wanted a wife to teach you how to be a lady."

"Why did he choose *you*?" the girl asked. "There's a long list of women—younger and prettier—that he could have chosen."

The insult hit her. "Perhaps I was the first one of that long list willing to face the challenge," Thea said, "and I can now see the enormity of it."

The girl's eyes narrowed with hurt. She might be insufferably uncivil, but that was no excuse for Thea to behave in the same manner.

As they reached the main doors, she spoke again. "Will you punish me if I don't do what you say?" Her voice had lost some of its confidence, and Thea detected a note of fear.

"It's not my place," Thea said.

"But Mrs. Ellis said…" the girl began, then she broke off.

A steady tap-tapping echoed from inside the house, and a woman appeared. With her black gown, thin frame, and sharp-nosed features, she reminded Thea of a corpse. One bony hand curled around the top of a cane.

"Mrs. Oake, I presume," she said. "Where's Mr. Oake?"

Thea ignored the demand. "Who are you?" she asked.

"I'm Mrs. Ellis—Rowena's governess and housekeeper."

The woman thought too much of herself if she believed she filled both roles—and Thea's husband had no idea how a home should be run.

"It looks as if I have much to do here," Thea said.

"You do," Mrs. Ellis agreed. "I'm glad that, at last, I'll have assistance in controlling the child."

Who the devil did this woman think she was?

"You'll be the one assisting *me*, Mrs. Ellis," Thea said sharply.

"Naturally," Mrs. Ellis said. "But Rowena's a badly behaved child at the best of times. She has much to learn about respect."

Defiance shone in the girl's eyes, but Thea spotted the bravado for what it was.

"May I return to the garden, Mrs. Oake?" she asked.

"If you wish," Thea said, "though there's no need to address me as Mrs. Oake."

"I won't call you 'mama,' if that's what you're wanting."

"Very well," Thea said. "Mrs. Oake, it is then."

The girl skipped off and disappeared round the side of the house.

"Come inside," Mrs. Ellis said. "There's tea waiting in the parlor, then I'll show you around."

Thea followed her into a parlor on the ground floor. Griffin's obvious wish to leave her the moment they'd arrived had cut her deeper than she cared to admit. A pot of tea might not compensate for a husband who'd declared he wouldn't love her, but it was better than nothing.

"That child will take advantage unless you're firm from the outset," Mrs. Ellis said, pouring a cup. "It's harder to discipline her if she believes she can continue unpunished."

"Unpunished?" Thea asked.

"I'm a firm advocate of the saying that if you spare the rod, you spoil the child."

Thea glanced at Mrs. Ellis's cane. "I trust you're speaking metaphorically."

Mrs. Ellis dipped a spoon into the sugar bowl. She lifted it to her nose and sniffed.

"Salt," she said. "Devil child! That's the second time this week. You see what wickedness I have to endure?"

"Just silly mischief, surely?" Thea suggested.

"That's not all she does," Mrs. Ellis said. "She smeared honey on the handle of my cane last month, and she knows I cannot bear to have sticky hands. And just last week, she…"

Thea looked out of the window, her attention wandering while the woman droned on. If Mrs. Ellis knew half the tricks Thea's nephews played, she'd have a fit. Last week, young Billy had managed to catch a grass snake and placed it in the flour. The cook's screams could be heard halfway across London.

A face appeared at the window.

Rowena. The girl pressed her nose against the glass and lowered her face until her nose was splayed out like a pig's snout. Then she poked her tongue out and crossed her eyes.

Thea lifted her teacup to hide her smile. The girl frowned, then stepped back and raised her skirts, displaying her petticoats. A mouthful of tea caught in Thea's throat, sending her into a fit of coughing.

"Mrs. Oake? What's the matter?"

Thea shook her head and waved away Mrs. Ellis's offer of assistance. By the time the coughing had subsided, Rowena had disappeared.

Mrs. Ellis stood. "Shall I show you round the house?"

Thea shook her head. She'd already had enough of the woman's company.

"No, I'm a little tired," she said. "When will supper be ready? Do I need to speak to the cook?"

"Mrs. Morris will serve it at eight like she always does."

"Mrs. Morris?"

"The cook."

"The *cook* serves supper?" Thea asked.

Dear Lord—what sort of house was Mrs. Ellis running, where she undertook the role of both governess and housekeeper—and the cook served the meals?

Even if she couldn't tame her stepdaughter or make her husband love her—she could turn Sandiford Manor into a well-run household.

Chapter Eleven

"HOW DO YOU find your new home?" Griffin asked.

His wife looked up from attempting to cut her steak.

"Very pleasant, thank you."

Pleasant. Ugh. Since he'd returned to the house that evening, she'd presented him with the dull, staid persona of the spinster aunt.

Where had the passion gone? During the ride to Sandiford, he'd watched her while she slept. She'd changed into her traveling clothes during a brief stop at her brother's townhouse before they continued on to Sussex. The plain gray gown had not quite concealed her form, but she'd covered herself with a shawl as if the thought of him seeing her body disgusted her.

But as she slept, the shawl had slipped from her shoulders to reveal her form.

Her very delectable form.

What might she look like spread before him?

Shortly before they'd arrived, she'd let out a soft moan. There was no doubt she'd been dreaming of a lover, the way the skin at the swell of her breasts turned a delicate shade of pink. He could swear he'd spotted two little peaks poking at the material just below her neckline, and his mouth watered at the prospect of suckling them.

Then she murmured a name.

"Hercules…"

Who the bloody hell was Hercules? Her lover?

He'd shaken her awake, his touch roughened by jealousy, and a glimmer of shame crossed her expression before she'd smoothed it away.

She resumed her attention on her steak, attempting to slice her knife through it. But Griffin had learned over the years that Mrs. Morris's steaks were tough enough to defend themselves against most items of cutlery.

"I trust Sandiford Manor isn't too—rustic—for your tastes," he said.

She slipped, and her knife clattered to the floor.

Rowe gave a snort of laughter. He shot her a warning look, but she pulled a face, then resumed her attention on the plate in front of her.

Dorothea held up her steak, impaled on her fork—which was now bent at the head—then she dropped it on the plate.

"The building itself is to my taste," she said. "As to everything else, I'll keep my opinions to myself for fear of giving offense."

Rowena pushed her plate away. "May I be excused?" she asked. "I'm not hungry."

"No," he said.

"But I'm tired!"

"Rowena, you must show more respect to your…"

"Let her go!" Dorothea snapped.

He opened his mouth to chastise his wife, then caught the distress in her eyes. It wouldn't do for Rowena to observe them arguing—and Dorothea had endured enough for today.

"Very well," he said. "But go straight to your chamber, Rowena. No more antics, or you'll be sorry."

She drew back her chair and exited the room. His wife sat, staring straight ahead.

"Mrs. Morris makes a good apple pie," he said. "Perhaps that'll be more to your taste."

She remained still, almost as if she'd not heard him, then she sighed. "There's much we need to discuss about the house."

"So, it's *not* to your taste?"

"Not in terms of how it's run."

"I don't understand."

"I can see that," she said. "For one thing, Mrs. Ellis shouldn't occupy both positions of housekeeper and governess. And the cook shouldn't serve supper."

"Why not?"

"Because it's not done!"

"Why? Because it's frowned upon by society?"

"The society into which you want your daughter to be accepted," she said. "Her education is not purely through instruction or discipline, but it also comes from the environment in which she's raised. I take it that not only do you wish for her to learn the manners of a lady, but you wish for her to be comfortable in a lady's environment?"

He couldn't argue with that, but did she have to explain it in such a condescending manner?

But then, he'd not shown her much civility or acted the gentleman himself.

"Clearly defined roles exist to enable perfection," she continued. "I rather wonder at Mrs. Ellis's skills in either of her roles. As for Mrs. Morris…" She nodded to her discarded steak as if to prove a point. "If she confines her role to the kitchen, she can perfect her skills there. Has it never occurred to you that, while she's serving the steak, her apple pie might be burning?"

"And you have the answer?"

"Of course," she said. "I'll need to inspect the ledgers and interview the rest of the staff to understand where need exceeds capacity, but this house is the same as my brother's townhouse, except that it's larger and therefore needs a larger staff."

"Do you intend to waste my money on staff we don't need?" he asked.

She tipped her head up, a determined set to her jaw.

"*Your* money?"

"Yes," he said. "I'm head of this family and should have the final say in how the money is spent."

"You couldn't wait to be parted from me the moment you arrived here," she said. "Why should I defer to you?"

"Because you're my *wife!*"

She flinched at his outburst, then sat back and nodded. "Forgive me for forgetting that our marriage is just another of my brother's business arrangements where I'm merely the goods."

Frustration laced her tone and something else.

Thwarted ambition.

"Dorothea..." he began, but she interrupted him.

"I'm tired," she said.

"Then I suggest you retire."

She opened her mouth to respond, then closed it again, nodded, and stood, scraping her chair back. She smoothed down the front of her dress, then exited the dining room, almost colliding with Mrs. Morris in the doorway.

The cook bobbed a curtsey, deposited the apple pie on the table, then cleared the plates.

At least he had the pie to himself, which he knew, from experience, he'd be able to eat without breaking his teeth.

Unlike that damned steak.

THEA DISMISSED HER maid and looked about the bedchamber. The burning fire couldn't disguise the tell-tale smell of mold.

At least the room was warm, and the bed a good size.

She flushed as her train of thought led her to the image of two naked bodies locked in passion beneath the covers.

Or might he take her on the floor? The hearth rug was large enough for two. Meggie had once let slip that Dexter had, on impulse, spent half the night loving her on the bearskin rug beside the fireplace and, despite complaining about friction burns on his knees, he'd enjoyed it enough to indulge in the activity several times since.

She tugged at the laces on her nightrail. Would her husband prefer her naked when he visited her? Or would he wish to undress her himself?

She approached the bed, drew back the covers, and gave a start.

A huge, brown toad sat in the center of the bed, staring balefully at her. She folded her arms and stared back, and the toad crawled backward.

The poor creature was more afraid of her than she of it.

She scooped it into her hands.

"Good evening, little fellow," she said. "There's no need to fear me. I'm a newcomer here, just like you."

The creature continued to stare out of its bulbous eyes.

"I fear you wouldn't thrive indoors," she continued. "While I relish the prospect of a fire and a warm bed, you'll be more comfortable near a pond or concealed beneath an obliging rock in the garden. Shall we go in search of one?"

The animal blinked.

"Very good," she said. "Perhaps you could teach my husband a lesson in communication—you're considerably more accomplished in the art of it."

She giggled to herself, then slipped on her shoes and tiptoed out of her chamber.

The house was quiet, save the occasional clang of pans. Most likely poor Mrs. Morris was in charge of cleaning the crockery, too. Thea's first task would be to find her some help. That steak was appalling, though the aroma coming from the apple pie had made her mouth water, even if she'd nearly sent it flying tonight when she'd bumped into Mrs. Morris.

What was Mrs. Ellis playing at? She had no idea how to keep a house—or, from what Thea had seen—govern a wayward child.

Though the sun had already set, the air was still warm. Thea slipped into the back garden and picked her way toward the far boundary, where the fading light found the smooth surface of a pond, broken by the occasional ripple of a fish. A perfect sanctuary for her new friend. She placed the toad beside the water's edge, and he crawled toward a rock. Then he let out a deep croak.

"You're welcome!" She laughed.

She looked back toward the manor and noticed a glasshouse built against one end, which had been invisible from the front entrance. A hothouse, perhaps? Tomorrow she'd explore the house on her own, to assess the enormity of the task which lay before her as its mistress.

Not to mention the task as Rowena's stepmother.

As she crossed the lawn on her return journey, a silhouette appeared in one of the upper-floor windows. She stopped and looked up, and the silhouette darted out of sight, then reappeared.

Smiling to herself, she slipped back inside the house, returned to her bedchamber, and waited for her husband.

An hour later, heavy footsteps approached her chamber, and a shadow appeared under the doorframe. Her skin tingled in anticipation of his hands on her, and she held her breath and waited. Her body grew warm, with the faint pulse in the secret place between her thighs.

Would he touch her—*there*?

The shadow moved, then it disappeared, and the footsteps receded.

His cold words the day he'd offered for her returned to taunt her.

As to the more intimate matters associated with marriage...I'll leave you be.

He didn't want her.

Chapter Twelve

GRIFFIN GAZED UP as his wife entered the breakfast room, looking even more disappointed than she had last night.

"Good morning, husband," she said. "And Rowena—I trust you slept well?"

His daughter shoveled a forkful of Mrs. Morris's scrambled eggs into her mouth and shrugged.

"Rowena," he growled.

"Good morning," she said, her mouth full.

Not particularly civil, but better than no response at all.

Dorothea took a seat, avoiding his gaze.

Had she expected him to visit her last night?

He wanted her—his body's reaction as he'd passed her chamber last night told him that. He'd had to use all his willpower to stop himself from charging into her room, spreading her legs, and fucking the prim schoolmistress out of her. But the last thing he wanted was a wife distracted by passion, when she needed to focus her efforts on polishing that little hellion into a lady.

The door opened, and Mrs. Morris entered carrying a platter of bacon. As soon as she left, Griffin's wife spoke.

"I'll make a start on drawing up a list of positions we need to fill in order to run the house properly."

Rowena glanced up and looked from Griffin to Dorothea, then

back again.

"Do we need more staff?" he asked.

"We need at least four footmen to tend to a house of this size," she said. "I'll reserve judgment on exactly how many until I've interviewed the current staff and understand their capabilities. And, of course, we'll need a butler and a housekeeper."

"We have Mrs. Ellis," he said.

"That woman isn't even out of her bed yet!" she cried.

Rowena let out a snort. He glared at his daughter, and she stared defiantly back.

"Dorothea," he said, fixing his gaze on his daughter, "has my daughter been courteous toward you?"

The defiance left Rowe's eyes, and she flushed scarlet.

"Rowena has been very civil," Dorothea said, "given that a stranger is now in charge of her home."

"Mrs. Ellis is no stranger," he replied. "She's been with us for five years."

Temper flared in her eyes. "I meant myself. *I'm* lady of the manor, whether you like it or not."

Rowena snorted. "That's told *you*, Papa."

"Dorothea," he continued, "last night, Mrs. Ellis mentioned several instances of bad behavior on your arrival. Perhaps you can elaborate, so I can decide whether my daughter needs to be punished."

Rowena glanced uncomfortably at Dorothea, who looked up and paused.

So, Mrs. Ellis had spoken the truth last night. Rowena *had* been up to something.

"I had a very pleasant evening after supper," Dorothea said.

Ugh—*pleasant*. Not that bland word again.

"I had no idea what an abundance of wildlife there was round these parts," she added.

"Wildlife?" he asked.

"I swear I heard a natterjack toad just as I retired."

She smiled at Rowena, a glint of devilry in her eyes. "I often confuse the toad's call with the sound of linen flapping in the breeze."

What the devil was she on about?

"Particularly," she continued, "the sound of ladies' undergarments which, of course, should be neither heard nor seen."

The color drained from Rowena's face, then Dorothea let out a laugh.

"Of course I jest," she said. "As to your question, I believe Rowena is an innovative young woman, and I look forward to discovering exactly how lively her imagination can be."

She rose to her feet. "And now, if you'll both excuse me, it's time I inspected the house."

Inspected it? She sounded like a sergeant on her way to a drill, ready to find fault with her soldiers.

She fixed her blue gaze on Griffin. "I would like to see the ledgers. Are they in your study?"

"Mrs. Ellis sees to them," he said.

"Not any more, husband."

Rowena's gaze flitted between the two of them, her lips curled into a smile.

"As you wish," he said. "But any decisions regarding expenditure must be run by me."

"Naturally." She nodded, then exited the room.

He glanced at his daughter. The expression in Rowena's face as she watched Dorothea was something he'd not seen in her before.

Admiration.

AFTER SURVEYING THE family rooms and the servant's quarters—which all needed a thorough refurbishment—Thea wandered round the back of the house, the ledgers tucked under her arm, and entered the kitchen.

Dirty dishes were piled in the sink at the window, almost completely obscuring the sunlight. A fire burned in the range—above which a pot was suspended with heaven knows what inside it—and her eyes stung with the smell of smoke.

The chimneys couldn't have been swept for years. How could anyone work under such conditions?

Mrs. Morris stood by the sink, strands of graying hair peeking out from beneath her cap. She picked her way through the pile of dishes but may as well have been an ant attempting to scale a mountain.

"Ahem."

Thea cleared her throat, and the woman glanced over her shoulder. The irritation in her eyes morphed into shock, and she dropped a plate. Thea winced at the sound of shattering crockery.

The cook wiped her hands on her apron and bobbed a curtsey.

"Ma'am," she said as if addressing royalty.

"Mrs. Oake will do," Thea said. "Might we discuss something over a pot of tea?"

"Begging your pardon," the cook said, "but if luncheon is to be ready, I can't spare the time for tea."

"If you please," Thea said, her voice firm.

"But Mrs. Ellis…" the cook began, and Thea interrupted her.

"Mrs. Ellis is no longer in charge." Thea glanced pointedly around the kitchen. "And not before time, by the look of it."

The cook turned her mouth into a frown, then she sighed and placed the kettle on top of the stove.

"Luncheon will be late," she said.

"So be it," Thea replied.

"But Mrs. Ellis…" the cook hesitated. "No matter. Will you want your tea in the parlor?"

"I'll take it here," Thea said. "I wanted to discuss a few matters with you..." she glanced around the kitchen, "...beginning with the fact that you're run off your feet."

"I've had no complaints from the master," the cook said, her tone defensive, "and I've been here three years."

"Three years!" Thea exclaimed. "And in all that time, have you had to cook, clean, *and* serve the meals?"

The cook nodded. "Mrs. Ellis says..."

"Mrs. Ellis knows less about managing a house than a horse knows about the principles of trigonometry," Thea said. "The biggest problem with having to do everything is that you end up doing none of it well."

"You're saying I can't cook?"

"Not under these conditions, Mrs. Morris," Thea said. "How can you be expected to cook to the best of your ability when your time is taken up with everything else?"

"There's Rosie. She comes once a week, on laundry day, and sometimes helps with the dishes. And Betsy, who cleans the house."

"Not very well, I'm afraid."

"She does her best."

"Only if her 'best' includes the dead mouse I discovered under the chaise longue in the drawing room," Thea said. "I'm afraid there's been little or no structured housekeeping, but now I'm here, that will change."

"You can't dismiss me!" Mrs. Morris cried, "I do my best. And Rosie and Betsy have no other means of income. A few hours a week is little to live on when they've families to support. Rosie's ma is sick and needs every penny."

"Which is precisely what I have in mind," Thea said. "A cook, one young man, and two girls coming in once a week is not enough to run a house. And I never want to have to endure a steak like last night's again."

"I do my best, Mrs. Oake."

"I'm sure you do," Thea said. "That is why it's imperative that you're given more time in which to perfect your cooking. I intend to give you a full complement of staff in the kitchen to undertake tasks you should never have been expected to perform alone. Would you like that?"

The cook's plump face creased into a smile, revealing a gap between her front teeth.

"Oh yes, ma'am!"

"Good," Thea said. "Now, if we employ Rosie and Betsy full-time, which of the two do you think is more capable of assisting you in the kitchen? Or would you recommend I search elsewhere?"

"You're asking *me*?"

"Yes, I'm asking you," Thea said. "Consider it the first step along the path toward accepting your new responsibility."

"They're both good girls and would appreciate the work," Mrs. Morris said. "Rosie's helped me with the pots. Betsy prefers to stay out of the kitchen."

"Rosie it is," Thea said. "I'll need to take a look at her before deciding, but I trust your judgment. Do you think the girls would object to living in?"

"On no! Rosie's da's right bad-tempered when he's drunk."

"Then I think we have a plan, Mrs. Morris."

The cook's face lit up into a smile. "So, I'm to be in charge of the kitchen?"

"It's not a responsibility to take lightly," Thea said, "but if you do, then you'll have a properly run kitchen in no time. I would, however, ask that you permit me to teach you how to cook a steak properly. As for scrambled eggs..." she wrinkled her nose, "...the worst you can do is overcook them. I can show you how to cook to the best of your ability."

"You can?"

"Of course." Thea smiled at the enthusiasm in the cook's expression. "I also intend to show Miss Rowena, though I suspect she'll prove a somewhat less enthusiastic pupil."

"She's not a bad child," Mrs. Morris said. "She's just unhappy, what with her da never being around. Perhaps now you're here, that'll change."

Unlikely—given that Thea's husband had left—presumably to spend the day at his inn—shortly after breakfast.

"We'll see," Thea said. "There's one more thing I wanted to ask you. What do you do with the pineapples?"

"The what?"

Thea opened the ledger and pointed to a page.

"An entry five years ago refers to the sale of a quantity of pineapples. There are regular entries in prior years, but nothing since. Given that a pinery can yield a substantial income, it seems a pity it was discontinued, unless the plants died. Have you've never served pineapple?"

"Is it a form of apple?" the cook asked. "The fruit in last night's pie came from the orchard beside the west wing. Pardon me, if I'd known we could sell them..."

"No, it's something else entirely," Thea said. "It's a bizarre-looking fruit, considered a delicacy and a status symbol—so much so that many families in London will hire one to decorate their dining tables to give the impression of wealth."

"Hire a fruit?" Mrs. Morris scoffed. "More money than sense, some of these folks." She glanced at Thea. "Forgive me. I meant no disrespect to your kind."

"Not my kind at all." Thea laughed. "I rather suspect you're a jewel, Mrs. Morris. We need to give you the opportunity to shine."

"I wonder..." The cook hesitated and shook her head. "No matter."

"Mrs. Morris, if you wish to ask something, I shan't object."

"Its poor Will—but it's not my place to say anything."

"I'll hazard a guess," Thea said. "Will undertakes all the duties of a male servant with no help, and he, too, is not given a day off." She shook her head. "It's a wonder this house hasn't crumbled to dust."

"I meant no criticism."

"I believe this is a circumstance where honesty is favored over diplomacy," Thea said.

"It's not the master's fault," Mrs. Morris said. "He's a good man, begging your pardon. Please don't blame him. But he doesn't understand..." she trailed off, her cheeks reddening.

"I wasn't assigning any blame to my *husband*," Thea replied. "Tell me—how did Mrs. Ellis come to take up her position here?"

Understanding dawned in the cook's expression. "Her husband was the parson in Sandiford, and he passed five years ago, about the same time the master bought the manor from Lord Gillingham. His lordship took the housekeeper with him but suggested the master hire Mrs. Ellis as her replacement. Or so I was told."

"You weren't employed here at the time?"

"No, ma'am. My predecessor left shortly afterward. She's with a family in Brighton now."

"And the rest of the staff?"

"They left also. Mrs. Ellis has a lot to say about economy in the home and the perils of frivolity."

"There's a difference between necessary expenditure and frivolity," Thea said. "I take it Mrs. Ellis lowered the wages and drove the staff into leaving without a reference, which left the house—and Miss Rowena—completely at her mercy."

The door opened, and Rowena appeared. "Mrs. Morris, I wondered if you had any..."

She spotted Thea and backed away. "I'll come back later."

"Stay," Thea said. "Mrs. Morris and I were just discussing how I was going to teach her some of my recipes. You can learn them also."

"I shall not," the girl said.

"I've an excellent recipe for shortbread," Thea continued. "My sister taught me…"

"I can think of nothing worse than being stuck in a kitchen, baking biscuits."

"As you wish, Rowena," Thea said, "but it's a poor lady who doesn't understand how her home is run."

"I don't want to run a home."

"Then, if you expect people such as Mrs. Morris here to wait on you, or…" Thea glanced out of the window, "…if you wish to play in the garden all day rather than take care of your home—you must find an indulgent husband or protector to furnish you with such a lifestyle."

"Like you did with my pa?"

Thea recognized the taunt for what it was. Bravado.

"I don't view your father as an indulgent husband," Thea said crisply.

Rowena laughed. "You're learning. He doesn't love anyone but himself. He never has and never will." She folded her arms and glared at Thea, but she hadn't been able to disguise the hurt in her voice.

How the devil was Thea ever going to communicate with her?

She must come to me on her own terms.

She rose to her feet. "Come on, Mrs. Morris," she said. "There's no time to indulge in idle chatter. Perhaps you'd show me the laundry? I'm anxious to see where the linen is washed."

She exited the kitchen, beckoning Mrs. Morris to follow.

Before she left, she glanced over her shoulder and winked at Rowena. She could swear she saw the ghost of a smile on the girl's lips.

Chapter Thirteen

T HE SIGN ABOVE the entrance to the White Hart creaked as it
swung in the breeze.

The hinges needed oiling.

Griffin's wife had said the same about the doors at Sandiford Man-
or, but he preferred them to creak—it prevented Rowe or Mrs. Ellis
catching him unawares. Though, in Mrs. Ellis's case, he always heard
that bloody cane of hers tapping on the floor before she accosted him
with yet another tale of Rowena's misdemeanors.

A fortnight had passed since he'd brought his wife home, and he
hadn't seen much improvement other than meals being easier on the
palate. Last night's steak presented no risk of pulling a tooth when he
bit into it. This morning's scrambled eggs, however, were runny. But,
on voicing his opinion, he was met with a lecture on how the French
cooked their eggs, while Rowena watched their discussion with
interest, no doubt plotting some nefarious scheme of her own.

He glanced up at the sign—a wild hart, prancing in a forest, its
white flank reminding him of his wife's skin, pale against her jet-black
hair.

She possessed a wild, passionate heart. He was sure of it. But she
kept it well hidden.

Perhaps that was for the best. Louisa had been a passionate woman—she'd driven him mad with desire until he realized how freely she

distributed her favors throughout the village.

He opened the door and, as he did each time, averted his gaze from the staircase leading to the guest rooms—the staircase at the bottom of which his late wife had lain, a crumpled heap on the floor, her neck broken.

He had no wish to bring Dorothea here. With her perceptive gaze, just like her brother's, she'd see the guilt which stabbed him every time he thought of Louisa.

What would she do if she learned the truth about Louisa's death? What would her brother do? On the day of Griffin's wedding, Sir Dexter had taken him to one side and threatened to repay him a thousandfold if he hurt so much of a hair on Dorothea's head.

It was plain to see that Griffin's wife had no idea of the depth of her brother's love for her. She must have spent most of her life believing that she was unloved and unwanted.

But Sir Dexter had not given Dorothea to Griffin out of necessity. A man that rich could weather scandal. He must have given her to Griffin because he believed him worthy of her.

He was a formidable man indeed. Why hadn't Griffin had a friend such as him, rather than...

He shook his head. There was little point dwelling on the past—or on Alex Ogilvie.

With his good looks and charm, Ogilvie had fooled them all. But he'd earned his just reward and now languished in Horsham Gaol, where he could no longer tempt his best friend's wife to part her thighs.

"Ah! Griff—there you are!"

Griffin turned his back on the scene of Louisa's death and joined his manager.

"All set for the fight this weekend, Ned?" he asked.

"Cellar's all stocked, though we'd draw a bigger crowd if you took part." Ned poured a glass of ale and handed it to Griffin. "Why don't you bring that pretty wife of yours?"

"The White Hart's no place for her."

"Too much of a society miss to dirty her hands?" Ned laughed. "Will you forsake your friends in your ambition to become a gentleman?

"A woman isn't going to change me," Griffin said. "Not again."

"Except where her fortune will be used to renovate this place," Ned said. "You must agree marriage has its benefits—and she's easy on the eyes."

Griffin tempered the flare of jealousy. "Has she been here?"

"I saw her at church on Sunday with your daughter," Ned said. "I didn't see you. Are you so free of sin that you've no need of absolution?"

Griffin shook his head. "We both know I've sinned so much, there's little point in asking forgiveness." He pushed the beer glass back to Ned, untouched.

Ned sighed and took the glass back. "What happened to Louisa wasn't your fault. Alex Ogilvie was to blame."

"He wouldn't have taken the goods had they not been offered so freely," Griffin said.

"You've taken enough yourself," Ned said. "Is that why you're not fighting this weekend? Because your wife's afraid you'll stray? She doesn't know you as I do, my friend. Why not bring her? I'm sure she'd love to see your talents displayed, and it might increase her..." Ned winked, "...*enthusiasm* for you, or does she need no help in that quarter?"

"That's none of your business," Griffin growled.

"You sound frustrated." Ned grinned. "She looked a little prim, sitting in church. Does she find the act so distasteful that she insists it's done under cover of darkness while she lays back and thinks of London?"

"Ned..." Griffin warned.

"Didn't you tell me that most women were whores underneath? Is your wife the exception? I'll wager ten shillings that you'll have her spreading her legs as soon as she hears you unbuttoning your breeches and screaming your name loud enough to wake the dead before the month is out!"

Anger simmered like a bubble and expanded in Griffin's chest. Ned's good-natured teasing never bothered him until now—when it was directed at Dorothea. How could he subject her to the crudeness of the White Hart? It was a place he loved—the first inn he'd owned. But it was no place for a lady. The notion of Dorothea turning her prim little nose up at the source of his pride was not something he could bear. He found himself unwilling to expose himself to the risk of having her disappointed in him.

More disappointed than she already was.

"I've no intention of finding out whether my wife is a whore or not," he said.

Ned let out a laugh. "You're leaving her be? Has the Mighty Oak lost his potency? Shall I help out? You wouldn't want an unsatisfied wife, and I like 'em posh."

The bubble burst. With a growl of fury, he reached over the bar, grasped Ned by the collar, and pulled him close until Ned's body was half sprawled over the bar. The beer glass toppled onto the floor and shattered with an explosion of brown liquid.

"Don't you dare touch her!" he roared.

Ned's face tuned pink, and he coughed and sputtered, clawing at Griffin's hands, his eyes wide with terror.

What the devil was he doing?

Griffin released Ned, who fell back, clutching his throat.

"Forgive me, Ned," he said. "I don't know what came over me."

But he did—and so did Ned.

It was jealousy. Primal, possessive jealousy.

Rather than the resignation he'd felt at Louisa's adultery, a searing pain ripped through him at the notion of another man touching Dorothea.

She belonged to *him*, and he'd kill any man who tried to take her away.

Including the man whose return he feared the most. Alex Ogilvie—the man who'd stolen Louisa's heart.

The man who was Rowena's father.

Chapter Fourteen

T HEA SAT AT the escritoire and began to write.

Dear Meggie,

Sandiford Manor is very pleasant, and I have much to do here. The gardens are larger than yours, and the apple trees need pruning. Shortly after I arrived, I discovered a pinery. You must come and visit so that I can show it to you. If Dexter can spare you, I should very much like you to come next month...

Coarse laughter echoed from outside. Thea lowered her pen and glanced out of the window.

Rowena was hanging upside down from an apple tree, her petticoats on full display.

It was no coincidence that the girl had chosen the tree within sight of the parlor window.

But at least Rowena noticed her.

Her husband barely spoke more than ten words to her each day—five to wish her good morning, and another five to bid her goodnight. Each night, like a lovesick fool, she waited, hoping he'd visit her. But as each night passed, she grew more assured of his disregard—that he viewed her as nothing more than a companion for his daughter.

There had been some progress with Rowena. Rather than force a relationship, Thea hoped that her silent, reassuring presence and touches of regard might make the girl soften toward her. She'd taught Mrs. Morris to make shortbread and, though Rowena had initially refused a piece, Thea spotted her stealing a biscuit when she thought nobody was looking. The girl needed to be *shown* that someone cared for her rather than be told. And, as with anything, showing always took longer than telling.

Rowena might pretend indifference, but Thea often spotted the girl watching her. And on many days—such as today—Rowena seemed to ensure that her misbehavior was within Thea's eyeline, often showing visible frustration when Thea didn't react.

Once Rowena learned—through experience, rather than being lectured—that Thea would ignore such nonsense rather than make a fuss about it, the wall she'd erected round herself might crumble and reveal the personality within. Rowena was like a tree, and a tree needed to bend and grow, not as Mrs. Ellis clearly wished, to have her branches savagely pruned until she broke.

Rowena valued her own space, and Thea had no wish to encroach upon it until she was invited. When Mrs. Ellis had taken her to the pinery, Thea had spotted the telltale signs of occupation—scuffs in the dust, a thumbprint on the glass of the door, and a blanket neatly folded in the corner with two books on top—a book of Byron's poems and, if Thea was not mistaken, the same book of anatomy she'd spotted Rowena procuring from the library.

Thea glanced at the words she'd written on the page, then scrunched up the paper and tossed it into the fireplace.

Bland pleasantries wouldn't fool Meggie. Thea needed to open her heart to someone, or she'd lose her mind.

And opening her heart in a letter meant that she had to admit to herself what she wanted—what she needed.

She wanted *him*. The Mighty Oak—her Hercules—the demi-god who'd strutted across the ground, wrestled his opponent into the dirt, then stood and roared his victory, like some great beast—the man who'd warmed her blood into a raging inferno of need.

She wanted him to want her back.

She wanted to experience the unbridled ecstasy that made women scream a man's name.

How could she articulate *that* in a letter?

Someone knocked on the door, and she called out. A young maid-servant entered, carrying a tray of tea. According to Miss Ellis, Betsy was a foolish and lazy girl. But since Thea had offered her a full-time, live-in position as housemaid, she'd found her intelligent and willing to work.

"Come in, Betsy," Thea said. "Put the tea on the table."

"Sorry I was late, ma'am. I was busy with Mrs. Ellis's tea. She wanted it earlier than usual, on account of her nerves."

Thea sighed. "Mrs. Ellis's nerves cause a great deal of work for everyone else. I'll speak to her."

"I wouldn't want to cause no trouble," Betsy said.

"It's no trouble," Thea said, "at least not for anyone other than Mrs. Ellis."

She rose and exited the parlor.

She found Mrs. Ellis asleep on a chaise longue. Judging by the smile on the woman's face, her nerves were in perfect working order.

Beside her on the table was a plate laden with shortbread biscuits.

The same biscuits Thea had spent yesterday afternoon baking for Rowena.

Thea stood in the dark of the doorway and cleared her throat.

"Ahem."

Mrs. Ellis's eyelids fluttered open, and she sat up, her face creased into sourness.

"How many times, Betsy, did I tell you..."

Thea stepped into the light, and Mrs. Ellis drew in a sharp breath.

"What did you tell Betsy, Mrs. Ellis?"

"I asked her to wake me when it was time for Rowena's next lesson."

"It's after four, Mrs. Ellis," Thea said. "Rowena's been outside since luncheon. Or did her lesson involve an exploration of the grounds while you slept?"

"She's been a tiresome child today, Mrs. Oake. I can only endure so much of her incivility."

"I've seen nothing more than the antics of a normal, spirited child," Thea said.

"If I'm permitted to be frank, Mrs. Oake, you seem ignorant to her faults."

Insolent woman! "Mrs. Ellis," Thea said, keeping her voice calm though she longed to scream at the woman, "I understand the difference between frankness and incivility."

Mrs. Ellis reached for her cane and stood. "I meant no offense."

"Nonetheless, your remark was received as such."

Thea fixed her gaze on Mrs. Ellis, and the two women stared at each other. At length, Mrs. Ellis averted her gaze. Like all bullies, she surrendered when someone faced her head-on.

"I trust you'll appreciate equal frankness from me," Thea said. "I fail to understand what Rowena could have done to drive you to languish on a sofa all afternoon while the rest of the household see to their duties."

"The master has no objection to me taking my rest," Mrs. Ellis said, a sulky tone to her voice.

"*I'm* in charge of the household and Rowena's welfare," Thea replied. "She strikes me as an intelligent young woman in need of a little understanding."

"She needs discipline—plain and simple. The tricks she's played on me—you wouldn't believe! She's defiled the portraits again!"

"Defiled?"

"It's disgraceful—and so lacking in respect of his lordship."

"His lordship?"

"Lord Gillingham."

"Lord Gillingham no longer lives here," Thea said, "so he can have no cause to take offense at anything Rowena does."

Mrs. Ellis tapped her cane on the floor in frustration—the adult equivalent of a stamping her foot. But in one aspect, she was right—if Rowena was to learn how to run a home, the first step was to *not* desecrate its contents.

"Let me show you," Mrs. Ellis said crisply.

"As you wish."

The gallery was on the first floor and spanned almost the entire length of the manor. The walls were covered in portraits that must have been crammed in over the years, displaying a variety of ancient-looking men and women, who stared oppressively out from their canvases.

Halfway along, Mrs. Ellis stopped and pointed upward.

"Look!"

The pictures were stacked in two rows. In the upper row—immediately above a landscape covered in so much grime that the features were barely visible save for a mountain and a bare tree in the foreground—was a portrait of a man.

Thea read the inscription.

"Augustus Theodore Baldwin Henry John Fortescue, eighth Lord Gillingham."

"The present lord's great-grandfather," Mrs. Ellis said, her voice a reverent whisper. "Just *look* what she's done to him!"

"Apart from the sour-faced expression, I fail to see anything amiss," Thea replied.

"Look closer."

Why did the woman see fit to order Thea about as if she were the servant?

She craned her head upward, then saw it.

A huge black mustache had been stuck onto the subject's face, in contrast to his thinning gray hair.

"Are you sure that was Rowena?" Thea asked. "The portrait's out of reach."

"Of course it was her!" Mrs. Ellis exclaimed. "Tiresome brat—it's not the first time. Last month she stuck a beard onto the seventh Lady Gillingham, but she denied it—the nasty little liar. I've never seen such outrageous disrespect!"

"The subjects are both dead, Mrs. Ellis," Thea said. "I'm sure that, wherever they are now, they've more important things to concern themselves with.

"It's so..." Mrs. Ellis gestured in the air, her breath catching, "...so *wrong*! The artist, if not the subject, would not welcome his work being defaced in such an inappropriate manner."

A wicked urge to laugh swelled within Thea, and she tried to hide her smile. "Should the mustache have been gray to match his lordship's hair?" she asked.

Mrs. Ellis gave an explosive snort of rage. "She continues to disrespect *me*! It's not the behavior of a lady, and Mr. Oake told me he married you primarily in order to turn her into one."

Had Griffin told Mrs. Ellis why he'd been forced to marry Thea? Did the woman gossip about her in church with all the other disapproving widows?

But, in one aspect, the woman was right. Rowena's behavior needed curtailing. But she clearly resented authority—and resented Thea even more.

As for Griffin...

He seemed to be doing everything he could to avoid her. He spent every waking hour at his inn—where all manner of women must be throwing themselves at him. How soon would a man of his raw sexuality surrender to the lifestyle he must have enjoyed before being shackled to her? Or had he already succumbed and was, this moment, in the arms of another?

Never did she need the counsel and gentle, loving company of her sister-in-law more than she did at this moment. Meggie would know what to do. Meggie was the one person in the world who truly loved her.

And despite the demands Dexter had placed on Thea's husband when drawing up the marriage contract, despite all the threats about using her dowry, about ensuring she was kept safe from harm…

Despite all that, Thea only wanted one thing.

To be loved.

⟫⟪

"I TELL YOU, Mr. Oake. Your wife is incapable of controlling the child."

Couldn't the woman even let him get inside his own house before accosting him?

Mrs. Ellis might have come recommended by that fool Gillingham as "a good, god-fearing woman" who could tend to his house and educate Rowena, but in reality, she was incapable of either.

She was the type of woman who made a show of attending church—preaching the morals of the sermons she heard there—but on the other six days of the week, she forgot the basic principles of loving her neighbors.

"You must speak to your wife," Mrs. Ellis continued, her voice reminiscent of a crow stuck in the chimney. "My nerves cannot take much more of the brat's disobedience."

"Does Rowena disrespect my wife?" he asked.

Mrs. Ellis let out a huff. "She's been disrespectful to *me*. Your wife spends little time in her company."

A shard of pain throbbed in his temple—as it always did when he had to listen to Mrs. Ellis for too long.

"Very well," he said, rubbing his forehead. "Leave me be, and I'll speak to my wife."

In truth, he'd been avoiding Dorothea. Women had a tendency to nag. And there was nothing worse than a nagging, discontented wife.

But Dorothea, in the weeks since he'd married her, had said very little. When she expressed discontent at something, she mentioned it once, then took action herself to address it.

Such as the steaks. He had to admit that he'd eaten last night's supper with relish. All his life, food had been a mere necessity to maintain his strength. But she'd taught him that it was also to be savored, enjoyed, and relished.

Like a delectable female form—to be devoured slowly, each bite filling his body with delicious sensations of pleasure.

He shifted position as his breeches tightened at the thought of unpeeling his wife's staid little gowns to reveal the figure underneath. Would she, like a ripe steak, reveal the succulent interior when he sliced through her prim outer form?

Then he shook his head. He'd not married her to rut her. His wife's role was to fashion Rowe into a lady. And while the food at his table was edible, and the house no longer smelled of mold—Rowena still had faults aplenty.

He left Mrs. Ellis standing in the hall and made his way to his wife's parlor.

He found her sitting at her writing desk. The last rays of the setting sun caught her hair, giving it a soft sheen. His fingers itched to remove the pins which kept her severe hairstyle in place, to tumble her hair about her shoulders.

What might she look like, her face framed by a wild abandon of tresses, flushed in ecstasy, mouth open, his name on her lips while he slipped inside her?

His gaze followed the line of her profile—a proud brow, perfectly formed nose, and those full, red lips which she'd once offered up to him for a kiss.

He licked his own lips at the memory of their taste—sweet honey with an undercurrent of the spice of passion.

Then she turned and focused her clear gaze on him.

Feeling as guilty as a schoolboy caught spying on an adult, he moved toward her.

"I hadn't expected you to come home so early," she said. "Supper won't be ready for some time."

Did he detect bitterness in her voice?

He nodded toward the pen in her hand. "What are you doing?"

"Writing a letter."

"To Lady Hart?"

"I've already written to Meggie," she said, turning her back and resuming her attention on the paper in front of her. "I invited her to stay. I trust that meets with your approval. Were you ever here during the day, I'd have asked you directly."

Yes—definitely bitterness.

"And now?" he asked.

"I'm writing to an employment agency in London."

"Whatever for?"

"Because I wish to employ someone."

Infuriating woman! Was she trying to goad him?

"No—I mean, why in London?"

"It's where the agency is located."

Were she directing her comments at another, he'd have laughed at their dryness—but they were directed at him, laced with an undercurrent of exasperation.

He placed a hand on her shoulder and glanced at the letter, which was written in a neat, elegant hand, as if a law-writer had penned it. She sighed, and his skin tightened as her warm breath caressed the back of his hand. He rubbed his thumb along the fabric of her dress, then moved his forefinger until his fingertip touched the skin of her neck. She caught her breath and shifted position, leaning almost imperceptibly toward him. Then she stiffened and straightened her posture, her rational mind conquering her body's instinct.

She had feelings but kept them suppressed. Perhaps she'd had her heart broken before.

His mind wandered to the rumor he'd heard about the Hart sister who'd taken a lover and been ruined before Sir Dexter had made his fortune.

Curse the man—whoever he'd been.

Griffin withdrew his hand. He needed to remember that he'd also had his heart broken.

"May I ask you something, Dorothea?"

She turned, and he caught a glimmer of hope in her eyes. Her lips curled up a fraction, and he found himself yearning to see her smile.

"I would ask you to consider hiring locally if you're wanting staff," he said, "rather than writing to London."

She frowned, and he caught a flicker of sorrow in her expression before the prim persona returned.

"If you want your home run efficiently in order to give your daughter an appropriate environment in which to learn what it is to be a lady, then you must permit me to hire an appropriate body of staff."

An appropriate body of staff? A soulless turn of phrase meant to intimidate others with her intellect.

"From London?" he asked. "Is that what you want?"

"What do *you* want?" she asked, fixing her gaze on him.

He hesitated. Was she asking about his wishes regarding the staff or asking for something more—to know his innermost desires?

He lowered his gaze, lest he betray those desires. "I would like you to give the villagers a chance."

"I..." she hesitated, "that is, *we*, need, at the very least, a butler capable of managing the rest of the staff. The benefit of an agency is that they'll have already vetted suitable candidates and can recommend someone to meet our requirements. I know very little of the villagers here—certainly not enough to determine whether they'd be suitable for such a post."

"*I* know them," he said. "Why don't you select a list of potential candidates, and I'll help you decide."

She turned her head away. "You mean, you'll decide for me."

"I'd merely advise you so you could make…" He hesitated. Damn it—what was the phrase? "…an *informed decision*."

Her mouth curved into a smile, softening her features, and he fought the urge to capture her lips in a kiss.

"Sometimes you remind me of Dex," she said.

Oh, dear. For all his excellent qualities as a businessman, Sir Dexter was an overbearing arse.

"How?" he asked, then shook his head. "No—don't tell me."

She let out a laugh, and her eyes widened as if she surprised herself. He met her gaze and smiled back. Her eyes sparkled against her pale face, like sapphires in the snow, and he felt a sharp pull deep within his soul.

"Do I amuse you?" he asked.

"Sometimes," she said. "You forget—two months ago, I had no thoughts of matrimony, let alone the prospect of finding a husband just like my brother."

She colored as she spoke. Was she ashamed of the notion of being married? Or did she blush for some other reason—perhaps the same reason which had led her to offer her lips to him that night on the terrace…

Those lush lips with the promise of sweetness elsewhere…

Lips which he only needed to lower his head a fraction to claim.

Then she looked away, and the moment was lost.

She picked up the letter and crunched it into a ball. "If you're willing to advise me," she said, her voice crisp and business-like, "then I'll make inquiries in the village."

"Give me a list of all the positions you wish to fill," he said.

"The senior staff can be trusted to assist with the rest," she said. "Therefore, we should begin with the butler and housekeeper."

"We have Mrs. Ellis," he said.

"I should like to hire someone else."

"Mrs. Ellis has been with us for five years and came recommended by Lady Gillingham."

"Lady Gillingham is no longer the lady of Sandiford Manor, is she?"

Why did she always have to take on that spinsterish tone of hers?

"Mrs. Ellis tells me Rowena exhibited further bad behavior today," he said, the mention of the woman reminding him of his original reason for wanting to see his wife. "She says you have yet to deal with the girl."

"I'll see to Rowena in my own time," she retorted.

"She's *my* daughter, Dorothea," he replied. "She's yet to show improvement, and you've been here almost a month."

She stiffened, and her voice grew cold. "A young woman cannot be fashioned into a lady overnight."

"Or at all, if she's left to run wild. Aren't you supposed to teach her how to behave? After all, that's why I agreed to marry you."

He regretted the words as soon as they'd slipped out of his mouth.

She jerked herself free from his touch, then stood and approached the window where she looked out, her face silhouetted against the evening sunlight.

"If you'll excuse me," she said. "I'll see you at supper."

"Forgive me, I shouldn't have…" he began, but she interrupted.

"I need no reminder of the circumstances which forced us together," she said. "You made it clear that you don't wish me to make any unnecessary—*demands*—on you. I will refrain from doing so, as best as I'm able, but it behooves me to say that Mrs. Ellis is not the paragon you believe her to be."

"Dorothea, I…"

"Please go."

Her voice wavered, and he caught a glint of moisture in her eyes.

Nothing he could say would appease her, so the best course of action was to retreat. With luck, her cold shell would reform by the time he had to face her at the supper table. Then he wouldn't have to be confronted by her disappointment in him—which was nothing compared to his disappointment in himself.

Chapter Fifteen

HOW DARE HE! Did he think himself the only unwilling party in this marriage? And how dare he accuse her of not dealing with his daughter?

Dealing with her—as if she were vermin to be culled!

After his footsteps faded, she ventured out into the garden in search of Rowena. The girl wasn't going to come to Thea of her own accord, and if Mrs. Ellis had taken to tale-bearing, it wouldn't end well for her.

The garden appeared to be empty, but Thea spotted a tree that quivered, though there was no breeze. As she approached it, she noticed the book of anatomy at the base of the trunk.

"May I speak with you, Rowena?" she asked.

No answer was forthcoming—though she hadn't expected one.

"I'm merely curious to know how it was done," she continued.

A foot appeared, followed by another. Then, with a rustle of leaves, Rowena jumped out of the tree and landed on the lawn.

"That's better," Thea said. "I prefer to see who I'm engaged in conversation with."

Rowena smoothed the front of her skirt, causing a smear of mud across the material.

"That'll need to be washed," Thea said.

"I don't care how I look," the girl retorted.

"Yes, I can see that," Thea replied. "But *I* care about the work Rosie has to undertake in the laundry. I understand you've refused to help her."

"I don't want to do domestic work," Rowena said.

"Consider yourself fortunate there's someone who does," Thea said. "But I'm not here to discuss dirty linen. I came to ask why you saw fit to furnish the eighth Lord Gillingham with a mustache."

Rowena opened her mouth as if to deny it, then she nodded.

"I saw it as a challenge."

"A challenge?"

"Mrs. Ellis said she'd have me sent away to school if I did it again. I wanted to prove that she couldn't."

"But *I* could," Thea said, and Rowena's eyes widened in fear.

"I won't, of course," Thea continued. A wave of compassion threaded through her as the girl visibly relaxed.

Rowena was adopting the tactics of any normal child faced with boundaries—testing their limits yet terrified of the consequences.

Thea reached for Rowena's hand, but she snatched it away.

"You're not my mother," she said. "I don't even like you."

"Good," Thea replied. "I don't like *you* either."

"Aren't you supposed to like me?"

"Why?" Thea asked. "Neither of us knows the other well enough yet. I prefer to wait until I can make an informed decision. But you've earned my respect."

"How so?"

"I can weather insults," Thea said, "for I've experienced many. But I will not tolerate being lied to."

The girl shifted on her feet uncomfortably, much as Thea's nephew Billy did when she adopted the same tone of voice.

"For telling me the truth about the eighth Lord Gillingham's rather impressive addition to his facial hair, you have earned my respect."

Rowena folded her arms. "What if I don't want your respect?"

"Nevertheless, you have it." Thea glanced toward the book on the ground.

"Now, forgive me, I must return to the house. I had hoped to teach you a little about Latin."

"Latin?"

"A fascinating language," Thea said. "Very logical in its construction. It helps with the study of anatomy and the finer points of the English language. But I've been too long occupied with your handiwork in the gallery. I now need to speak to Mrs. Morris about supper. Would you like to help?"

"No."

Rowena flinched a little as if expecting a reaction. But Thea smiled.

"As you wish," she said. "I'll see you at supper."

Rowena hesitated, then picked up the book and flicked through the pages. Then she glanced up and watched Thea leave. By the time Thea had reached the house, Rowena still stared after her.

The girl wanted to learn—her behavior was the product of a lively and curious mind—but she was afraid to ask.

What made her so scared? Was it something to do with her mother?

Why did Griffin always get so angry when his late wife was mentioned? What did he have to hide?

Chapter Sixteen

T HE NEXT DAY, as Griffin approached the breakfast room, he spotted his wife in her parlor, opening a parcel.

So that explained the hoofbeats outside at some unholy hour of the morning.

And a bloody awful morning it was to be out. The air was thick and oppressive, and he'd woken with a headache, which still throbbed behind his temples.

"What's that?" Griffin pointed to the parcel.

"It's a parcel."

Why did she always have to be so damned logical?

He folded his arms and leaned against the doorframe. "Thank you for enlightening me."

Her mouth twitched into a smile. "I've been expecting it," she said. "It's from Lilah."

She looked at him expectedly, as if he ought to know who the devil Lilah was.

"My youngest sister, Delilah," she said, reaching into the parcel and pulling out a book. "Her second set of poems has been published, and she'd promised to send me copies."

She held the book up to the light. The gold embossing on the cover glinted in the sunlight, and her face broke into a smile of pride. Her eyes shone in the sunlight, a vivid blue that reminded him of the bluebells that graced the woodlands of Sandiford in spring.

She was a beautiful creature when she wanted to be! Her features may not be striking, but they had character—the firmness around the mouth which conveyed strength and resilience, the sharp intelligence in the sparkle of her eyes, and the pride in her smile—pride in a sister she loved.

Most women would be jealous of a younger sister who'd secured the hand of a duke and realized her career ambitions. But not Dorothea. Such a capacity for selfless love was not often to be found.

Would she ever be proud of him—or love him—as much?

She opened the book and flicked through the pages. Then she gave a little gasp, and a tear splashed onto her cheek.

He took her hand. "Is something wrong?"

"No," she said, closing the book. "It's time for breakfast—the eggs will curdle if we delay." She withdrew her hand and moved to the door.

"May I have a copy?" he blurted.

For a moment, he thought she'd refuse—grab the parcel and conceal it in her room, the same way she concealed her heart. Then she nodded.

"Of course," she said. "Rowena can have one also if she wishes. Lilah's sent enough."

She exited the parlor, and he reached for a book, tracing the letters of the title with his fingertip.

My Heart's Completion.

What the devil did that mean? Was that what had upset her?

He flicked through the book, stopping at a page at random, and his gaze wandered over the lines...

> *Hard against the granite wall, we seek fulfillment in the pleasure of the earth...*

Bloody hell! There was no way he'd let Rowena read *that*. He read on, his blood warming at the raw passion of the verse. They were just words on a page, but they had the power to evoke such need—and stiffen his cock. He closed his eyes, relishing the notion of taking a woman against the rock of the Highlands. He hardened at the image of his wife's face—lips parted as she cried his name…

Then he opened his eyes and drew in a sharp breath. It wouldn't do to be caught with a cockstand in the middle of the parlor.

He flicked to the front of the book, and his eye caught the dedication.

> *To my darling Thea, whose capacity for love inspired me to write this book. May your heart find the true completion it deserves.*

The touching, heartfelt words in the dedication were in sharp contrast to the raw, unbridled passion in the verse. Dorothea's sister was a wordsmith indeed—those few words of dedication said more about Griffin's wife than she had revealed herself.

That she yearned to love—and to be loved.

Snapping the book shut, he followed his wife into the breakfast room.

⋙⋘

BY THE TIME Griffin arrived at the White Hart, the dull ache which plagued his head during breakfast had intensified until it felt as if the Sandiford blacksmith was using his skull for an anvil. He'd not been fit for anything, and eventually, he succumbed to Ned's insistence that he spend the remainder of the day at home.

As he trudged along the path adjoining the garden, he caught sight of his wife. She stood beneath the canopy of a tree and seemed to be talking to it.

No—she was talking to a pair of legs that dangled from the leaves.

She folded her arms and set off in the direction of the orchard, and, shortly after, a body appeared to accompany the legs, and Rowe leapt onto the lawn. She stared after her stepmother, watching as she stopped beside one of the apple trees.

Then Will's voice echoed across the garden, and Dorothea waved, hailing him with a smile and a laugh. Griffin loosened his collar in an attempt to ease the effects of the heat. The air really was oppressive today—and why the devil couldn't his wife smile and laugh with *him*?

Dorothea glanced over her shoulder toward Rowe with a smile but made no attempt to speak to her, and she resumed her conversation with Will, pointing at the apple tree and gesturing with her hands.

Rowe crossed the garden to stand a little distance away from Will and Dorothea, watching them, her eyes dark with concentration. She made no attempt to engage in the conversation, nor did Dorothea try to draw her in.

He stood back and continued to watch, swallowing the surge of jealousy at the easy conversation and gentle laughter.

She circled the apple tree, pointing to the branches. He moved forward, then concealed himself behind a bush, unwilling to disturb them. Eventually, they ceased conversation and crossed the garden together, leaving Rowe standing alone. He shrank back as they neared the bush, and he caught their conversation.

"The pinery hasn't been used for years," Will said.

What the bloody hell was a *pinery*?

"We can have it up and running in no time," Dorothea said. "The plants are still alive, and we can get them to yield fruit next year if we tend to them now—maybe this year if we're lucky. The returns could be considerable."

They passed the bush, and Griffin watched their retreating backs as they walked toward the abandoned hothouse.

So *that* was the pinery.

"Are the fruits that valuable?" Will asked.

"There are people willing—or foolish—enough to pay huge sums of money to hire one for an evening," she said. "My brother once spent ten guineas for the privilege of displaying one as a centerpiece for a dinner party in order to impress a titled client."

"Did it work?"

She laughed. "No, it didn't! According to my sister-in-law, the fruit was so rotten that the guests were far too eager to finish their meal and leave as soon as possible to get away from the smell."

"It seems rather a waste, begging your pardon."

"I agree," she said. "Dexter learned a valuable lesson. The next time he purchased a pineapple outright and served it to his guests. He gained three large accounts in a single evening. After all, fruit are meant to be eaten, not handed around the tables of London society until they rot."

"Have you eaten one?"

"Meggie was kind enough to save me a piece," she said. "An exotic taste, which I look forward to enjoying again. If the pinery yields any fruit, we shall all share the first one."

"That's very kind of you."

"Nonsense!" she said, her schoolmistress tone coming to the fore again. She gave an exasperated little sigh and swatted at the air.

"Curse these flies!" she cried. "They're everywhere today."

"They're storm flies," Will said. "Can't you feel it in the air? There's a storm coming."

They reached the hothouse, and their voices faded as they slipped inside.

Griffin jumped at a voice from behind.

"Don't you know it's rude to eavesdrop, Pa?"

He turned and saw Rowe, standing next to the bush, a sneer on her lips.

"Spying, are you? Do you think she fancies the gardener?"

"Don't speak nonsense, child!" he retorted. "And if I hear any more talk of that sort, I'll take my hand to you."

"I'd like to see you try!"

He reached out to her, and she darted back, a flash of fear in her eyes. Did she really think he'd *hit* her? He might be a brute, but he only hit opponents in the ring—not women, and certainly not his child.

She folded her arms, and the mischief returned to her expression.

"Have you heard her sing yet?"

"Sing?"

Her expression turned to triumph. "You haven't, have you?" she laughed. "She sings to herself in the upstairs parlor when she thinks nobody's listening."

"Spying, were you?" he said.

Her face fell.

Curse it! Just because she behaved like a petulant child, there was no excuse for him to do the same.

"Forgive me, Rowe," he said, "I didn't mean…"

"No," she said. "You *did*."

Before he could respond, she turned and ran across the lawn in his wife's wake.

Chapter Seventeen

WHY COULDN'T SHE find a cool spot in the bed?

After a day spent clearing the pinery, Thea had sunk, gratefully, into the bath which Betsy had drawn. The faint aroma of lavender still clung to her skin as she lay in her bed. But sleep eluded her.

A low rumble echoed outside, and she climbed out of bed and crossed the floor to the diamond-paned window. A flash illuminated the landscape, and she counted, under her breath, until she heard another rumble.

The next flash lit up the sky with a jagged, vertical streak of white fire. Two breaths later, the telltale sound of a crack overhead was followed by an explosion in the air.

A scream ripped through the air—a high-pitched wail of pure terror—and the skin tightened on the back of her neck. She drew her shawl round her shoulders and went in search of the source of the scream.

Thea wasn't afraid of storms, but they had the power to cause considerable damage. When she was a child, a bolt of lightning had felled a tree near her home—and a rumor circulated about a stable-hand who'd been struck while out walking and turned to ash.

Another scream tore through the air—from Rowena's room.

Thea broke into a run and entered Rowena's bedchamber.

The light of a solitary candle threw sharp shadows across the chamber, picking out the shape of the bed and the vase of flowers on the table beside the window.

But the bed was empty.

"Rowena?" Thea called out. "Are you there?"

A soft whimper came from the far corner.

"Rowena, sweetheart?"

Thea moved forward and found her huddled in the corner, her gaze fixed on an imaginary object in front of her.

Thea had heard tales of children walking in their sleep. Doctor McIver always said it originated from some past event that the child was incapable of dealing with while awake. Had something happened in Rowena's past?

She crouched beside her and took her hand.

The girl's eyes cleared and focused on Thea. Almost immediately, she pulled free.

"Leave me alone."

"Rowena, dear," Thea said. "I…"

A flash illuminated the room, and a crash ripped through the air. Rowena let out a scream and pitched forward.

"The storm!" she cried. "I can't bear it!"

Thea placed her shawl round Rowena's shoulders and drew her into her arms. This time, the girl made no attempt to resist.

"Hush," she soothed, rocking her to and fro. "I'll not let any harm come to you."

Another flash illuminated the room, and Rowena gave another cry. Thea counted one…two…until the telltale rumble.

"The storm's moving away," she said.

"H-how can you tell?"

"By counting after each flash. The number you reach is how many miles away the storm is."

She stood and held out her hand. "Let's get you up."

Ignoring the proffered hand, Rowena struggled to her feet. Then, another flash lit up the room.

"It's coming back!" she wailed.

Thea took her hand. "Let us count," she said. "One...two...three...four...five..."

A low rumble sounded.

"There!" Thea said. "Five miles. It was only two before, so it's moving away. There's no need to be frightened."

"I'm not frightened."

The tremor in the girl's voice contradicted her words.

"There's nothing to be ashamed of in fearing a thunderstorm," Thea said.

"I don't..." Another flash interrupted Rowena, and she gave a low cry and bit her lip.

"Storms can be dangerous when they're directly overhead," Thea said. "But the noise isn't the problem—it's the lightning, which can damage anything tall, such as trees and towers. That's why you must never shelter under a tree in a storm—and it's why the tallest buildings have lightning rods."

"What's a lightning rod?"

Thea smiled. Curiosity was the best antidote to the girl's fear. "It's a device which helps lightning travel to the ground," she said.

"What do you mean—travel?"

"Lightning wants to get to the ground, so it has to travel there," Thea said. "Much like your papa when he's traveling home to you in the carriage. With a carriage, it's safer for everyone if it sticks to the road. You wouldn't want to be wandering in the woods and be run down by a coach and four. It's the same with lightning."

"So, it's like a road for lightning?"

"Exactly!" Thea said. "Lightning likes to travel through metal. So if rods of metal are placed on the tallest buildings, they'll attract the lightning and prevent it from striking anything else nearby. Sandiford

Church has one—I'll show it to you on Sunday."

"How do you know all this?" Rowena asked.

"I studied the works of Benjamin Franklin," Thea said. "If you like, I can order copies of his publications for you to include them in your study. Science is there to explain what might otherwise frighten us— such as thunderstorms." She gave Rowena a playful nudge. "Of course, when I was a child, my brother teased us about thunderstorms being the Almighty moving his furniture about. I swear that last rumble was Him tossing a longcase clock down the stairs!"

Rowena giggled, then stopped herself. "That's blasphemous!"

"I hardly think we'd incite condemnation for conquering our fear with laughter."

"Miss Ellis says that lessons are best learned through fear and discipline."

Good Lord! What nonsense was that woman teaching Rowena?

"What else does Mrs. Ellis say?"

Rowena looked away. A rumble echoed in the distance, and she stiffened.

"Rowena?" Thea prompted. "You can tell me—I won't say anything to Mrs. Ellis."

"It's nothing."

"Is she unkind to you?"

The girl hesitated, then shook her head. She drew the shawl tighter around her, and Thea caught a glimpse of a bruise on her wrist.

"Your poor wrist!" she cried. "What have you done to it?"

"I fell out of a tree. I'm always doing it."

The answer sounded a little over-prepared.

"My sister-in-law has a liniment for bruises," Thea said. "I'll write and ask her to send me some. I wish I'd had it when I was a child—I was always falling out of trees."

"You climbed trees?" Rowena fixed her wide-eyed gaze on Thea.

"I was quite proficient."

"I bet you're not as proficient now."

Thea laughed. "If that's a challenge, then I accept."

Rowena's smile disappeared. "All adults say that. They make promises which they don't fulfil. You'll be no different."

"My nieces and nephews would beg to disagree with you," Thea said.

"My mother..." Rowena began, then she shook her head and looked away.

"You can speak of your mother if you wish."

"She *always* kept her promises. She took me out for picnics every Sunday after church."

"*Every* Sunday?"

"Yes, that's right," Rowena said, her tone defensive.

"We can do that," Thea said. "I'll ask Mrs. Morris to make up a basket for us. What did you like to eat on a picnic?"

Rowena hesitated, then shrugged. "I don't know."

"Where did you go? Did your mama have a favorite spot?"

"I can't remember."

"But she took you there every Sunday!"

"Yes, she did!" Rowena cried. "And she sang me lullabies. Every night. She was always there. She sang all my favorite songs."

She folded her arms and stared at Thea as if daring her to challenge.

"I have several song-sheets I brought here with me," Thea said. "They might include some of your favorites. We could sing them to honor your mama. What songs did you sing together?"

Rowena frowned. "I can't remember the names."

"Perhaps you could hum a melody?"

Rowena closed her eyes, then shook her head. "I can't remember, but I know I loved them. I loved them very much. They were my favorite."

Why did the girl feel the need to repeat herself?

"Don't you believe me?" Rowena asked.

"Of course I do, dear," Thea said. "I just find it a little strange that you cannot remember the details."

"It's true," Rowena said. "My mama...oh!" She broke off as she glanced toward the door.

"Rowe?" a deep voice spoke.

Griffin stood in the doorway. "Is everything all right?" he asked.

"Yes," Rowena said a little too quickly.

"I thought I heard screaming," he said. "And the storm—I know you dislike storms."

"Your daughter is well," Thea said. "We've been discussing lullabies and picnics, haven't we, Rowena? I thought we might take a picnic tomorrow once the weather clears. I hear you used to enjoy them."

A frown rippled across his brow, then he nodded. "Every Sunday after church. And lullabies every night."

"Perhaps *you* remember the songs?" Thea asked. "I could see if I have them in my collection."

He shook his head. "I'm not sure."

"Of course not," Rowena said. "*You* were never there, were you?"

She climbed into the bed and drew the blanket round her. "I'm tired now," she said. "May I be excused?"

"Rowe..." Griffin began, but Thea placed a hand on his arm.

"Leave her be," she whispered. "The storm's passed. She'll be fine."

He retreated, and Thea followed, closing the door. When she turned to face him, he was already halfway down the corridor.

"Husband?"

"What is it?"

"Rowena's troubled by something. Do you know what it is?"

He wiped his brow, and for a moment, she caught a flash of sorrow and regret in his eyes.

"Griffin?"

He let out a sigh, and on impulse, she took his hand.

"She's all I have in the world," he whispered. "Nothing matters except her."

"I know," she said. "Rest assured, I'll take care of her."

She released his hand, then returned to her chamber.

Nothing matters except her.

Thea climbed into her bed and drew the covers around her.

But still, sleep wouldn't come, not now she understood—he loved his daughter, but he would never love *her*.

⟫⟫⟫⟫⟪⟪⟪⟪

WHY DID HE have to stick his bloody great feet into the mire once more?

The stricken look on his wife's face as she turned from him almost matched the fear in Rowe's eyes when she saw him in the doorway.

He seemed doomed to always say the wrong thing at the wrong time.

He'd woken to the crash of thunder and been plagued by the image of Louisa's body, broken and twisted, illuminated by the lightning. Rowe's scream had taken him back to that night—so like her mother's scream when she'd known she was falling to her death.

And her face—the ashen face staring up at him with the dark, dead eyes. When Rowe was angry or stressed, she became the mirror image of her mother—an image he recoiled at.

Yet his wife had taken his daughter in her arms and comforted her while he'd watched unobserved.

In a few short weeks, Dorothea had shown Rowe more love than her real mother had ever done.

At all costs, Rowe must be protected from the truth.

Chapter Eighteen

THE RAIN PERSISTED through the night, and by midmorning the next day, it still battered against the windows.

There was no chance of venturing outside, let alone a picnic.

After breakfast, Thea excused herself and retired to her parlor. The light was so poor that she needed a candle to continue her letter to Meggie.

Shortly after, she heard the familiar trudge of her husband's footsteps on the gravel drive.

Not even the rain deterred him from visiting his beloved inns. Why he didn't take up permanent residence there, she did not know.

Then she scolded herself for being so ungenerous. Few husbands preferred to spend time with their wives over friends or business associates. Even a husband who loved his wife would struggle to maintain his affection if forced to spend every waking hour with her.

And Griffin had made it plain from the beginning that their marriage wouldn't be based on love.

She picked up her pen and began to write.

Dearest Meggie,

I find myself in need of your company and your advice.

I have a lovely home and am fortunate to be married to a good man with a lovely young woman for a daughter. But I confess I'm lonely.

She glanced up at a noise and saw movement in the passageway outside.

"Who's there?"

No reply came, but she glimpsed the hem of a lace petticoat through the gap in the doorway.

"Rowena? Is that you?"

She heard a sigh, and the door opened to reveal her stepdaughter.

"Is there something I can help you with, Rowena?"

The girl fidgeted with her hands, picking at her thumbnail. Then she shook her head.

"Never mind," Thea continued, forcing a smile. "I'm glad you happened to be passing, for I wanted to speak to you."

Rowena glanced over her shoulder.

"There's nothing to be concerned about, my dear," Thea said. She gestured to a chair. "Why don't you come in and sit over there?"

"It's *my* home. I'll sit where I please."

"Of course," Thea replied. "I merely suggested what I felt was the most comfortable chair."

Rowena took the chair furthest from Thea and sat, her body stiff with tension. She scratched her thumb again, and Thea noticed how the skin was reddened and inflamed around the nail.

"What do you want?" Rowena asked.

"I was going to send for Mr. Franklin's works and wondered if there was anything else we could study together."

"We?" Rowena frowned.

"I understand the rudiments of arithmetic," Thea said, "and it's an essential subject to master if you wish to manage your own home." Rowena rolled her eyes, but undeterred, Thea continued. "And there's the sciences, of course. We could discuss the matter further when we have our picnic."

For a moment, Thea thought Rowena might smile, but she lowered her gaze to her hand and continued to pick at the skin around her thumb.

"You can't replace her."

"Who?" Thea asked. "Mrs. Ellis?"

Rowena lifted her thumb to her mouth and sucked it. The action raised her sleeve, and Thea caught sight of a dark mark on her arm.

"Rowena, have you been hurt?"

"I..." Rowena hesitated, then sighed and turned her head toward the window. "I fell out of my tree. I'm always doing it. See?" She raised her other hand and pointed to the bruises on her knuckles.

Thea remained silent.

"Don't tell Papa," Rowena said.

"He wouldn't want you hurt."

"I don't want him thinking I'm a nasty liar."

"A nasty liar?" Thea exclaimed. "That's a horrible name to take to yourself."

She crossed the floor and took Rowena's hand. At first, the girl tried to withdraw, then she curled her fingers round Thea's.

"I'm not here to replace your mother, Rowena," Thea said.

Rowena nodded, then she withdrew her hand. "May I go now?

"Of course, but I'd like you to consider my offer. I was wondering if you might help me with a scientific experiment later today."

Rowena cocked her head to one side. "Isn't science for boys? Miss Ellis says..."

"Miss Ellis says a great deal too much about things she understands too little," Thea said crisply. She patted Rowena's hand. "The offer's there, my dear—but you're under no obligation to take it."

She returned to her writing desk and resumed her letter to Meggie, aware of a pair of dark brown eyes watching her.

"Whatever you may think of me, Rowena," she said, maintaining her focus on the letter in front of her, "I'm here to fight for *you*—and I'll fight whoever I need to."

At length, she heard soft footsteps cross the floor.

"Thank you—Dorothea," a quiet voice said.

Thea let out the breath she'd been holding and turned round.

Her stepdaughter stood in the doorway. She gave Thea a quick, tight smile before disappearing.

It was progress, if only a little.

BY THE TIME Griffin returned home, the storm had cleared.

At least the storm *outside* had cleared. What about the one brewing inside? Rowe seemed to hate him more each day. And his relationship with his wife looked to be moving in the same direction.

Why weren't women easier to understand? They were a different species entirely. They said what they didn't mean and didn't say what they wanted. In a marriage, the rules regarding the woman seemed to change for no explicable reason, yet the man was expected to know and understand them at any given time.

Unlike a fight. There, the rules were simple. Tonight's fight at the White Hart promised to yield a considerable profit. Johnny Tighe had arrived from London that morning, and several small fortunes had changed hands as his followers placed their bets. Ned had tried to persuade Griffin to fight, but he'd refused. If he were to become a respectable husband, he must rise above his basest urges—including the urge to beat another man to a pulp—to show his wife he was capable of becoming a gentleman.

But not all physical urges could be easily conquered.

As if to prove the point, he caught sight of his wife hurrying toward the kitchen. Her hair in disarray, face flushed with exertion. She bore the wild look of a woman ripe for pleasuring—a sharp contrast to her usual spinsterish air.

The severe style of her gown could not completely conceal her figure—the womanly curves she did so much to hide and the lovely round arse beneath the folds of her skirt.

He followed her to the kitchen, where she was setting out a number of vials on the table. Then she approached the stove and dropped a white cloth into a pot, suspended over the fire.

What the bloody hell was she doing?

"Dorothea."

With a yelp, she jumped and turned to face him. She patted her hairs, trying to tame the stray tendrils.

"You needn't do that on my account," he said. "I prefer it when you don't look like a spinster aunt."

A flicker of hurt crossed her expression. "What do you want?"

He gestured toward the pot. "I wondered what you were doing."

"I'm preparing an experiment for Rowena."

He peered inside the pot, which contained a mush of red cabbage. She pressed her spoon onto the cloth and stirred it.

"Are you conducting an experiment on which of the two substances—cabbage or cotton—is a tougher meal?" he asked. "Is this to be my punishment for not eating all my vegetables last night?"

Her lips curled upward as she continued to stir.

"Ah—a smile!" he cried. "Perhaps I should conduct an experiment of my own to find out how I can stop my wife from appearing so discontented all the time."

The smile disappeared.

Bugger. He'd done it again.

"Forgive me," he said. "I'm not clever enough to know the right thing to say. Would you be kind enough to explain your experiment?"

She grasped a pair of tongs and lifted the piece of cloth from the pot, which was now stained a soft pink.

"It's something I tested at home in London," she said.

"Your home is *here* now," he said quietly, "and I'm glad of it."

The smile returned—his reward for repairing the earlier damage.

"I'm testing the acidity of different liquids," she said. "The pigment in the cabbage changes color when mixed with liquids of differing levels of acidity. The effect is more easily seen when the liquids are dropped onto a cloth stained with the pigment."

"Differing levels of acidity?" he asked. "I thought a liquid either was an acid, or it wasn't."

"There are differing degrees," she said. "Some liquids are strongly acidic and burn the skin. Others less so, and just cause a mild sting or, in the case of vinegar, a sour taste on the tongue. It's the same as people. Some are so disagreeable that you cannot bear their company. Others are only mildly irritating."

He threw back his head and laughed, and her eyes widened in surprise.

"You have a peculiar way of explaining things, Thea," he said. She turned her head away, but not before he caught her shy smile at his use of her name.

"Are you doing this for Rowe?" he asked.

She nodded. "I find it's often easier to learn through practical application rather than sitting at a desk and reading. And Rowena cannot sit still for long—she needs to be kept occupied."

At that moment, the subject of their discussion entered the kitchen, carrying an armful of flowers and grasses, and humming a melody. She caught sight of Thea and Griffin and stiffened.

"Oh," she said. "I can come back later."

"There's no need, Rowena," Thea said. "I've been preparing our experiment." She nodded toward the grasses in Rowe's arms.

"They're very pretty."

"You like them?"

"Yes, I do," Thea said. "Grasses are more interesting than flowers."

"Are they?" Griffin asked, voicing his curiosity even though he didn't wish to interrupt.

His wife focused her sapphire eyes on him. "Flowers attract one's attention immediately through their bright colors," she said. "Grasses, on the other hand, exhibit more subtle hues, which require deeper observation. To the untrained eye, they're plain and uninteresting. But to those of us who take the time to *look*, they give us a greater insight into the concept of beauty."

She might as well have been speaking of herself. Most of society thought her dull—that had been clear from his observations in London. Yet, the more he looked at his wife, the more he noticed her beauty.

She colored under his scrutiny, then addressed his daughter.

"Rowena, my dear, may I have some of those grasses for my chamber? They'd look very pretty there."

"Of course," Rowe said. "I'll find you a vase."

Griffin raised his eyebrows in astonishment. Since when had Rowe been so obliging?

Dorothea frowned at him as if admonishing him for his lack of faith in his daughter.

She was perceptive as well as beautiful.

"Rowena's been of great use today," she said.

"Mrs. Ellis will be pleased to hear that," Griffin said. "She always says…"

"Let us not speak of Mrs. Ellis," Dorothea said, glancing at Rowe, who'd visibly stiffened.

"May I be excused, Dorothea?" Rowe asked.

"Of course. Supper is at eight."

Rowe gave Dorothea a smile—an actual smile!—then she exited the kitchen.

"You're doing well with Rowe," he said. "She was almost civil just then."

"Your daughter's a lovely young woman," she replied. "She appears to have been misunderstood for most of her life—or at least, the last few years." She turned to face him, the directness of her gaze unsettling. "I intend to get to the bottom of what's troubling her."

"For what purpose?"

The last thing he wanted was his wife meddling about with the past, destroying the memories of a loving mother that he'd constructed so carefully.

Her eyes widened at his sharp tone.

"To give her peace of mind," she said.

"There's nothing wrong with her mind," he said. "You shouldn't interfere in matters which aren't your concern."

"Your daughter's welfare *is* my concern!" she cried. "Isn't that the sole reason you condescended to marry me?"

Bloody hell—he'd said the wrong thing again.

"No," he said quietly, "that's not the sole reason."

"Do you regret our marriage?"

Her words came out like a taunt, but her voice wavered, and her hands shook as she plucked at the grasses in her fist. Her expression conveyed defiance, but he saw something else.

A yearning to be valued.

He grasped her shoulders.

"No," he said. "Dear Lord, no—I shall never regret marrying you."

Her eyes widened, and for a moment, they stared at each other.

Then, unable to resist the craving which had burned from the moment he'd seen her disheveled form, he pulled her to him and placed his mouth over hers.

She stiffened in his grip, like a frightened woodland creature needing to be coaxed into submission. But she made no move to push him away.

Which he took as a good sign.

He lifted a hand and caressed her hair, then he peppered her mouth with tiny feather-light kisses until she began to soften in his arms.

A sigh escaped her lips, her breath a warm caress, and his whole body tightened with a surge of need. He ran his tongue along the seam of her lips, probing, teasing, begging entry while his manhood strained against his breeches.

She parted her lips—an invitation borne of instinct, and the aroma of herbs, which always lingered in the kitchen, sharpened into something else—the unmistakable, sweet scent of raw female need.

Dear Lord, she tasted like no woman he'd tasted before!

He opened his eyes to find her staring directly at him, the pupils dilated until they were almost black—deep pools into which he could plunge and take pleasure like never before. The raw desire in their expression shone like tiny stars deep within her soul.

Then she touched his tongue with hers—tentative at first, but she grew bolder and swept her tongue across his, engaging in a seductive dance. The hands which once held him at bay now clung to the fabric of his jacket.

What other woman kissed in such a wanton manner, other than the most accomplished whores? Most women closed their eyes to preserve their modesty and mystery. But the woman in his arms now stared right into him, her eyes conveying the basest, most primal need.

The need to be thoroughly and completely bedded.

In one move, he could bend her over the kitchen table, spread her legs, and rut her into the next county…

What the bloody hell was he doing!

Dorothea…" he said. "Forgive me. I have no idea what came over me."

She stared back at him, lips swollen from his kiss.

Shame replaced the desire in her eyes.

Damn it! He should have left her alone—sought relief at his own hand, or doused himself with a bucket of cold water.

"I'm sorry," he said.

"There's no need to explain," she said, her voice tight. "Please go."

He moved toward her, and she held up her hand. Then she lowered her gaze to his groin and let out a cry.

That was a first. No woman had cried at the sight of his erection before.

Finding himself dismissed, he retreated. Then, his mind made up, he crossed the main hallway and strode outside. Stopping only to tell a surprised-looking Will that he would not be coming back until late, he set off for the White Hart.

There was only one way to ease his torment—there had only ever been one way.

A bloody good fight.

Chapter Nineteen

WHAT THE DEVIL was her husband playing at?

He'd not turned up for supper, and a shamefaced Will had said he'd gone to his inn for the evening. There was little chance of him returning before her usual time for retiring, and she'd be damned if she would hang around waiting for him like some lovesick fool.

She blushed at the profanity, even if only uttered in her mind. Rather than turn her husband into a gentleman and his daughter into a lady—she was turning into a wanton.

Whatever he might have said earlier, it was plain that he regretted their match. There was nothing else to do tonight other than retire—perhaps with a glass of brandy to ease the ache in her head, if not the one in her heart.

As she crossed the hallway, the main doors crashed open, and a man staggered over the threshold. Untamed blonde locks curled over his shoulders. With his shirt half undone, exposing a broad muscular chest, and a necktie hanging loose, he looked like a ruffian.

He lifted his head, and she let out a yelp.

"Griffin!"

A bruise was already darkening on his face, and one eye was swollen almost shut. He lumbered toward her, and she caught the stench of male sweat and the familiar, metallic odor of blood.

He lifted a hand to steady himself, and she caught sight of his knuckles—swollen in places, red droplets blooming where the skin was missing.

He was hurt!

"Were you attacked on your way home?" she cried. "Who did this to you?"

"Johnny Tighe."

She clasped his sleeve as he reeled sideways.

"But the Mighty Oak felled him once more."

Thea recoiled in disgust as realization dawned on her.

"You've been fighting, haven't you!" she cried. "Is this why you were so eager to abandon your family tonight, to indulge in a brawl?"

"I won."

"That's not the point! You could have been hurt."

"*Johnny* came off worse. He won't get the better of me."

"Judging by the state you're in, I'd say he *did* get the better of you!"

"Is this what I come home to?" he growled, "A henpecking harridan?"

"Whereas you're nothing more than a brutish barbarian!"

Curse him! He wasn't the only one who could use alliteration as an insult.

He let out a crude laugh. "If I recall, you've looked upon this brutish barbarian with relish. What does that make you?"

She recoiled at the insult. "I was going to tend to your injuries, Griffin," she said. "But for *that*, you can see to them yourself."

She gave him a push, and he let out a yelp.

"Don't be such a baby!" she snapped.

Men were worse than children—overly eager to get into fights to prove their prowess but the first to cry for their mamas the moment they sustained a scratch.

He clutched his chest, and a red stain spread across the fabric.

Sweet heaven—he really *was* hurt!

She pulled his shirt back to reveal a deep gash on his chest, which glistened with a darkening red liquid.

She touched it with her fingertip, and he flinched.

"Was there nobody at the inn to tend to injuries?" she asked.

"Whatever for?"

"Silly me," she huffed. "I suppose you'd consider sending for a doctor to be an act of weakness."

"Have you finished, woman?" he growled.

"Not with *you*, I haven't. Can you walk unaided?"

"Of course. What do you think I am?"

"*That* question's best left unanswered," she said sternly. "Like it or not, those wounds need cleaning."

"They're nothing to speak of," he said. "Leave me be."

"Don't be a fool," she said. "Go and wait in the drawing room, and I'll tend to you there."

"Henpecking me again?"

"Oh, you're unbearable!" she cried. "But much as I'd prefer to leave your wounds to fester—if only to teach you a lesson in manners—you'll be even more unbearable tomorrow if I do."

"Do what you like," he said. "My head hurts so much, it's easier to yield."

He might be The Mighty Oak, but a few sharp words felled him better than any blow from Johnny Tighe, whoever *he* was. He was worse than her young nephew.

Ten minutes later, she entered the drawing room, carrying a tray laden with bandages and supplies. But he was nowhere to be seen.

He'd slunk off to his chamber to hide and sulk. Well, he wasn't going to escape.

When she reached his chamber door, she hesitated. There seemed to be an unspoken rule that a husband's bedchamber was his sanctuary, and a wife must wait to be invited inside.

But, tonight, he'd lost all rights to obedience. She pushed open the door.

The room was furnished in deep, masculine colors. Dark wood paneling lined the walls, which were unadorned except for candle sconces. A huge bed occupied the center of the room, thick, carved wooden posts supporting a canopy of dark green velvet, with frayed edges which needed mending.

She wrinkled her nose at the faint smell of damp.

The chamber must have been elegant in its time, but now it looked forlorn and neglected. It was, most certainly, the room of a barbarian.

And the room of a lonely man.

He lay on the bed, seemingly asleep. As she moved closer and placed her tray beside the bed, he let out a groan.

"Hell! That hurts."

She recoiled at the profanity.

"You've only yourself to blame," she said.

He let out a snort. "Are you here to plague me?"

"I'm here to dress your wounds," she replied. "Take your jacket off—or must I do it for you?"

He sat up, his eyes narrowing in pain, then hesitated, glancing at his chest.

"There's no need for shyness," she said. "I think I'm capable of restraining myself while I clean you up. Here—let me." She tugged at his sleeve and, with a sigh, he yielded and let her peel off his jacket and shirt.

The aroma of man grew stronger, and she lowered her gaze to his chest. Her heart thudded and her cheeks warmed as she followed the contours of his muscles.

She reached for the cloth and dipped it into the bowl of water, releasing the soft aroma of the herbs she'd sprinkled over the surface.

He wrinkled his nose. "What's that?"

"Lavender," she said, dabbing the cloth on his chest. "It's good for wounds and for masking unsavory smells."

"Are you saying I smell bad?" He looked up at her, and she was met with the full force of his gaze—a clear green, like an exotic ocean—an ocean she would willingly drown in...

"Ouch!" he winced. "That's devilish painful."

She arched an eyebrow. "Devilish?"

He gave a wry smile. "I can hardly curse in the presence of a lady."

"It hasn't stopped you before," she said, returning the smile. "Here..." She reached for a small vial and uncorked it.

He wrinkled his nose. "What's that?"

"Laudanum," she said. "It'll be less troublesome—for you and for me—if I can clean your wounds while you're half-conscious and free from pain."

"As you wish." Like an obedient child, he opened his mouth when she held the spoon to his lips.

She placed the bottle back on the tray, but before she could resume her work, he caught her hand.

"Thank you," he said.

"I'm doing what any wife would do."

"Not in my experience."

He closed his eyes, and she tended to him in silence, washing the grit out of his wounds and pressing the cloth against the bruises. By the time she'd finished, his breathing had grown steadier.

She placed her hand on his chest and caressed the skin, following the planes of his muscles with her fingertips. His body shuddered, and a smile curved along his lips.

"Mmm..." he murmured. "Delectable creature. I could rut you all night."

She froze. "What did you say?"

"That lovely arse of yours," he continued. "Two ripe, round globes, just made for my hands. I could part them and mount you from behind, while you howled like a cat in heat."

Sweet Lord!

"And your breasts…" he sighed, and his voice grew fainter, "…oh, those breasts. So sweet, so pink—how I long to taste them!"

Who was he speaking of? Some harlot from the White Hart?

"I want you," he whispered.

Tears stung her eyes, and she wiped them away.

"I want you…my Thea."

She froze.

"You want me?" she whispered.

But no answer came, for he'd fallen asleep.

Chapter Twenty

THEA SIFTED THROUGH the shortlist of names for positions in the household. Her husband had left for his inn before she could speak to him about it. He'd said nothing at breakfast about their encounter last night.

Had he forgotten what he said before he'd fallen asleep? That he wanted her?

Was it such a shameful thing to want a woman—or was it just shameful to want her?

During breakfast, he'd focused all his attention on Rowena. The girl seemed high-spirited. And from Thea's experience, a greater-than-usual sign of high spirits was the precursor to mischief.

"Mrs. Oake!"

She jumped at the voice, which seemed to be calculated at the exact pitch to convey dissatisfaction.

She turned to the newcomer. "What do you want, Mrs. Ellis?"

"I wish to discuss the child."

The child—Mrs. Ellis almost spat the words out.

"What's she done?" Thea asked.

"It's more what *you're* going to do," Mrs. Ellis said. "It's time she was sent to school. You must see it's in her best interests."

"You mean *your* best interests, Mrs. Ellis."

"You've not had to endure five years of her wickedness."

"Mrs. Ellis, you forget yourself," Thea said. "I won't have you speaking of Rowena in that manner."

"You forget *yourself*, Mrs. Oake," Mrs. Ellis said. "Like most second wives who cannot understand what it's like to be a mother, you're incapable of controlling a child who's not your own. I only speak out of a wish to be of use to you. I have a greater understanding of these matters."

This time the woman had gone too far.

Thea rose to her feet. "If you'll excuse me, Mrs. Ellis, I'm very busy."

The woman either didn't take the hint or chose to ignore it, and she followed Thea out of the parlor, her cane tap-tapping on the floor.

"Don't you have duties to attend to, Mrs. Ellis?" Thea asked. "I'm sure this can wait. In fact..." She met the woman's gaze. "I wish to take tea in the morning room, now—alone. We can discuss Rowena later."

Mrs. Ellis's mouth creased into a scowl. But Thea didn't care. The woman had seen fit to assume the morning room belonged to her.

"It's time for *my* tea, Mrs. Oake," Mrs. Ellis said.

"Then, take it in the kitchen."

From the look of horror on Mrs. Ellis's face, anyone would think Thea had asked her to parade naked to church on Sunday.

Thea swept into the morning room. Undeterred, the woman followed her.

"Really, Mrs. Ellis, I must protest!" As Thea spoke, she heard a small gasp. She glanced round the room and saw a curtain twitch at the far window. Perhaps Rosie had left the window open.

"I insist you take my advice on Rowena," Mrs. Ellis said. "The girl has a wicked soul."

"What utter rot!" Thea said. "Rowena's a bright young woman, in need of nothing more than a little guidance—and, I might add, love."

"She needs *discipline*," Mrs. Ellis said, "especially if you want her to become a lady. Mr. Oake will listen to my concerns, even if you refuse to."

How dare she! It was all Thea could do to prevent herself from smacking that pious expression off the woman's face.

"Rowena's welfare is not your concern, Mrs. Ellis," Thea said, "nor, from what I've seen, has it ever been."

"With all due respect..." Mrs. Ellis began, and Thea let out a snort.

"In my experience, the phrase *with all due respect* is the precursor to an insult." She folded her arms and met the woman's gaze. "You're on dangerous ground, Mrs. Ellis. Please do me the courtesy of remembering you're an employee—and not the mistress—of this house."

"I'll not stand here to be insulted," Mrs. Ellis said. "Mr. Oake will have something to say about this."

"Be my guest," Thea said. "I believe he's at the White Hart all day—much the same as any other day."

"Then I'll speak to him tonight," Mrs. Ellis said. She crossed the floor to the door opposite which was half-open. "If you need me, I'll be in the kitchen."

Thea heard another gasp from the direction of the twitching curtain. She glanced up and froze. Balanced on the door leading to the kitchen was a small wooden bucket.

Mrs. Ellis placed her hand on the door handle.

"Watch out!" Thea cried.

But it was too late. Mrs. Ellis pulled the door, and the bucket wobbled, then toppled over. Water poured onto her head as the bucket caught a glancing blow off her shoulder, then rattled to the ground.

Mrs. Ellis let out a shriek.

"What in damnation is this?" she cried.

Water dripped off her hair and shoulders, a dark stain spreading across her dress.

"Bloody brat!" she screamed. "I'll wring her neck!"

Thea recoiled at the force of her anger.

A snort came from behind the curtain. Miss Ellis strode to the window—surprisingly agile for a woman who professed to need a cane—and pulled it back.

Rowena stood in the alcove, shaking with laughter.

"You ungodly little bastard!" Mrs. Ellis cried. "You should be beaten for this—and I'll gladly be the one to do it!"

Before Thea could stop her, Mrs. Ellis raised her cane and brought it down hard on Rowena's shoulders. Rowena gave a howl of pain.

"No!" Thea cried. She rushed toward the window, but not before Mrs. Ellis landed another blow. Rowena crumpled to the floor, fending off the older woman with her hands.

Mrs. Ellis raised the cane again.

"You—spawn of the devil!" Mrs. Ellis cried. "How many times must I do this!"

Thea grasped the cane. "Stop!"

Mrs. Ellis turned, and Thea flinched at the hatred in her eyes.

"Give me my cane!" she cried.

"I most certainly won't," Thea said. "You've no right to treat Rowena like a dog. How long have you been beating her?"

"I've only done what any God-fearing woman would do."

"That's rot!" Thea cried.

Mrs. Ellis yanked at the cane, and Thea lost her balance.

The two women crashed to the ground, wrestling for the cane. Thea rammed her knee into Mrs. Ellis's chest. The act made the other woman lose her grip, and Thea wrenched the cane free. She struggled to her feet, then poked Mrs. Ellis in the chest with the tip of the cane.

"Get up," she said coldly.

Mrs. Ellis propped herself up with her arms. "I'll need my cane."

"Your cane is forfeit," Thea said. "You've shown that you only have one genuine purpose for it, and I'll not tolerate that in my house."

She glanced at the cowering girl in the alcove.

"Rowena, my dear, would you fetch Will? Mrs. Ellis will need help vacating the manor."

Rowena reacted to the calmness in Thea's voice and nodded. Then she retreated through the door.

Thea raised her eyebrows in challenge. But Mrs. Ellis, like all bullies, knew when she'd been cowed.

"Mr. Oake will hear of this," she said.

"That he will," Thea replied, smiling. "If I were you, I'd make sure you're several miles away by the time he learns the truth about how you've been abusing his daughter. And if he doesn't believe *her*, I've seen the bruises—and today's little demonstration of how you inflicted them leaves no doubt in my mind." Thea folded her arms and cocked her head to one side. "I wonder if the local magistrate would join me for tea tomorrow afternoon?" She glanced at the clock again. "My offer won't last forever, Mrs. Ellis. I'm inclined to let you have only five months' wages. One more word of protest, and it'll drop to four."

Shortly after, Rowena returned with Will.

"Ah! Excellent!" Thea said brightly. "Will—Mrs. Ellis is in need of an escort. She's visiting Reverend Flight, and I'm afraid she's lost her cane. So she'll be in need of assistance on her journey if you'd be kind enough to walk with her and carry her belongings."

"Very good, ma'am."

"Dear Mrs. Ellis, in her eagerness to appear independent, is averse to being given any help," Thea continued, "but I won't take no for an answer, Will. You must take her all the way to the reverend's door. There's no accounting for the ruffians who prowl the streets these days. Nobody is safe—not even in our own homes. Isn't that right, Mrs. Ellis?"

The woman nodded, her shoulders slumped in defeat.

"Perhaps you'd be so kind as to wait outside her door, Will, while she changes her attire, just in case she changes her mind also."

Will bowed to Thea, then held his arm out. Mrs. Ellis took it, and they shuffled out of the room.

As soon as the door closed behind them, Thea drew Rowena into her arms. The girl didn't resist but began to weep while Thea rocked her to and fro.

No words were necessary. Rowena cried, not only for the hurt she'd suffered but out of relief—that her torment was over. Thea saw no need to ask why Rowena hadn't asked for help before. In her own way, the girl *had* been asking for help in the manner by which she strove to gain her father's attention.

Her father...

What would Griffin say?

As if she read Thea's mind, Rowena stiffened in her arms.

"What will Pa do when he finds out?"

"You needn't worry about your papa," Thea said. "I'll explain it to him."

"Why didn't *he* punish me? I tell him I hate him, but he never beats me."

"Surely you don't *want* him to beat you?" Thea asked. "Do you want him to only see you as a wicked child—like Mrs. Ellis does?"

"Better that than not see me at all."

Thea's heart broke at the words of a young girl who just wanted to be noticed.

"Will *you* beat me?" Rowena asked.

"I don't advocate physical discipline," Thea said. "I can think of worse punishments to teach good behavior."

A ripple of fear glittered in Rowena's eyes.

"What could be worse?"

"The very worst punishment is that which we inflict upon ourselves," Thea said.

"Ourselves?"

"To reflect and understand the consequences of our actions—who we've hurt, what they're compelled to do to ease their pain. Often, the knowledge that the joy in someone's life is extinguished at our hand is punishment enough."

"What if I don't care?"

"I think you *do*," Thea said. "And though you may believe otherwise, your father *does* see you. And he loves you.

"He doesn't love me," Rowena said, "and he certainly doesn't love *you*."

Ignoring the stab of pain, Thea smiled.

"You know, Rowena—despite your best efforts, I'm beginning to like you."

"So, you won't punish me for what I did to Mrs. Ellis?"

"I didn't say that," Thea said. "You need to understand the consequences of your actions, and I have something in mind."

The fear returned in Rowena's eyes.

"With luck, you won't see it as a punishment," Thea said. "But it may not be easy for you." She held Rowena at arm's length.

"I don't expect you to like me, Rowena, but will you promise, from now on, to trust me enough to tell me the truth whenever I ask it? Sometimes confessing can be frightening, but it can save a lot of hurt."

Rowena met Thea's gaze, then the fear left her eyes, and she nodded.

"Good," Thea said. "And now, perhaps after your ordeal, you'd like a little solitude. Do you wish to spend the rest of the morning in the garden?"

"Yes," Rowena replied. "Do you mind?"

"Of course not. You may go."

Rowena approached the door, then hesitated.

"I'm sorry."

"What for?" Thea asked.

"For saying that Papa doesn't love you. It was unkind—when you've been nothing but kind to me."

Thea smiled. "Consider it forgotten, my dear."

Rowena returned the smile, then exited the room.

Poor child—how she must have suffered! And the more so for having nobody she could trust to speak of it. It was too painful to consider how long Mrs. Ellis had been beating her—but at least Thea had sufficient evidence to rid them all of that woman for good.

But as Thea watched her stepdaughter run across the lawn, she couldn't help but believe that what she'd said in the heat of the moment was true.

That her husband didn't love her—and never would.

Chapter Twenty-One

A S GRIFFIN TRUDGED up the driveway, he knew something was wrong. Will—whose demeanor was usually cheerful, ran out of the main doors, looking ragged.

"What's the matter, Will?"

"Mrs. Ellis has gone."

"Where?"

"The mistress dismissed her this morning."

What the devil had his wife done?

"*Dismissed* her?"

Will nodded. "I've never seen her so angry!"

"Mrs. Ellis—or my wife?"

Will colored and cast his gaze down. "Both."

"Both?"

"The mistress demanded I take you straight to her as soon as you returned."

What the bloody hell did she think he was? A wayward schoolboy to be summoned for a scolding?

Will set off toward the house, then glanced over his shoulder.

"Begging your pardon, sir, but are you coming?"

Heaven help him! She'd even got Will trotting after her.

Griffin thrust his hands into his pockets and followed Will inside. The law and the church might require the wife to pledge a vow of obedience, but in most marriages, it was the man who signed his life away to servitude.

He found his wife on the staircase, polishing the wooden banister.

"Shouldn't the servants be doing that?" he asked.

She stopped and fixed him with her intense gaze, her mouth creased into a frown. Recognizing the danger, Will muttered something about tending to the woodpile in the back yard and disappeared through a side door.

Coward.

Dorothea watched him, then shook her head in the manner of a disappointed teacher and resumed her attention on Griffin.

"I daresay Will told you what happened today," she said. He opened his mouth to speak, and she raised her hand.

"Permit me to finish before you present your excuses."

This was bad.

"I've endured the circumstances in this house for some weeks," she said, "and my suspicions were confirmed today. I've decided that enough is enough."

Had she decided to give up on him? Infuriating woman she might be, but a life without her was not to be borne.

"Are you leaving?" he blurted.

She frowned, then shook her head. "I don't know where you got that notion from," she said crisply. "Like it or not, this is my home, and I've no intention of leaving. I'm sorry to disappoint you."

Oh, Lord—he'd done it again. "No," he said. "I didn't mean…"

He broke off as she held up her hand again.

"Mrs. Ellis has left," she said.

"I know."

"I take it Will told you, though I ordered him not to," she continued. "But I half-expected him to disobey me, so I'm not surprised—only disappointed."

"Why did you dismiss her?" Griffin asked.

"The situation with Rowena became untenable," she replied. "While you were frittering away your time at your inn, you failed to notice what was going on in your house—the shameful and, frankly, wicked behavior of one who should know better."

Was she plotting to rid herself of Rowe?

"You can't send her away," he said. "I forbid it."

"Oh, you do—do you?" she said, her eyes flashing.

"I know she's a willful child," he said, "but you mustn't give up on her. Give my daughter a chance—please!"

Her eyes widened. "You think I want to send *Rowena* away?"

"Don't you?"

"Of course not! What the devil do you take me for?"

"I thought..."

She curled her lip in disgust.

"You thought I was some selfish creature who wished to dispose of your daughter so that I might have you all to myself?" She snorted. "Don't flatter yourself. And how dare you think I'd give up on your child? Don't you have the slightest notion of what's been going on here?"

She was talking in riddles again. Why did women never speak plainly enough for a man to understand?

"I can tell by the vacant expression on your face, you have no idea what I'm talking about," she said. "Let me spell it out for you—Mrs. Ellis has been abusing your daughter."

"How do you know?"

"Rowena's a forceful young woman," she said, "but she always seemed afraid of Mrs. Ellis. Nothing obvious—*you* clearly missed it— but I noticed how she watched the woman as if constantly seeking to gauge her temper. When I saw the bruises..."

"What bruises?"

"The bruises on her arms."

"Mrs. Ellis was *beating* her?"

"I caught her in the act this morning."

Rowe—his child—being beaten in his home?

"How long have you suspected?" he asked.

"A week or so."

"And you said nothing to me?" he asked, his voice rising.

"How could I? I wasn't sure myself. Besides—you're hardly here."

"That's no reason," he retorted. "Just because I'm not in the house all day, because I have to earn my living, unlike a London fop—doesn't mean you couldn't have told me!"

"I wasn't going to accuse someone until I was certain of their guilt!" she cried. "Rowena said her bruises came from falling out of a tree, and at first, that seemed a plausible explanation because most of them do. But today, when I caught Mrs. Ellis taking her cane to Rowena, I understood what's been happening."

"You should have accused Mrs. Ellis earlier!" he said. "It doesn't matter whether she's innocent or not."

"It *does* matter!" she countered. "My brother was tried for a murder he didn't commit! He was almost hanged because the authorities couldn't be bothered to search for evidence. I'll never—*never*—put anyone through a fraction of what he suffered!"

"But you…" he began, but she interrupted him.

"And what about you?" she asked. "You should have noticed! But you always think so highly of Mrs. Ellis. Is it any wonder your daughter couldn't speak to you?"

"You're the one who's supposed to be taking care of her," he said. "That's why I married you. But instead of focusing on her, you see fit to henpeck me."

She recoiled at his words "How dare you! You think I wanted this? Marriage to a man who, at best, views me as an inconvenience and who cannot see how unhappy his daughter is? I didn't take you for a brainless knucklehead, but I was wrong. Your daughter's been suffering for years because the two things she wants most in the world are denied her."

"And what are they?" he asked.

"She wants to be loved. And she wants her mother."

Bloody Louisa again! Why did she continue to plague him from beyond the grave?

"She *is* loved," he said. He moved to go past her, and she caught his sleeve.

"The time has come to discuss her mother," she said.

"I'll *not* discuss my late wife!" he snapped. "I've asked you several times not to plague me on the subject."

Guilt stabbed at him as hurt flashed in her eyes. Then she sighed, and her expression took on the steely determination of a woman, which never boded well when directed at a man.

"I merely wish to point out that Rowena's pain, in all likelihood, stems from your inability to be completely truthful with her about her mother."

"What female nonsense is that?" he exclaimed. "Rowena's mother is none of your business."

"But Rowena *is* my business," she said. "She's my child by marriage, even if..." her voice cracked, "...even if I'll never have a child of my own."

She blinked, and the despair in her eyes stabbed at his heart.

Rowena wasn't the only one who was deeply unhappy.

A tear spilled onto her cheek, and she wiped it away with an angry gesture, but when she spoke, she'd forced her usual calmness into her voice.

"Rowena is your child," she said. "She's in the world because of you. She didn't choose this life. Whereas I—I married you by choice, in full possession of my wits, and I must live with that choice, however much I may come to regret it."

Her voice caught once more, and she drew in a shuddering breath before resuming, as if forcing her emotions to recede. "You profess to love your daughter. But she needs you to *show* her. And you must begin by telling her the truth. However distasteful that may be for you—if you truly love her, then you owe it to her, even if you don't love…" she turned her head away, "…even if you have no wish to tell *me* the truth."

The sorrow in her voice pierced his heart, all the more because she fought to conceal it.

"And now," she said, "if you'll excuse me, I've duties to attend to."

She turned, and her foot slipped. With a cry, she tumbled down the stairs, and, for a moment, the memory of Louisa paralyzed him—the image of her body—lifeless and broken at the foot of the stairs.

"Dorothea!"

He raced after her, almost tripping in his desperation to reach her—but he was too late. She landed on a heap on the floor, her skirts round her waist.

She tried to stand.

"Don't move!" he roared.

She froze, her eyes widening as he approached her. He offered his hand, and she took it, curling her fingers round his.

"Are you hurt?" he asked, helping her up.

She winced. "My ankle."

"We must get you a doctor."

She shook her head. "It's just a sprain—and it doesn't hurt that much. There's no need to make a fuss."

The expression in her eyes said otherwise.

"There's every need," he said, and he scooped her into his arms. "Hold onto me, and I'll take you to your parlor and get Rosie to fetch you some tea."

"No…" she protested.

"Please," he said. "Let me take care of *you* like you've taken of me, and…" he hesitated, "like you've been taking care of Rowena."

He looked into her eyes and uttered a silent plea—one he could not bring himself to voice, asking her to give him a chance.

The irritation in her expression melted, then she lifted her arms and wrapped them round his neck.

"Very well," she said. "Just this once."

"Thank you," he whispered. "And, for what it's worth, I'll *never* have cause to regret our marriage."

He dropped a swift kiss on her forehead, then carried her up the stairs and along the portrait gallery, toward her parlor.

Halfway along, he glanced up at one of the portraits.

The eighth Lady Gillingham if he recalled. A woman with sharp yellowing eyes, a gray pallor, and, on closer inspection, a huge black beard that had been stuck onto her chin.

Mrs. Ellis had always complained about Rowena—her adornments to the portraits and her disrespect for the esteemed Gillingham family. And what had the woman said about his wife?

She seems to think it as much of a joke as the brat.

He hadn't thought that of any consequence until now.

He could have ended up with a wife like many other society ladies—sour-faced and only concerned about her social status—the kind of woman who cast a shadow on any merriment.

But Dorothea was not like any other. Beneath that exterior lay a wicked sense of humor to match Rowe's. And, out of everyone, she understood how Rowe was feeling.

In short, she was the best woman Fate could have chosen for him, and he was very much in danger of falling in love with her.

But the last thing he wanted to do was risk his heart—not after Louisa had ripped it to shreds.

Louisa's last words still haunted him, as if she'd cursed him from beyond the grave.

You're a big ugly brute, who doesn't deserve to be loved, Griffin. You don't know what it is to love another, and you never will. The day you die, there will be nobody to mourn you.

Was he doomed to suffer the fate she had decreed?

If Dorothea, and Rowena, ever discovered the truth, then he probably was.

Chapter Twenty-Two

"Would you like a bread roll, Rowena?" Thea handed the plate to her stepdaughter, who took one with a smile. "Thank you."

"I made them with Mrs. Morris, especially for our picnic," Thea said. "We added herbs and cheese to the mix. What do you think? They're still warm."

"It's delicious," Rowena said.

Thea looked around her, taking in her surroundings—the apple trees which had begun to blossom in the warm summer air, and the babbling stream which danced over rocks and stones, the clear water twinkling in the sunlight. The urge to climb one of the trees needled at her, as did a desire to paddle in the stream. She slipped her shoes off, rolled down her stockings, then stepped into the stream.

The water was cold, but she relished the refreshing feel of the stones beneath her feet.

Rowena finished the roll, then wiped her hands on her skirt and wrapped her hands round her knees.

"Did you have hot bread rolls when you had picnics with your mother?" Thea asked.

Rowena frowned and stared into the distance. "I can't remember."

"Do you remember anything about her?"

"Papa doesn't want me to talk about her."

"But *I* don't mind," Thea said. "We should always remember our loved ones—especially those who are no longer with us."

"Papa said she died when I was young."

"Don't you remember?"

Rowena closed her eyes. "I remember hearing voices—shouting. And screaming." She opened her eyes again and shook her head. "There was something else, but I can't quite grasp it."

"Do you remember what she was like?"

"Papa once said that Mama was a free spirit."

"You've certainly inherited that," Thea said, smiling. "I wonder if she doused her governesses with buckets of cold water, too?"

Rowena colored and looked away.

"Mrs. Ellis got what she deserved," Thea said. "I hear Reverend Flint is most relieved that she's gone to live with her sister in Hertford-shire. She won't be bothering us again."

She kicked her foot in the water, sending a splash toward Rowena. "Why don't you come in? The water's lovely."

Rowena grinned, then she slipped her stockings off and joined Thea in the stream.

"Damn—that's cold!" Rowena cried. Then she gasped. "Oh, for-give me!"

Thea laughed. "You should hear young Billy curse!"

"Billy?"

"My nephew—Meggie's son. I adore him."

"Who's Meggie?"

"My brother's wife," Thea said. "I've invited her to stay—I do hope she comes."

"Will she like me?" Rowena asked.

"She'll *love* you!" Thea said. "She's a free spirit, as well. Did you know, my brother once came upon her half-naked, swimming in a lake? He was furious! But, last summer, Meggie persuaded him to swim in the lake himself. I wish I could have seen it!"

"Weren't you there?" Rowena asked.

"I remained in London to mind the house." Thea sighed, remembering Dexter's townhouse, empty and forlorn with only her in it. Meggie had asked her to accompany them to the country, but she'd chosen to remain in London. She loved seeing her brother and his wife so happy together—but sometimes, she had to quietly turn away from it.

A hand caught hers, and she looked round to see Rowena's chocolate brown eyes watching her, bright with sympathy.

"Don't frown," Rowena said. "You were smiling before. You should smile more often."

"Should I?"

Rowena nodded. "Even at your age, you look quite pretty when you smile—not that being pretty is something anyone should aspire to."

Thea laughed. "I *think* I'll take that as a compliment."

Rowena colored. "I've said the wrong thing again, haven't I? Mrs. Ellis was always admonishing me for it."

"You spoke the truth," Thea said. "Whether or not that's something others wish to hear is their problem, not yours. But..." She cocked her head and raised an eyebrow. "You'll have to learn the art of diplomacy if you're to triumph in London."

"Diplomacy—what's that?"

"Being polite to people you don't like."

Rowena withdrew her hand. "Why must I go to London?" she asked. "I won't like it."

"Your papa wishes it."

"I don't want to go."

"Don't you want to try new things?" Thea asked. "Have you thought about what you want to do in life?"

"Not really," Rowena said. "Why should I?"

"You'll have to consider it at some point," Thea said. "Better to decide sooner rather than later when the choice may be taken from you. You're fortunate enough to have a choice, and you have a father who loves you enough to let you make that choice—if you'll give him a chance."

"He won't listen to me," Rowena said.

"Perhaps he'll listen to both of us."

"Why would you help me?"

Thea took Rowena's hand and patted it. "Because there's nothing more tragic than unfulfilled potential."

She blinked, and tears pricked at her eyelids. Rowena stared at her, understanding in her expression as if she knew that Thea was speaking about herself.

It was time to change the subject. Thea gestured toward the picnic basket.

"There's shortbread in there," she said. "Would you like me to show you how to make it?"

Rowe opened her mouth to protest, but Thea continued. "Consider it part of your education."

"In the domestic servitude of a woman?"

"My brother-in-law bakes it often," Thea said, "and he's a duke."

"A duke?" Rowena's eyes widened with interest. "What's he like?"

"Very affable, for all that he has a title—and he loves my sister Lilah with all his heart, which is admirable given that she's even more of a hellion than you are."

Rowena gave a laugh, which warmed Thea's heart.

"Lilah is so like you," Thea continued. "Fraser, her husband, is magnificent. A real Highlander, like the ones you see in paintings, with flame-red hair and a booming voice, you can't help liking him..." She closed her eyes, drawing on her memory for the image of two cherubs, so full of life and laughter. "...and little Flora and Campbell. How you'd love them! Perfect in every way and always so sweet to their old aunt."

"Do you want children of your own?" Rowena asked.

Thea blinked back a tear. "I have you, have I not? You're not a child anymore, but I can try to help you as best I can."

"To bake biscuits and keep house—like a servant?"

"Making biscuits needn't represent a loss of liberty," Thea said. "It's about being self-sufficient, so you don't need a husband to pay someone to do it for you. You might think managing a home a dull occupation, but it requires skill and good judgment, and I had to acquire both on my own, for I had nobody to show me. I even learned to chop wood."

Rowe's eyes lit up. "You did? Papa chops wood. But he never lets me help."

"Perhaps we can persuade him—together," Thea said.

"I'd rather chop wood with Papa than bake biscuits with you."

Thea ignored the stab of hurt. "As you wish—we don't all have to like the same things."

She stepped out of the stream and sat on the blanket, wiping her feet. Shortly after, Rowena joined her.

"May I have a piece of shortbread?"

"Of course," Thea said. "Have as many as you like."

She lay back and closed her eyes, relishing the warmth of the sun on her face and the delicate, musical babbling of the stream—gentle sounds, infinitely preferable to the bustle of London.

She heard Rowena rummaging about in the hamper, followed by crunching as she helped herself to a biscuit.

"Dorothea?"

"Mmm-hmm?" Thea murmured, unwilling to open her eyes, as she drifted into a doze.

"This shortbread is delicious."

"Don't eat it all, Rowena, or you'll not do justice to supper."

"If I do eat it all," Rowena said, "you must show me how to make more—if you have no objection."

Thea smiled to herself. She may never know the love of a child of her own, but the olive branch her stepdaughter offered was something to nurture.

"No, Rowena, my dear," she said. "I have no objection at all."

Chapter Twenty-Three

A s Thea entered the breakfast room the next morning, her husband and Rowena were already seated at the table.

An envelope was propped up against Thea's teacup. The sight of her name, written in a familiar hand, swelled her heart with hope and love.

"Meggie…"

She traced the direction with her forefinger, following every curve of the letters. Then she set it aside.

"Why don't you open it?" Rowena asked.

"I'll wait until after breakfast," Thea said. "It's not polite to read during a meal."

"Is that something I must learn for when we go to London?"

"Do you want to go?" Thea asked.

Rowena glanced at her father, then she nodded. "You'll come, too, Dorothea, won't you?"

"Of course she will," a deep voice said. Thea glanced up to see her husband looking straight at her. "We'll be going together—as a family."

Then he smiled. "Read your letter, Dorothea," he said. "I know how much you miss your sister. Of course…" he hesitated, "…you'll want to read it in private."

She opened the letter. "I can read it now—I have no secrets."

He glanced at Rowena, discomfort in his expression.

Thea opened the envelope and let out a cry of joy as she read the first paragraph.

"Oh! She's coming to stay next week—that is, if you've no objection."

"None at all," he said. "We'll do all we can to make her welcome—won't we, Rowe? If you help Dorothea with the house, I'll see to the estate. There's a huge pile of logs needing chopping."

"*I* can chop firewood," Rowena said.

"I don't know," he said. "I…"

Thea cleared her throat. He glanced toward her, and she raised her eyebrows.

Then he smiled and nodded. "Of course you can help."

Rowena smiled. "Thank you, Papa!"

He reached for Rowena's hand. She hesitated, then took it. The surprised smile on his face tore at Thea's heart. Unwilling to intrude on the tenderness of the moment, she rose to her feet.

"I should see to Mrs. Morris in the kitchen," she said. "There's much to be done before Meggie arrives."

>>><<<

"IT'LL BE GOOD to have a guest in the house!" Mrs. Morris said as she sprinkled water onto the flour mixture and stirred it with her hands.

She squeezed the dough into a ball and lifted it up. "Is this the right consistency?"

"It needs to be sticky," Thea said. "A wet dough makes a lighter bread, though the kneading's a little messy."

"How can you tell when it's sticky enough?"

"You throw it at the wall," Thea said. "If it sticks, then it's just right. Shall I try it?"

"Mrs. Oake!" the cook exclaimed. "You wouldn't waste a good

dough, would you?"

"Of course not," Thea laughed. "Now, can you remember how to plait it, like I showed you?"

"Show me again."

Thea split her dough into three, rolled each part out, then folded them over each other.

"This is Meggie's favorite," she said, "particularly if there's rosemary in the mixture. Well, perhaps her *second* favorite, behind my shortbread."

Rowena appeared at the kitchen door. "What are you doing?" she asked.

"Baking bread for Meggie's visit," Thea said. "I'm making shortbread next."

"May I help?"

"Weren't you going to help your papa with the wood?"

Rowena's voice took on a note of shyness. "I—I'd like to help *you*, if you'll let me."

"Then you shall," Thea said. "Mrs. Morris, I'll keep an eye on the loaves. Perhaps you'd like to take the rest of the day off?"

"Can I?" the cook asked. "I could visit my niece. Her confinement's any day now, and she needs all the help she can get, with her twins being such a handful."

"Good, then that's settled," Thea said. "Once we have a full complement of staff, you must spend more time with your niece. Why don't you take her a slice of that meat pie from the store?"

"Thank you, ma'am!" The cook bobbed a curtsey, then disappeared, singing to herself.

Rowena remained in the doorway while Thea set out the ingredients. Though the girl seemed to have made progress, Thea still had no wish to force a relationship.

What was it Dexter always said when negotiating a business deal?

Always let the bid come to you.

Thea tipped flour into a bowl, followed by pieces of butter, then rubbed them together with her fingertips.

Soft footsteps approached, and Rowena appeared at the opposite side of the table.

"She's happier since you came to live here."

Thea sprinkled sugar over the mixture. "You mean Mrs. Morris?"

Rowena nodded. "I think *everyone's* happier." She gestured toward the bowl. "What can I do?"

Thea tipped the mixture onto the table and fashioned it into a ball. "You can cut out the biscuits if you like. My nephew likes me to cut it into the shape of a lion—which isn't as easy as it sounds."

"It's easier than chopping wood."

"Did you help your father with the logs?" Thea asked.

"Papa let me try, but he said my technique was so bad that I was in danger of taking a limb off."

"That's not very kind of him," Thea said.

"Oh no—he was right!" Rowena exclaimed, and Thea smiled at the girl's defense of her father. "I narrowly missed his hand. He pointed out that, unlike an apple tree, he only had two upper limbs, neither of which would grow back."

"A woman needs to master the technique all the more than a man," Thea said, "due to her lesser physical strength."

"Are we always to be the weaker sex?"

"Physical strength isn't everything," Thea said, rolling out the biscuit dough. "There's wit, intelligence, and strategy. Men think they have the upper hand, but the trick is in getting them to do your bidding while simultaneously convincing them it was their idea."

"Is that what you're doing with papa?"

"Heavens, no!" Thea laughed. "Nobody can convince your father to do anything he doesn't want to."

Certainly not me.

She picked up a knife and sighed. A slim hand touched her wrist, and she looked up. Rowena's eyes shone with compassion.

"Let me do it," she said.

Thea handed Rowena the knife, then wiped her eyes. "Why don't you cut the dough into whatever shapes you like, while I clear away the bowls?

"Isn't that a job for servants?"

"It does no harm to understand what the work entails," Thea said. "I did all the cooking and cleaning when we were growing up before we could afford servants."

"What was it like being poor?" Rowena asked. "Was it really dreadful?"

Thea poured water into the sink. "Life was simpler then—our needs were simpler."

"How so?"

"All we wanted was enough food so we'd not go hungry—and enough coal so we wouldn't freeze." Thea smiled at the memory. "We had each other, which was all that mattered—Dex was away most of the time."

"Dex?"

"My brother, Dexter."

"That's Papa's banker, isn't it? Sir Dexter Hart?"

"The very same."

"But he has a title!"

"Dexter earned his knighthood through hard work," Thea said. "Until he married Meggie, he didn't understand what matters in life."

"And what's that?" Rowena asked.

"Love," Thea said. "Meggie taught my brother how to love."

"How?"

"By being herself," Thea said. "You'll understand—when you meet her. There's something about Meggie that makes you want to love her."

"What?"

"I think it's because she wants everyone to be happy—and in love."

Even me.

Thea wiped her eyes, then turned from the sink to face her stepdaughter. "How are you getting on with those biscuits?"

Rowena said nothing but cleared her throat nervously.

"Rowena?"

The girl colored and set the knife down, suppressing a giggle. Thea looked over the dough, recognizing the shapes. Rowena had, indeed, been busy with the knife. How a girl of fourteen could draw the outlines with such accuracy was beyond her. But Rowena was an intelligent young woman, and she'd clearly put that anatomical reference book to good use.

Rowena had cut the shortbread into the shapes of male parts.

"What do you think?" Rowena asked, her voice tight with apprehension.

A bubble of mirth swelled inside Thea. "I applaud your attention to detail," she said. "What's that supposed to be?" she asked, pointing to the markings indented along the shape.

"Veins."

"Oh, my sweet Lord!"

Rowena's eyes widened, and she took a step back. "Are you angry?"

"Angry at what?" a deep voice said.

Rowena let out a shriek.

Griffin stood in the doorway.

"What's that?" he asked.

"Shortbread," Thea said. "For Meggie."

"May I try some?"

"We need to bake it first."

He stared at the dough, then raised his eyebrows.

"May I be excused?" Rowena asked. Without waiting for a response, she fled.

Griffin approached the table. "If they're supposed to be life-size," he said, a glint of amusement in his eyes, "then I should be affronted."

"I wouldn't know, would I?" Thea asked bitterly.

He took her hand. "Thea, I..." He hesitated, then drew close, lifting his free hand to her face. With a touch that was surprisingly delicate, he traced the outline of her face with his fingertip, then placed his palm against her cheek, and he stroked her skin with his thumb.

Her skin tightened with need as a rush of warmth flooded her body. How could such a giant of a man elicit such tenderness with a single touch or ignite such a burning need within her?

Then he lowered his hand and withdrew.

"I should see to the wood," he said. "Will felled a tree yesterday, and it'll take weeks to chop into logs."

She nodded and turned away, not wanting him to see the disappointment in her eyes. By the time she turned back, he'd already gone.

Chapter Twenty-Four

T HE CARRIAGE DREW to a halt, and a diminutive woman stepped out, dressed in a fashionable gown of bright orange.

"Welcome to Sandiford Manor, Lady Hart," Griffin said, offering his hand. She looked up and smiled.

"Thank you, Mr. Oake."

Griffin's wife stood in the doorway next to Rowe.

"Meggie!" she cried.

"Thea!"

The two women ran toward each other and embraced.

Tears of joy ran down Dorothea's face. "You've no idea how much I've missed you."

Dear Lord—was his wife that unhappy?

"And I, you, darling Thea," Lady Hart said. "What a beautiful house you have! Are you happy here?"

"I'm well, Meggie, as you see," Dorothea said.

Not very encouraging.

Lady Hart glanced toward Griffin. "I trust you've been taking good care of my sister, Mr. Oake."

He shuffled on his feet uncomfortably. Did every woman in this damned family wish to chew his balls off? What could he say? That his wife was unhappy, and there wasn't a damned thing he could do about it?

"Of course he's taking care of me, Meggie!" Dorothea exclaimed. "He's a good husband."

There was a little too much insistence in her voice. But if Lady Hart noticed it, she gave no sign.

"You must show me around, Thea," she said. "If this house is half as beautiful on the inside as it is on the outside. I shall be obliged to call it the most delightful house in the kingdom."

She looked at Rowe. "You must be Rowena—how delightful!"

Rowe had stood, fidgeting in the doorway, while Dorothea embraced her sister. Now, under Lady Hart's scrutiny, her mouth downturned into a scowl. She looked like a thundercloud about to break.

But Lady Hart was not to be deterred.

"Thea's told me so much about you, Rowena. I feel I know you already."

A ripple of panic crossed Rowe's expression, and she glanced at Dorothea, who let out a laugh. "There's no need to worry, Rowena. Meggie's not Mrs. Ellis."

"Ugh—Mrs. Ellis!" Lady Hart wrinkled her nose. "She sounded a right miserable old hag. I've met women like her. All prim and proper but an evil old witch beneath all that respectability—there's plenty to be found in London."

"Are there?" Rowena asked.

"They're like rats," Lady Hart said. "You're always within ten feet of one."

"But unlike rats, they're not so easily disposed of," Dorothea laughed.

Griffin's skin tightened at the mirth in her voice. She threw back her head, and her eyes sparkled in the sunlight. She was a beautiful creature when she smiled like that!

Lady Hart offered her free arm to Rowe. "Would you join us for tea?"

Rowe glanced at Griffin, uncertainty in her expression. Then she lowered into a curtsey.

"Lady Hart, welcome…"

"Oh, that's enough of that!" Lady Hart laughed. "I'd like to think among friends I never have to hear that awful name. *Lady Hart!* Makes me sound like a fat, dowager fossil."

"How should I address you?" Rowe asked.

"Aunt Meggie will do nicely."

"*Aunt* Meggie?"

"Why not? On your papa's marriage, you gained a new family—and I'm one of them. Now—take my arm. Perhaps *you'd* be so kind as to show me around."

To Griffin's relief, Rowe smiled. She took the proffered arm, and the three of them went inside. After giving instructions to Will to take Lady Hart's trunk to her chamber, Griffin followed in their wake.

⟫⟩⟨⟨

"WOULD YOU LIKE some coffee, Lady…I'm sorry…Aunt Meggie?"

Griffin watched as Rowe reached for the coffeepot. The lid rattled—the only indication of her apprehension.

How did she come to be so civil? Not a single profanity for the whole of the day! As for dinner—he'd never seen such table manners.

"I trust you've had a pleasant afternoon, Lady Hart," Griffin said.

"Wonderful, thank you," she replied. "I found the picture gallery particularly interesting." She winked at Dorothea, who smiled back.

He couldn't remember ever seeing his wife this relaxed. Not even at her brother's house in London.

"Supper was delicious, Thea," Lady Hart said. "Steak's so difficult to cook—all the more because it has the illusion of being easy. I must commend the excellence of your cook."

"Rowena oversaw supper tonight," Dorothea said. "Mrs. Morris acted under her direction. Didn't she, Rowena dear?"

Rowe blushed and smiled.

"Then you're as talented as Thea said in her letters," Lady Hart said. "My sister's not prone to exaggeration, but I have to admit a little skepticism when I read her letters. I hardly dared believe such a paragon existed."

Rowe glanced at her stepmother. "You wrote good things about me?"

"Her letters are full of you, my dear," Lady Hart said. "I've so looked forward to meeting you—and I cannot wait for you to come to London."

Rowe picked up a plate laden with shortbread and handed it to Lady Hart, who took one and placed it on her saucer.

Griffin's heart fluttered. *Ye gods!* Was that the one shaped like…

Dorothea let out a squeak, but Lady Hart seemed not to notice. She sunk her teeth into the end of the shortbread, and Griffin winced as he felt a twinge of pain in his groin.

Rowe let out a snort, and she lifted her hand to her face as if to hide her smile.

Bloody hell.

"I can't wait until Madame Dupont sees you," Lady Hart said.

"Who's she? A French teacher?"

"She's a modiste—she makes dresses. She'll rave over you—I can imagine her now, as soon as she sees the color of your eyes." Lady Hart threw out her hands in an exaggerated gesture and wiggled her nose. *"Ooh la la! Chocolat liquide!"*

Dorothea laughed. "You look like a squirrel, Megs! Madame doesn't speak like that—or twitch her nose."

"I dare say she twitches her nose a good deal when Easton takes his unfortunate wife to see her."

"Easton?" Rowe asked. "Who's that?"

"The Duke of Easton," Dorothea said. "The stench of cabbage

always lingers around him."

"And a cloud of flies," Lady Hart added.

"So, he's found someone to marry him?" Dorothea asked. "Not that dreadful Francis creature! What was her name—Sarah? Atalanta *loathes* her."

"And well she might. She gave me the cut direct when I first came to London," Lady Hart said. "Not that I mind—I'd hate to feel obliged to be civil toward her."

"You couldn't be uncivil if you tried, Meggie, darling." Dorothea smiled. "Leave that sort of thing for Lilah."

Rowe let out a yawn, then she gasped. "Do forgive me!"

"No—you must forgive *us*," Dorothea said. "Your Aunt Meggie and I have so much to catch up on."

"Come along, Rowe," Griffin said. "We'd better leave these two ladies to their gossip."

Dorothea colored and rose "Griffin, I..."

He placed a light hand on her shoulder. "I was jesting," he whispered. "I know how fond you are of your sister-in-law, and I also know that you're too considerate to demand to be left in peace to spend time alone with her." He stroked the skin of her neck with his thumb.

"Let me grant you that peace."

She looked up and rewarded him with a smile.

"Thank you."

It was the first time she'd turned her smile on him—a genuine smile of gratitude and pleasure.

It was a smile that touched his heart.

And if he could, he'd see that smile on her face every day for the rest of his life.

"ANOTHER SHORTBREAD, MEGGIE?"

Thea leaned across the picnic blanket and handed her sister-in-law the plate. Meggie was to be at Sandiford less than a week. The days had flown by, and Thea only wished she could stay for longer.

"They're delicious," Meggie said. "Though I can't say the shape would be acceptable in Dexter's drawing room. Imagine the look on Lady Cholmondeley's face!"

"Or Lord Cholmondeley!" Thea giggled. "It might give him a sense of inferiority if he held it against his breeches."

"Really, Thea, you're getting quite crude!" Meggie laughed. "I'm seeing a different side to you here. I don't know whether it's because you're now mistress of your own home, or..." A tone of mischief entered Meggie's voice, "...whether it's due to that husband of yours."

"Griffin?"

"He's quite something," Meggie said. "He seems friendlier than he was in London. And he's easy on the eyes, of course. I swear I saw that woman salivating in church on Sunday."

"What woman?"

"The one who looked like she'd stepped in a cowpat," Meggie said. "You said she once owned Sandiford Manor?"

"Lady Gillingham?" Thea shrugged her shoulders. "I take little notice of her."

"She wrinkled her nose as soon as she saw me." Meggie sighed. "No doubt the story of my birth has reached her. I was half-hoping she'd insult me to my face to give me leave to reciprocate. But perhaps it's for the best. One must never call another woman a sharp-nosed old sow—at least not in church."

Thea giggled. "You're quite irreverent, Meggie, do you know that? Nothing like the timid creature Dex brought home to London. Don't tell him I said so, but Dex is good for you—and you are for him, of course."

"I could never have imagined I'd be so happy!" Meggie said. "Sometimes, I wake up in the morning and wonder if it's all a dream.

Then I feel the bed move, and he's right beside me."

"He…" Thea hesitated, unwilling to let the jealousy bleed through into her voice, "…he visits you every night?"

Meggie colored and nibbled on her biscuit. "Forgive me. It's not done to speak of such things." She gestured toward the house.

"You must be happy here," she said. "At least I can reassure Dexter on that front. Your husband adores you."

"Does he?"

Meggie sat up. "You don't see it?"

Thea shook her head. The tears, which always seemed just out of reach, now threatened to make an appearance.

"Oh, Thea!" Meggie cried. "You must have noticed the way he looks at you? And—if you'll permit me to speak of such things—the surest way to tell whether a man wants you is how often he visits your bed."

Thea turned her head away and focused her attention on the apple tree at the entrance to the orchard. The blossom, tiny dots of pink, gave a soft contrast to the pale green leaves. If the warm weather continued, there would be plenty of apples to fill the cold store.

A light hand touched her arm.

"Thea? Have I said anything wrong?"

Thea shook her head. "No, Meggie. It's my fault."

The confusion in Meggie's eyes turned to understanding.

"He's not visited you, yet?"

"No," Thea said. "Did you have to invite my brother to your chamber?"

"When have you ever known Dexter wait to be invited? He knocks loudly, then crashes through the door, regardless—but your husband is different."

"Is he?"

Meggie laughed. "Of course! Despite having the appearance of a primitive, Mr. Oake is far less likely to take what he wants than

Dexter. He lacks that streak of ruthlessness. But he's a fool to leave you alone. Perhaps he's shy."

"Shy? A man like Griffin?"

"Big, powerful men often are," Meggie said. "And when they value the prize, they become flustered in the struggle to attain it. I dare say your husband thinks you're too much of a lady for him, so he has no idea what do to with you."

"But he's my husband!" Thea burst out. "Why doesn't he just take what he wants?"

"Do you *want* to be taken?"

An uncomfortable heat bloomed in Thea's face. Her face must be as red as the strawberries they'd eaten last night for supper.

"There's no shame in wanting your husband to make love to you," Meggie said.

"And how do I achieve that?" Thea asked.

"You must seduce him!"

"Like a wanton?" Thea asked. "Did *you* have to seduce Dexter?"

"Not at first," Meggie said. "But I soon learned that he takes much pleasure from being seduced—and gives me much pleasure in return."

Thea blushed again. Her cheeks felt as if they were on fire.

"Thea! Do I embarrass you?"

Thea shook her head. "No—I just wonder why you never said anything before, about..." she hesitated, bushing again, "...about relations between a man and a woman."

"You're married now," Meggie said. "Before, I saw no reason to speak of something which you might never experience."

"I might still never experience it."

"Nonsense!" Meggie cried. "Your husband just needs a little encouragement."

"Like what?" Thea asked. "How do you encourage my brother?"

Now it was Meggie's turn to blush. She leaned toward Thea and lowered her voice, though there was nobody around to hear them.

Rowena was in the kitchen helping Mrs. Morris—she'd promised to bake a pie for supper before Meggie left for London tomorrow—and Griffin was in the yard, chopping wood.

"Sometimes I strip for him," Meggie whispered.

"Strip?"

"I remove my garments. Not all at once—he takes pleasure in what he *cannot* see. A man possesses a vivid imagination where a woman's body is concerned."

"You think I should *strip* for my husband?"

"Not all at once," Meggie said. "Start with your..." she glanced over her shoulder, "...start with your breasts."

Thea drew in a sharp breath and lifted her hand to her throat. "My..."

Meggie nodded. "Dexter loves to caress them—and you cannot believe how much I like it. The sensations he brings about are quite astonishing. My whole body comes alive, not only with the sensation but with anticipation of what's to come."

Thea's breath caught in her chest. "Oh, dear,"

"There's no need to be embarrassed, Thea. You have a lovely figure, though you keep it hidden. You should be proud of your body."

"Pride is a failing, Meggie," Thea said. "It leads to an exaggerated opinion of one's worth."

"That's vanity, Thea darling, and you're the least vain creature I know. There's nothing wrong with taking pride in your body."

"I have no wish to make myself look pretty for a man," Thea said.

"A commendable philosophy," Meggie said, "but with one failing."

"Which is?"

"It leads to self-loathing. You must love yourself for others to love you. There's nothing wrong with having confidence in who you are."

"I wouldn't want to be a slattern," Thea said.

Meggie threw back her head and laughed. "A slattern! You're the last person in the world I'd call slatternly."

"Nevertheless, I doubt I'll be able to seduce my husband."

"All you need is a little courage," Meggie said. "Something to soften the hard edges of inhibition. I suggest brandy."

"Brandy?"

"Or whisky, if you're averse to drinking your husband's brandy. I know Lilah gave you a bottle when you married. Or does your husband keep his liquor under lock and key?"

"He hardly touches it," Thea said. "I've never seen him drink, except a little wine at mealtimes. He showed no interest in Lilah's whisky. In fact, it's still in my chamber."

"Excellent!" Meggie said. "All you need do is drink some, then you're ready to seduce him."

"How much should I drink?"

Meggie shrugged her shoulders. "Two—maybe three glasses? Enough to swell your courage, but not so much as to lose your reason."

"Will it work?"

Meggie laughed. "Of course it will! If a man looks at a woman the way your husband looks at you, all you need do is show him a little flesh, and then he'll be under your spell."

"Are you sure? I don't want to do anything I'd regret."

Meggie took Thea's hand and kissed it. "Trust me," she said. "When you've discovered the pleasures of making love, the only regret you'll have is that you didn't do it sooner."

"THE CARRIAGE IS ready, Lady Hart."

"Thank you, Will. You've looked after me admirably during my stay."

Griffin watched as the young man blushed, then scuttled outside to wait beside the carriage. Will was smitten with Lady Hart.

She was no ordinary society woman—and she was all the better for it.

As was Griffin's wife.

During Lady Hart's stay, Dorothea had never seemed happier. Rowe, too, had relaxed in their guest's company, her initial shyness having disappeared as soon as Lady Hart had taken her into her arms and kissed her warmly on both cheeks. One couldn't help being disarmed by her innocent charm. Sir Dexter was a damned lucky bastard.

As was Griffin.

They reached the carriage, and Rowe approached Lady Hart, a parcel in her hand.

"Something for your journey, Aunt Meggie."

"I hope it's something sweet," Lady Hart replied. "Four hours in a carriage is too long to go without something to eat."

"It's shortbread," Rowe said. "I made it myself. There's enough for you and Sir Dexter—and your children."

Oh no...

The last thing Griffin wanted was Sir Dexter in a rage when he opened the packet to find cock-shaped biscuits.

"My favorite!" Lady Hart cried. "I trust you've fashioned them into interesting shapes?"

Rowe had the grace to blush—the little hellion!

"I've cut them into stars and flowers," she said. "I thought the children would appreciate them."

Beside him, Thea visibly relaxed and exhaled. She met Griffin's gaze, and he winked. The smile she rewarded him with ignited a flame that threatened to burst in his breeches.

"I mustn't open them until I'm home," Lady Hart said with an exaggerated sigh. "Once I do, I'll not be able to stop eating them—and Dexter would be most disappointed."

"My brother can weather a little disappointment," Dorothea said.

"It wouldn't do for him to get his own way all the time."

"But," Lady Hart said, "if I return with a little treat for him, then he'll reward me in other ways."

Was he imagining it, or did her eyes glimmer with a hint of wickedness? Did this innocent-looking little thing hide a passionate heart?

"I wish you didn't have to go," Dorothea said.

"It's not forever," Meggie replied. "You'll be coming to London very soon. And, Rowena, my dear, don't forget, you're to address my husband as Uncle Dexter."

Dorothea giggled. "I hope I'm there to see his face when that happens!"

"Oh dear," Rowe said. "Perhaps I oughtn't."

"You most definitely *ought*," Lady Hart said. "My husband might growl at strangers, but among family, he's gentler than my pug—though I wouldn't recommend setting him on my knees, and I know for a fact that he dislikes being scratched behind his ears."

"Meggie!" Dorothea laughed again.

Bloody hell! Did she do it deliberately to ignite Griffin's passions until he could no longer contain them? If she threw back her head one more time to laugh—exposing that long throat of hers, and stretching her gown across her breasts—he'd spend in his breeches like a teenager in a brothel.

As it was, he could see her ripe, round form through the thin fabric of her gown—the delicate turn of her ankles, moving up to her beautifully proportioned calves, then widening out into shapely thighs, which begged to be parted...

Lady Hart turned her attention to Rowe once more.

"Don't forget, my dear, as soon as you arrive in London, you must go straight to Madame Dupont to see about your wardrobe. Then I'll introduce you to my friends. Lady Stiles is charming, and she paints excellent likenesses. Would you like to sit for your portrait?"

"I don't know," Rowe said.

"I'm sure *your* likeness would do a much better job of gracing the portrait gallery here at Sandiford," Lady Hart said. "The Gillingham family were a gruesome-looking lot, were they not? I daresay the beard I spotted on Lady Gillingham's portrait was a marked improvement, seeing as it hid all those chins."

Rowe giggled, and Lady Hart embraced her. "My children will *adore* you." She turned to Griffin. "Billy is eager to meet the famous Mighty Oak—my brother Devon has spoken of little else. I'm afraid you'll find yourself obligated when you come to London."

"Obligated?" he asked.

"You promised to teach him an uppercut—not that I know what *that* is."

"It's a move during a fight," Dorothea said. "A punch which travels upward at force and connects with the chin." Her tone grew breathless, her eyes bright. "When executed properly, it can fell an opponent with a single blow. It can only ever achieve success at close range, so it requires daring as well as skill." She let out a sigh. "I've never seen anything so magnificent. I…"

She broke off and blushed.

Dear Lord—the passion with which she'd spoken—it was enough to drive a man wild with need! It wasn't the feigned interest that doxies used in order to secure coin. It was the raw, unbridled passion of a woman who took pleasure from the mere physical prowess of another.

Lady Hart cleared her throat. "I can see why Devon wishes to master the move," she said. "And now, I must take my leave. I don't want to be on the road when it's dark."

She held out her hand to Griffin, and he kissed it.

"I look forward to seeing you in London, Mr. Oake," she said, her face taking on a note of steel. "Dexter is most anxious to see you again—to be assured that you're taking good care of Thea. Now— permit me to say goodbye to my sister."

Considering himself dismissed, he bowed, then stepped back. Lady Hart drew Dorothea into her arms.

"'Til we next meet, darling," she said. *"Courage."*

She whispered something, and Dorothea glanced at Griffin, then nodded.

Then Lady Hart climbed into the carriage, and it set off. Before long, the hoofbeats had faded into the distance.

"Come along, Rowena," Dorothea said, her voice catching. "Shall we take a turn round the garden before supper? I'm sure those strawberries we spotted yesterday will have ripened enough to be picked."

Rowe took her arm, and they disappeared into the garden.

What had Lady Hart whispered into his wife's ear when they parted?

Griffin thrust his hands into his pockets and returned to the house. The tension in his body needed to be eased—and what better way than to spend the evening chopping wood? With luck, the physical exertion would take his mind off the burning need to bury himself between his wife's thighs.

Chapter Twenty-Five

G IVE HIM A *chance…*
Meggie's whispered words echoed in Thea's ears as she
dipped the cloth into her washbasin. Now her sister-in-law had left, the
house was quiet again. Who'd have thought the timid little woman
Dexter married would be capable of bringing such life to Sandiford
Manor? But Meggie's sheer joy in her existence rubbed off on the
people around her. Rowena had seemed more relaxed, and even
Griffin had laughed.

Griffin…

The sounds of the evening filtered through the open window—the
cows lowing in the nearby field and the distant church bell ringing out
nine times.

A dull, continual thud reverberated around the air.

Griffin was chopping wood again.

He'd be alone—Will had gone to help Mrs. Morris in the kitchen,
and Rowena had retired to bed with a headache and a cup of cocoa.

Thea's chance had come.

She stripped to the waist, until she wore nothing but her petticoat,
and ran the cloth over her body, watching in the mirror as the water
beaded on her skin and trickled down her body, following the
contours of her breasts.

She placed a hand over a breast. Meggie said she liked it when

Dexter touched her breasts, and... Thea blushed as she lowered her gaze...when he touched her *down there.*

As she ran her thumb over her nipple, it hardened into a bud, and Thea flushed at the image of her husband touching it, or even suckling it.

Then she shook her head. She couldn't act in such a wanton manner. She simply *couldn't!*

But what if the reward surpassed the fear? If what Meggie said was true, unimaginable pleasure awaited her—if she were brave enough to take the first step.

She looked out of the window.

Her husband was in the yard, holding an axe. In a smooth, fluid movement, he swung it over his head. His shirt was open to the waist, and the movement revealed his chest—the solid muscles she'd caressed in her dreams. Then he brought the axe down on a log, splitting it in two.

Her mind returned to the first time she'd seen him, flexing his muscles as he paraded round the ring to the deafening chant of the crowd.

The Mighty Oak...

The man every woman in that inn wanted that night—including her.

And, now, he was hers for the taking—if she had courage.

She reached for the whisky bottle and poured a glass. Wrinkling her nose at the sharp, smoky aroma, she tipped it up and swallowed. The liquid burned her throat, and she coughed and spluttered. But the warm sensation increased. Not unpleasant—it spread through her bones and fueled her courage.

She poured a second glass and drank it, wiping her mouth when, in her eagerness, a little spilled onto her chin. Then she covered herself with a shawl and exited her chamber.

Tonight, she'd finally learn why everyone made such a fuss about the act of love.

As she descended the stairs, she heard Will scratching about in the dining room, and she tiptoed across the floor. It wouldn't do to be caught seducing her husband. She'd never survive the shame.

She let out a giggle at the thought of Will's face if he caught her naked in Griffin's arms...

Those strong, muscular arms...

Her body jerked as she hiccoughed, and she slipped on the bottom step.

"Oops!"

Whisky might be the cure for fear, but it wreaked havoc on her sense of balance.

She slipped through the doors and made her way across the yard. The sounds of wood splitting had ceased, and, as she rounded a corner, she saw why.

Griffin stood by the water pump, his back to her. The muscles on his back rippled as he pumped the handle up and down while liquid spilled into the trough. He dipped his hands in and splashed water over his chest, then he ran his hands through his hair, the shaggy, untamed mane which, now unrestrained by ties, gave him a primal air.

A small whimper escaped Thea's lips, and her skin tightened at the sight of his hard, muscular frame, glistening with sweat and water. How could any woman resist such glorious temptation?

The ache which had been coursing through her veins, now centered deep within her body, and she squeezed her thighs together to ease it.

She moved closer, and he tensed. He reached for a cloth hanging from the pump handle, wiped his hands, then turned to face her.

Her cheeks warmed at the intensity of his scrutiny. But the whisky fueled her courage, and she moved closer until she caught his scent— sweat and wood—the earthy, musky scent of man.

"Why are you here, Dorothea?"

She loosened the shawl, then let it fall to the ground, exposing her body. Her skin tightened as the air brushed across her breasts.

He continued to stare at her, his eyes darkening. His nostrils flared, and his chest rose and fell as he drew in a deep breath.

"I came to ask you something," she said.

"Y-you did?" His words came out in a hoarse rasp. He parted his lips, and his tongue flicked out. Hunger blazed in his eyes.

Meggie was right—it was working.

She moved closer, loosening her hips in an exaggerated gesture, then curled her mouth into a seductive smile.

"Do you want me, Griffin?"

He lowered his gaze to her breasts, which felt heavy and warm. Emboldened by the raw need in his expression, she took another step, until her nipples brushed against his chest. His body vibrated with need, but he made no move.

"Will you touch me?" she whispered.

He lifted his hand to her breast and brushed it with his knuckles. Need fizzed through her, and she let out a low mewl. She arched her back, pressing her breast into his palm, and tipped her face up, offering her lips.

He gripped her arms and pulled her against his chest. Then he lowered his head and brushed his lips against hers. She closed her eyes, savoring the sweet sensation and the anticipation of the bliss to come.

A rush of warmth flooded her body, and she became aware of her heartbeat in her ears—the rapid flutter of anticipation and apprehension.

Would it be as wonderful as Meggie had told her?

Then he tightened his grip, and he pushed her away.

"You've been drinking," he said.

She opened her eyes. Lust still shimmered in his expression, but a new emotion had come to the fore.

Anger—and hatred.

"Griffin, you're hurting me."

"Have you been drinking?"

"Griffin, I..."

"Don't deny it, woman—I can smell it on you!"

His body vibrated with anger, and she squirmed in his grip.

"Let me go!"

"Not until I answer your question."

"W-what question?" she stammered.

He bared his teeth. "You asked me whether I wanted you. Do you want my answer?"

"No! I want you to let me go!"

"You should have thought of that before you threw yourself at me," he said. "No—I don't want you. The very last thing I want," he added, his voice rising, "is a drunken whore for a wife!"

He released her arms and shoved her back.

"Cover yourself up, for fuck's sake," he growled. She stumbled backward, then picked up the discarded shawl.

For a moment, regret flickered in his expression, then he curled his lip in disgust.

"Go."

She clutched the shawl to her chest and fled. Her foot caught in a stone, and she fell forward onto her hands and knees.

He called out, but she scrambled to her feet and continued toward the house. Her humiliation couldn't get any worse—she had to get away from him as quickly as possible.

Sobbing, she ran inside and dashed across the hallway, where she collided into a solid figure.

"Mrs. Oake? Is something the matter?"

Will stood before her. He glanced at her disheveled form, and his face flushed.

"Forgive me," he stuttered, I-I..."

Not waiting for him to finish, she fled up the stairs and ran to her chamber, where she shut the door and locked it.

Sobbing, she tore at the shawl until it ripped into shreds.

How could she have been so foolish—thinking that she was even remotely desirable?

GRIFFIN BUTTONED HIS jacket and glanced out of the window. A thick morning mist shrouded the land in gray—to match his mood.

What had come over her last night? What had turned his staid little wife into a wanton?

Was it just the liquor—the root of so many evils? Louisa had always tried to seduce him when she'd drunk too much. Or, more often, after she'd spread her legs for another man. She'd sashay up to him, stinking of gin and the men she'd been with.

When he'd smelled the liquor on Dorothea's breath, the memory of Louisa had been too strong to conquer. Within a year of their marriage, she'd fallen into the same pattern—bed another man, then offer herself to him in order to pass off any bastards as his. But near the end, she didn't even bother to do that, laughing at him when he'd caught her in all manner of sordid positions with all manner of men—most notably, Alex Ogilvie.

He'd hoped Dorothea was different.

But he recalled the tales he'd heard in London of the Hart sister who'd ruined herself and borne another man's child.

Perhaps, deep down, all women were harlots.

As he strode along the corridor toward the breakfast room, he stopped as he passed the door to his wife's chamber.

On impulse, he pushed the door open. The room was empty.

The bed had been made—there wasn't a crease in sight on the cover—and an array of bottles and jars formed a neat pattern on the dressing table. Beside the window was a table with a washbowl and jug and a vase of wild grasses and flowers.

The only evidence of the room's occupation was a discarded piece of cloth on the floor beside the fireplace. He picked it up.

It was a silk shawl—the one she'd worn last night—embroidered with tiny pink and purple flowers in an intricate pattern. A large rent ran through the body of the shawl, the silk threads fraying at the edges. A name had been embroidered in one corner, using the same thread as the flowers, in an elegant script.

Dorothea Hart 1815

She must have made it when she was a young woman.

He traced the letters with his fingertip, imagining the love with which she'd made every stitch…

…and the heartbreak she must have felt when she ripped it in two.

He exited the chamber, stopping to drop the shawl in his study, and encountered Will halfway down the stairs.

"You have a letter, sir. Shall I take it to your study?"

"No, give it here."

"The mistress is in the breakfast room," Will continued. "She…forgive me…she seems a little out of sorts."

"Out of sorts?"

"I encountered her last night." Will blushed and averted his gaze. "She was very distressed. I-I sent Rosie to tend to her, but her door was locked. I hope I did right to tell you."

"Is my daughter with her?"

"Miss Rowena's still in her chamber. Her health is delicate this morning."

Griffin dismissed Will with a wave. He had no wish to be subjected to any more detail about his daughter's monthly state of health.

He couldn't imagine anything worse than two females suffering from a delicate state of nerves.

He tore open the envelope, pulled out a card, and read the inscription.

Shit.

That was the last thing he needed. A dance—with the bloody Gillinghams.

He rammed the invitation into his pocket, then entered the breakfast room and braced himself.

His wife was sitting at the table, spooning sugar into her tea. Most unlike her—she usually took her tea plain.

Her eyes widened as she saw him. Her hand shook, and she set the spoon down.

"Good morning, husband."

Her voice might be calm, but he wasn't so blind that he didn't notice how her hand trembled—or the dark circles under her eyes.

In the cold light of day, the fog of his anger had dissipated, and he saw his wife for what she was. An unhappy woman who, in her awkward way, had reached out to him, using liquor to fuel her courage and feed her hope.

And he'd crushed her hope underfoot.

He wasn't just a savage. He was an unfeeling boor who'd humiliated the woman who worked tirelessly to turn his house into a home—the woman who had brought light and life back into his daughter's heart.

He took his place at the table, and the envelope fell out of his pocket and onto the floor. He picked it up and placed it on the table, aware that pair of pale blue eyes watched his every move.

Then she sighed and resumed her attention on the plate in front of her—pushing the food around without attempting to eat it.

"Dorothea. We need to talk."

She looked up, and he caught a flicker of pain before the neutral expression returned.

"Yes," she said quietly. "We do."

"If I hurt you, in any way, I…" he began, but she interrupted him.

"There's much to discuss regarding the appointments of the various positions in the household," she said. "I consider myself capable of selecting the right individuals, but if you wish me to defer to your judgment, I'd be obliged if you could voice your opinion."

"That's not what I wish to speak of," he said.

"Nevertheless, it's what must be discussed," she replied. "As I have already said, we must begin with the housekeeper and butler. If you have no wish to concern yourself with such matters, I can make the decision myself—perhaps with Rowena's help. I understand enough of the duties attached to both positions to be able to make an informed choice."

"Dorothea, I..."

"There's no need to concern yourself with the expense. The fruit from the pinery will generate sufficient income and, in future years, it may yield a sizeable profit."

He opened his mouth to speak, and she continued, increasing the pitch of her voice. "The fruit is highly sought after in London. My brother has several contacts, and..." her voice wavered, then she continued, fixing her gaze on her plate, "...it may even be possible to send one to the royal household. As a gift, of course, but it would be a great honor for us, and while I set little store by such things, I must concede that it would help greatly with Rowena's come-out if she wishes to have a season in London."

He stared at his wife. Most women filled the silence with an overabundance of speech as if they believed their worth was in proportion to the number of words they uttered. But Dorothea was not one of them. She usually spoke only when she had something meaningful to say. But this morning, she seemed anxious to speak as much as possible, as if she wished to fill the silence with inanities to prevent him from speaking.

"And," she continued, "there's also the matter of your valet."

"A valet?"

"You'll need assistance in selecting a suitable candidate," she continued. "Given how—personal—such a service is, I cannot help with your choice. I can ask Dexter—by all accounts, his valet is an excellent man."

"Then I'll ask his advice when we see him in London."

"You still wish to go?"

"Of course," he said. "Why would you think I'd changed my mind?"

She colored and shook her head. "No reason." She resumed her attention on the plate in front of her but made no attempt to eat.

"If you continue to push those eggs around the plate, they'll become dizzy."

She frowned at his weak attempt at humor, then she set her fork down and pushed her plate to one side.

"Dorothea," he said. "About last night…"

She slid her chair back. "I should see to Rowena. She's still unwell today and might appreciate some sweet tea. Please excuse me."

Without waiting for a response, she moved toward the door. As she passed, he caught her hand.

"May I at least be given the opportunity to apologize for my behavior last night?" he asked.

"There's no need," she said. "I will ensure that I don't place you in such an unfortunate position again."

Such an unfortunate position? The cold manner of delivery belied the pain in her eyes. She tried to withdraw her hand, but he only squeezed it tighter.

"Unhand me, please."

For a heartbeat, he fought the urge to pull her into his arms, but she curled her lip in distaste, and he released her. She wiped her hand on her skirt.

What had he expected? Trickery? Cajoling?

It had never bothered him before. The harlots he'd rejected over the years had played games to punish him for rejecting their advances. But Dorothea wasn't trying to punish him. She was withdrawing from him. He'd rejected her and, rather than use stratagems to secure his affection, she'd simply surrendered, as if she didn't care whether he wanted her or not.

But she did care. He'd seen it in her eyes last night. Perhaps she withdrew from him not to punish him—but to protect herself.

"It's Louisa!" he cried. "Last night—what I did—what I said…it's because of her."

She froze, her back to him, then she turned to face him.

"Your late wife," she said. "I thought as much. Was she often drunk?"

How did she work that out? Were all women that perceptive—or just his wife?

"She…" he hesitated, afraid to disclose any more in case Rowena came upon them. Then he shook his head. "I don't want to speak of her."

"As you wish."

He picked up the envelope. "We've been invited to a ball," he said. "At the Crown Inn—at the other end of the village."

She eyed the invitation, arching her eyebrow. "Have we?"

"By Lady Gillingham."

"Do you wish me to write with our apologies or shall you?" she asked.

"I thought we should go," he said, "provided you have no objection."

She sighed. "I have no objection."

Ye gods—she sounded *bored*!

"Lady Gillingham has arranged it in our honor," he said. "If we're to move among society in London, I must learn how to behave. I've not been to many parties, as I'm sure was apparent by the way I behaved at your party in London."

She blushed but said nothing.

"At least if I make an arse of myself in Sandiford," he said, "you can point out my faults before I make an arse of myself in London."

Her expression softened, but she didn't smile. How could he make her smile?

"*I* want to go," he said. "I could show my beautiful wife off. You'll outshine Lady Gillingham and her friends, and I'll be the envy of all the men."

She rolled her eyes, and once again, he was acutely aware of his gaucheness.

"As you wish," she said, "but I cannot dance."

"I thought all women knew how to dance."

"Dexter never felt the need to teach me," she said. "I have no wish to embarrass myself by attempting to learn now. I really must see to Rowena." She exited the breakfast room, closing the door behind her.

His clumsy attempt at flattery to make up for his appalling behavior last night had failed.

Chapter Twenty-Six

"MRS. OAKE! I'M so glad you're gracing us with your presence."
Lady Gillingham descended on Thea, her gown a riot of color—eye-wateringly pink, with flashes of bright green.

The woman was determined to present herself as the premier lady of Sandiford, even if she no longer resided at Sandiford Manor. In all likelihood, she loathed Thea for being mistress of what she considered to be her rightful property.

The unfortunate Lord Gillingham, standing beside his wife, gave Thea and Griffin a stiff bow.

"Oake," he said, making it sound like an insult. "I trust you're taking care of the manor."

Thea folded her arms. "I wasn't aware you took such an interest in the maintenance of our home, Lord Gillingham," she said.

He turned his yellow gaze on her. "I don't believe I've heard of your family, Mrs. Oake," he said. "Hart—is that the name?"

"My brother's Sir Dexter Hart," Thea said.

"A baronet?" Lady Gillingham's eyes glittered with spite. "A lowly title, but acceptable all the same."

"He's a knight, not a baronet."

Lord Gillingham wrinkled his nose. "So, he's engaged in trade?"

"He owns the Hart Bank," Thea replied.

Lady Gillingham shook her head. "I've not heard of it, but the older families such as ours are very particular about who we bank with. The Gillingham family has banked with Coutts for years. They're more discerning when it comes to selecting their clients."

"As is my brother," Thea said. "He requires a minimum level of financial competence in his account holders—which is probably why you've never heard of him."

Lady Gillingham gestured toward the main parlor. "Do go through," she said. "You'll find plenty of comfortable chairs. When you're a little older than most brides, dancing can be rather strenuous."

Thea merely smiled. Lady Gillingham had a lifetime's experience of insulting subordinates, and Thea was no match for her. If only Lilah were here! She didn't care what people thought, and she'd think nothing of smashing a vase over the woman's head.

Lady Gillingham placed a possessive hand on Griffin's arm.

"Mr. Oake, you must oblige me with the first dance."

"Me?"

"Quite so. And you must partner my niece afterward. I've promised you to her."

Griffin glanced at Thea and raised his eyebrows in question.

"Come, come, dear sir!" Lady Gillingham cried. "You mustn't defer to your wife. A man of your—virility—shouldn't be seen hanging onto his wife's skirts. It's most unbecoming."

Could she be any more obvious? Thea half-expected to see her salivate.

"Lady Gillingham," he began, "I…"

"My husband can partner your wife," she continued, lowering her voice. "The opportunity to partner a viscount is an honor I'm sure she'll have no wish to pass on."

Griffin smiled—he actually smiled! Didn't he realize Lady Gillingham had just insulted her? Or didn't he care?

"I'm not inclined to dance at present," Thea said stiffly. "Perhaps

I'll go in search of a comfortable chair."

Lady Gillingham resumed her attention on Griffin. "How's that daughter of yours, Mr. Oake, now poor Miss Ellis is no longer in charge of her education? A gross injustice, but I understand *you* weren't entirely to blame. I hear she's now with her sister. Perhaps, one day, she'll find a situation where her qualities will be better appreciated."

How dare she sing the praise of that woman!

"I'm taking her to London," Griffin said.

"But you have no acquaintance to speak of."

"I'm sure she'll make do."

"You cannot settle for *making do!*" Lady Gillingham cried. "One word from me, and you'll have some of the best society in London."

Really! If Griffin wasn't going to stop her...

The musicians began tuning their instruments, and Lady Gillingham pulled him onto the dance floor without so much as a backward glance.

A footman walked past carrying a tray of champagne glasses. Thea took one, then made her way to a seat in the corner.

For the first two dances, Lady Gillingham partnered Thea's husband, while Thea remained sitting, refusing every offer to dance. She only wanted to dance with one person, and he was occupied. Griffin may not know it, but Lady Gillingham would be fully aware of the gossip that would ensue from the special attention she paid him.

Was this why Lady Gillingham had invited her? To teach a lesson to the woman who presided over her former home? Clearly, she considered Sandiford Manor her property. The question in Thea's mind was whether she also considered Griffin her property.

Judging by the pointed looks in the couple's direction and the sympathetic looks toward her, the whole company was asking itself the same question.

No longer wishing to watch, Thea rose and slipped out of the dance room, finding solace in the quiet of a side room.

When the music stopped, the chatter rose, accompanied by the familiar sounds of crockery as the guests helped themselves to the buffet. Shortly after, Thea heard Lady Gillingham's familiar shrill tones.

"...no talent on the dance floor to speak of. That's why she refuses to dance."

"I can't think why you arranged this in her honor, Caroline. A woman like that—whose position is so markedly beneath yours."

"Mr. Oake might be uncouth," Lady Gillingham said, "but I can't think why he offered for her, unless the rumors are true."

"Rumors?"

"Oh, my dear Letitia, didn't you hear?" Lady Gillingham let out a titter. "She compromised herself in order to secure him!"

"Women of her sort can be cunning when they want to."

This was not to be borne! Thea approached the group of women, Meggie's words echoing in her mind.

Courage...

"We all know Mr. Oake's not very particular about where his money comes from," Lady Gillingham continued. "The poor man thought he was gaining a wife when, in reality, he's shackled to a woman of a certain age who dresses like a governess.

"I say, Caroline, aren't you being a little unfair?"

"Oh, Letitia! You saw the dreadful ensemble she's wearing! I heard her fortune's thirty thousand, yet she can't even run to a new gown. I daresay he's regretting his choice, though it wasn't really a choice if he was tricked into it by a..."

An explosion of crockery interrupted Lady Gillingham mid-sentence.

"What the bloody hell's going on!" a voice roared.

The crowd parted to reveal Thea's husband—a shattered plate and what looked like a chicken thigh, at his feet. Lady Gillingham's niece stood beside him, trembling. He pushed her to one side, then strode forward until he was inches away from Lady Gillingham. Hands clenched, body shaking, he looked like he was about to strangle her.

"What the devil have you been saying about my wife?"

"I-I thought you were with the gentlemen."

"That much was apparent," he hissed through gritted teeth. His hair had worked loose, and his eyes flashed with fury. "Would you care to repeat what you said about my wife?"

Lady Gillingham grew pale, and he moved closer.

"Well?"

"I—I was asking my friends why you married her."

"Shall I satisfy your curiosity?"

"There's no need."

"There's *every* need, Lady Gillingham," he said. "I married her because she's the one woman in the world who can make me happy. She's intelligent, caring, and kind. And I happen to think she's beautiful—all the more because her beauty comes from within. Whereas you..." He curled his lip as if he'd just encountered a particularly bad smell. "You've no right to insult a woman who surpasses you—and every other woman in the room—in every quality that matters. Not a day goes by that I regret taking her for my wife, and I'll thank you to show her greater courtesy."

He glanced up, and his eyes widened as he spotted Thea.

"I think it's time the dancing resumed," he said, "and *this* time, I wish to dance with my wife, if she'll have me."

He offered his hand to Thea. Lady Gillingham turned and gasped as she saw her. Whispers threaded through the crowd. Thea wanted nothing more than to run out of the room—but with everyone's eyes on her, she had no wish to give Lady Gillingham the satisfaction of witnessing her shame.

She took his hand, and he led her to the center of the floor.

"I don't want to dance," she whispered. "I wasn't lying when I said

I don't know how."

"Then we're well-matched," he said. "I cannot dance either. I trod on Lady Gillingham's foot at least five times. Though, given her little speech earlier, I have no regrets and can only hope that it swells to the size of a watermelon." He hesitated, uncertainty in his expression. "Or, perhaps, that it goes green and falls off?"

She sighed. "I want to go home, Griffin. Can't we leave these dreadful people?"

He lifted her hand to his lips and kissed it. "There's nothing I want more than to take you home. But I ask you to oblige me this once—so we can show Lady Gillingham we're not afraid of her."

"Afraid?"

"I've met men like her in the ring," he said, "bullies who pick on someone they perceive to be weaker. But they crumble at the slightest show of strength. This ball is supposed to be in our honor, even if Lady Gillingham's objective was to insult you."

Thea shook her head. "I didn't realize you'd understood that."

"Not at first," he said, "but as the evening wore on, it became clear what the woman was about."

"Then why must we stay?"

"To show Lady Gillingham—and everyone else—that we have every right to be here."

She allowed herself to smile at the earnestness in his voice. "Perhaps you *are* ready for London," she said.

He held her close and moved across the dance floor. His steps might be clumsy, but she barely noticed as she looked into his eyes, her heart swelling at the pride in their expression.

His pride in her.

As the party drew to a close, Griffin issued a stiff goodbye to Lady Gillingham. Then, taking Thea's hand, they set off together on the short walk back to Sandiford Manor.

"Thank you," she said.

"What for?"

"For defending me."

He smiled. "It's my duty as your husband."

"Your duty."

"And my pleasure."

He stopped walking and drew her close—so close that she only needed to tip her head up, and their lips would meet. He parted his mouth and flicked his tongue out, moistening his lips. She clung to him, her heart hammering, fighting the burning need to kiss him.

Then she lowered her gaze. He may have defended her against Lady Gillingham, but the wound inflicted by his rejection of the other night had not yet healed—and she had no wish to be rejected again.

She pulled herself free.

"We should get going," she said. "I'm uneasy about leaving Rowena on her own for so long."

A lame excuse, but he gave no objection, and she set off. She thought she heard him sigh, then his footsteps followed her home.

Chapter Twenty-Seven

THE CARRIAGE DREW to a halt, and Griffin looked out of the window.

"We're here."

His wife and daughter stirred but remained asleep. Rowe nestled against Dorothea with the instinctive gesture of one who understood from whom they can seek protection.

It warmed his heart to see it—even if Rowe still occasionally turned hostile eyes on him.

As for Dorothea…

She seemed to have forgiven his appalling behavior of the other night, particularly after the Gillinghams' ball. But his rejection of her in the yard had created a wall between them. His only hope was that he could chip away at it, piece by piece.

"Dorothea?"

His wife opened her eyes and stretched. For a moment, he saw contentment in her expression then, as she rubbed the sleep from her eyes, the familiar hunted look returned.

She placed a hand on Rowe's arm.

"Rowena, my darling, we've arrived."

Rowe opened her eyes, then glanced out of the window.

"This doesn't look like an inn."

"I've taken a townhouse for the month," he said. "In Connaught

Street. Your brother thought it a good location."

"You've been writing to Dexter?"

"I have," he said. "He negotiated the rent on my behalf and has offered to assist me with purchasing a townhouse in the future."

"He'll make a tidy profit if he offers you a loan."

"I'd gladly see him make a profit out of me," he said, "given that he gave me his greatest treasure."

"Which was?"

"You."

It was a crass compliment, but she took it with grace. Rowe, on the other hand, rolled her eyes and snorted.

A footman approached the carriage door and opened it. Griffin climbed out, then helped his wife. She looked up, taking in the building.

He found himself wanting her approval more than anything else.

"Do you like it?" he asked. "I wanted a house large enough so you could invite as many of your friends as you wish, and Sir Dexter said in his letter that it's within walking distance of Grosvenor Street."

"Near Devon's house?" Her eyes sparkled.

"I thought you'd appreciate being close to your family," he said. "I'll confess a certain selfishness in wanting to further my acquaintance with your brother, who I see as a friend..."

He hesitated at the memory of Alex Ogilvie—the man he'd once called friend. "I've learned that good friends are rare—and should be cherished."

She smiled at his praise of her brother, and he took her hand.

"I have also learned that good women are equally rare—if not more so."

He lifted her hand to his lips, and to his relief, she did not resist.

"I trust I did well?" he asked, fearing her answer. "I know you had a right to be consulted—but I wanted it to be a surprise—for you."

"For me?" She shook her head. "In my experience, surprises are usually unpleasant."

"Forgive me," he said. "If you don't like it, I'll find another house."

"Oh, no!" she cried. "You misunderstand me, Griffin. I *love* it."

"You do?"

"I love it because *you* chose it, and a lot of thought went into your choice." She lowered her head and placed a soft kiss on the back of his hand.

"Thank you." She held his hand against her cheek. The gentle, loving gesture touched his heart more than any declaration of love.

Then, she stiffened and released his hand.

The barrier between them still existed. What would it take to gain her trust?

Rowe climbed out of the carriage.

"Good heavens—it's enormous!" she cried.

Dorothea slipped her arm through Rowe's. "Shall we take a look inside?"

The main doors opened to reveal a row of servants dressed in a variety of uniforms.

Surely a London house didn't need this many servants? What was he supposed to say to them all? Would they think him a savage if he did—or said—the wrong thing?

His wife gave him a smile of reassurance, then she addressed each servant, one by one, encouraging him to follow suit, until they reached the end of the line, where a gray-haired woman and equally gray-haired man stood, side-by-side.

"Mr. and Mrs. Bowes, at your service, ma'am," the man said.

"Oh, you're married!" Dorothea said. "How delightful."

She handed her pelisse to one of the maidservants, then, after issuing Mrs. Bowes instructions to attend her an hour before supper, she dismissed them, and they trooped across the hallway and disappeared through a door beside the staircase.

Trust her to know exactly what to do!

She crossed the floor to a wide-rimmed porcelain bowl on a side table, then reached in and plucked out a handful of cards.

"Meggie's already called," she said. "Anne Pelham...Atalanta..." she tutted. "What's she doing out so soon after her confinement—oh, I long to see them!"

"We must invite them all to dinner," he said. "Perhaps next week? That is...if you could manage it."

"Of *course* I can manage," she huffed.

He smiled. He'd piqued her pride, and it warmed his heart to see her feistiness.

"Supper for four couples presents no challenge," she said. "I take it we have a dining table which seats eight?"

"Nine," he said, "including Rowena."

"Rowena isn't out yet, though I could make an exception for an informal supper." She glanced at Rowe, who frowned.

"In which case," Dorothea continued, "we must see to Rowena's wardrobe. With your permission, I'd like to visit Madame Dupont as soon as possible."

"Of course," he said, "on one condition."

Her face fell.

"You'll like my condition," he said. "At least, I *hope* you will."

He stroked the back of her hand with his thumb. "You must commission a new wardrobe for yourself."

"Must I?"

"Yes," he said. "And none of this starched governess nonsense. You hide your beauty—when it should be admired."

She frowned.

He'd done it again—insulted her when he'd intended to give her a compliment. Most women relished a man's flattery. But she valued greater things than physical appearance.

It was a quality to be admired, but it meant that his attempt to show he cared had fallen flat on its arse.

"Starched governess?" She arched an eyebrow. "Is that how you see me?"

Oh, bloody hell.

He braced himself for the admonishment, then her lips curled in a smile.

Was she teasing him?

"Very well," she said. "I'll endure a few pretty gowns for your sake. And now—would you mind if I called on Atalanta this afternoon?"

"You don't want to rest first?

"I rested during the journey," she said. "I long to see baby Francine. She must have grown so much since I last saw her, and babies grow far too quickly..." she broke off. "Forgive me—if you prefer, I'll stay here."

He caught her hand. "There's no need to ask my permission for anything. You're a free woman, my love, and I hope you'll come to learn that I'm not a monster."

She curled her fingers round his hand.

"I already know that."

The smile on her face was enough to melt his heart—then he realized what he'd called her.

My love.

Chapter Twenty-Eight

"OH, LOOK AT you, little Francine—haven't you grown!"

Thea placed a kiss on her niece's head, breathing in her beautiful baby smell.

"I've missed you, sweet one," she whispered. "Oh, Atalanta, you must be so happy."

"I am," her sister-in-law replied, "though I look back with fondness on days when I could indulge in a full night's sleep."

"Perhaps we should go and let you take your rest," Thea said.

"No, stay—Lizzy can see to Francine while we take tea."

A young woman dressed in a neat uniform deftly plucked the baby from Thea's lap. Thea watched as she exited the parlor, her heart aching with longing.

"Time for tea," Atalanta said, rising to her feet. She crossed the floor to the bell-pull by the fireplace. She might have emerged from her confinement two months ago, but she'd regained her figure. Her slim, well-bred form was in sharp contrast to Thea's own dowdy frame. No wonder half of London had been madly in love with Atalanta—yet she'd had eyes only for Thea's brother.

And her gown was the most exquisite thing Thea had seen. Pale cream silk trimmed with lace.

Five years younger than Thea, titled, independently wealthy, and adored by all—Atalanta was everything Thea was not.

And she had children—two beautiful children.

Rowena sat beside Thea, scratching the skin around her thumbnail. Thea placed her hand over Rowena's and caressed the skin with her thumb.

"We don't want to put you to any trouble, Atalanta," she said.

"Nonsense!" came the reply. "I'm in need of congenial company, and you can't take Rowena away from me so soon after our introduction. Besides, your brothers are due back any moment, and they'd never forgive me if I let you leave."

Shortly after, a maid arrived with the tea things and set them on a table. Atalanta dismissed her and poured the tea.

"Some shortbread, Rowena?" She held out a plate. A glint of mischief shone in her eyes. "Sadly, my cook lacks your flair for fashioning the biscuits into interesting shapes."

Rowena blushed.

"Meggie gave me one of her biscuits when she returned from visiting you," Atalanta continued, "and she dared me to give it to Devon."

"Sweet Lord!" Thea cried.

"Don't worry," Atalanta said, "I ate it myself. I had no wish to give him a sense of inferiority with regards to its size."

Rowena erupted in a fit of coughing and set her teacup down. Thea patted her on the back until the coughing subsided.

Atalanta burst into laughter. "The look on your face!" she cried. "Do forgive me, Rowena. I suppose Dorothea has told you how elegant I am and how you must act appropriately at all times and not to speak unless spoken to."

Now it was Thea's turn to blush. Atalanta had repeated Thea's instruction to her stepdaughter, almost word-for-word.

"She's right when referring to London society," Atalanta said. "But, among family, we can speak more freely. I'm so happy you're here, and I speak for both Devon and myself when I say we'll be delighted to accept your dinner invitation."

A door opened and closed in the distance, and footsteps approached. Shortly after, Devon entered, followed by Dexter.

Atalanta leaped to her feet and embraced her husband.

Thea stood to greet her brothers, and Rowena followed suit. As Devon approached, Rowena stiffened and openly stared at him.

To his credit, Devon didn't react. He must be used to the stares by now, but it still pained Thea to see it—knowing that the world judged him by his appearance.

"Thea, it's so good to see you," Devon said. "And this must be Rowena. We've heard a lot about you."

Rowena continued to stare at Devon. Behind him, Dexter scowled.

Then Rowena dipped into a curtsey, just as Thea had taught her.

"Pleased to meet you, Major Hart."

"The pleasure's all mine," Devon said, smiling. "Meggie has been telling me about your studies, and I know Attie is keen to show you her medical journals and teach you a little of medicine."

"You are?" Thea addressed her sister-in-law.

"If that's what Rowena wishes," Atalanta said. "But I wouldn't want to impose."

"I'd love that," Rowena said. "Thank you, Lady Atalanta." Then she resumed her attention on Devon.

"Your scar..."

Devon stiffened—almost imperceptibly, but Thea noticed it. So did Atalanta, who squeezed his hand.

"I've never met a real soldier," Rowena continued. "You must have been brave to be injured like that. Did it hurt?"

"It hurt like hell—and still aches, especially in cold weather."

"Is there nothing you can do?" Rowena asked.

"Attie's given me an ointment, which helps," he replied, "though it'll never completely heal, of course."

"How awful!" Rowena cried. "Don't people stare at you?"

"That's quite enough, young lady," Dexter growled.

"I'm only asking!" Rowena retorted.

Devon's eyes widened. Both he and Thea knew that few people answered Dexter back without suffering the consequences.

"You're being unbelievably rude!" Dexter said. "If I were your father, I'd take my hand to you!"

"It's just as well you aren't then, isn't it?" Thea said. "Rowena's only saying what most people are thinking."

"Quite right," Devon said. "I prefer a frank question over whispered gossip. And there's no need for decorum among family."

He gestured toward Dexter. "This is your Uncle Dexter, Rowena. *I* might be the one with the appearance of an ogre, but my brother has the character of one."

"*Uncle* Dexter?" Rowena asked.

"Yes," Devon said. "Don't forget the uncle—he insists on it. In fact, he prefers Uncle Dex."

"Don't tease the poor girl, Devon darling," Atalanta said. "Do forgive us Rowena—what must you think of us!"

"You're not as bad as I was expecting," Rowena said.

Dexter's scowl returned, but Devon laughed.

"I think we can take that as a compliment," Attie said. "The benefit of uncles and aunts is that they're more willing to be indulgent than parents. As a consequence, they're often loved to a greater degree. I daresay I shall envy Thea when Sebastian and Francine show their marked preference for *her* because she can spoil them, knowing that she'll hand them back to me to dampen their joy with parental discipline at the end of the day."

Thea tried to smile, but Atalanta's words cut her more deeply than she could have imagined.

If only Attie knew how much Thea envied her!

"How right you are, Atalanta," Dexter said, "Meggie's told me how much Lillian's looking forward to seeing her Aunt Thea again, and she never shows the same degree of enthusiasm after Meggie returns from a day out. There's a big difference between a child's mother and her aunt, isn't there?"

Devon met Thea's gaze, then took her hand.

"As for Billy..." Dexter began, but Devon interrupted him.

"I hear there's a pinery at Sandiford, Thea!" he exclaimed, his voice overly bright.

Dexter frowned and opened his mouth to continue.

"You must tell me all about it," Devon added. "I once tasted pineapple while serving in the militia. Fossett said it was the most disgusting thing he'd ever tried. You remember Fossett, don't you, Thea?"

"I do," Thea said. "Is he well?"

"He's now a brigadier general," Devon replied. "He always was a better soldier than I. He's yet to take a wife—in fact, he's shown little interest in courting anyone. I had thought he'd do for you at one point, but it all worked out for the best. How is your husband, by the way? I've not forgotten his promise to teach me a few moves."

Dexter moved toward the window and stared out, his hands clasped behind his back.

"Rowena, dear, shall I show you our library?" Atalanta asked. "I've set aside some works I think will be of particular interest to you. I understand you're proficient at Latin—and anatomy, of course."

Rowena hesitated, then rose and took Attie's proffered hand, and the two of them left the parlor.

"Dexter, you needn't stay on our account," Devon said. "I'm sure you'll want to get back to the bank."

"I consider myself dismissed," Dexter said. "I'll see you at your dinner party, Dorothea. We can talk then."

Almost as soon as Dexter left, the atmosphere warmed.

"Forgive him," Devon said. "He has the emotional maturity of a boiled egg. He doesn't know how much you've wanted a child. And besides," he took her hand, "now you're married, you're bound to have children of your own."

"At *my* age?"

"Thirty isn't old!" he laughed. "The Duchess of Westbury is older, and she gave birth to twins last year." He lowered his voice. "Given the reputation the Mighty Oak has amassed over the years regarding his...er...*prowess*, you're bound to announce a happy event very soon."

Thea blinked back a tear.

He squeezed her hand. "What's wrong? Is your husband unkind? Dex might be an arse, but he'll help me flatten Oake if he treats you poorly."

"He's a good husband," Thea said. "It's just, he doesn't...I mean, he hasn't..."

His eyes widened in understanding, then he patted her hand. "Shall *I* speak to him?"

"Good Lord, no!" Thea cried. "Do you want to further my humiliation? Besides—what could you possibly say to him?"

"That he's neglecting his wife?"

She shook her head. "He's very attentive—and thoughtful. But he..." Unable to articulate her feelings, she made an aimless gesture in front of her. "Oh—I don't know—perhaps he doesn't want me."

"Then he's a fool," Devon said. "Perhaps all that pummeling has softened his head."

He gave her a sympathetic smile. Soon, his expression would turn to pity—which was something she couldn't bear.

"Rowena seems an interesting young woman," he said.

"Oh yes!" Thea said. "She's extremely intelligent."

"She's lucky to have *you*,"

"I'm very fond of her," Thea said. "I love her, even—perhaps as much as I would have loved a child of my own."

"It's plain to see she adores you."

"Really?"

"Yes," he smiled. "You've always been so perceptive when it comes to others, but you lack such insight with regard to yourself. I saw how she looked at you when you defended her against Dex. You've made a difference in her life. You're preparing her for the world, so that she may strike out as an independent woman and thrive. Isn't that what every parent wants for their child?"

"I suppose you're right, Dev," she said, "but I can't help wanting a child of my own. I always have."

"I know how much you want a child. But unfulfilled dreams lead to despair. You have much to be thankful for."

"Such as a brother who understands me."

The door opened, and Attie returned, with Rowena, carrying an armful of books.

"Look what Aunt Attie has lent me!" Rowena cried.

The enthusiasm shining in her stepdaughter's eyes warmed Thea's heart.

Devon was right—she had much to be thankful for. She had a daughter. Maybe not one of her flesh, but Rowena had secured a place in her heart.

If Griffin didn't want another child—then she owed it to Rowena and to him to do the best for the child he had.

Chapter Twenty-Nine

"A H! MADEMOISELLE HART! Or should I say Madame Oake, now? How thrilled I am to see you!"

"It's been a long time, Madame Dupont," Thea said.

"Too long. I last saw you when you came with Mademoiselle Delilah for her trousseau," the modiste said. "I said to myself the next time I see Mademoiselle Dorothea, it will be her turn—and then I find you're married and whisked away to the country without so much as a new gown!"

"Well, I'm here *now*, Madame."

"*C'est vrai.*" The modiste turned her attention to Rowena. "And, *this* must be Mademoiselle Rowena! What a beauty—those eyes, they're like chocolate, no? I have some lavender silk, which I've set aside for my most special customers—it would complement your eyes to perfection. Come here—let me look at you!"

Rowena stepped forward, discomfort in her expression.

"She's a beauty, *n'est pas*? She could find a husband tomorrow."

Thea almost burst out laughing at the look of horror on Rowena's face.

"We're not quite ready to see Rowena paraded in front of suitors," Thea said, "but we do, of course, want her to look her best on her introduction into society."

"*Naturellement.* Now—let us take her measurements. How many gowns were you thinking of?"

"Two evening gowns and three day dresses," Thea said.

"And for yourself?"

Thea hesitated, then Rowena gave her a pointed look, nodding in encouragement.

"The same for me, also."

"*Tres bien*. I have a beautiful blue silk to match *your* eyes."

The modiste busied herself with measuring Rowena, nodding, and writing in her notebook. As she was finishing off, Rowena gave her a shy smile.

"Could you make me a lace petticoat, Madame Dupont?"

"I can make anything you wish, Mademoiselle. Perhaps, if I may be so bold, I could suggest a pair of drawers? They're the very latest in undergarments and *très* comfortable."

"I should like that." Rowena turned to Thea. "You'd like some drawers, too, wouldn't you, Mama Thea?"

Mama...

Thea drew in a sharp breath. Moisture swelled in her eyes, and she blinked and averted her gaze.

"Have I said something wrong?" Rowena asked.

"No, my darling," Thea said. "Quite the opposite."

Madame finished writing down her measurements, then hung her tape measure round her neck and pocketed her notebook.

"All done!" she said in her sing-song voice. "Now, let me fetch that lavender silk—and I recall, I have a beautiful orange which would do for you, Madame, as well as the blue. Would you like to see it?"

Thea nodded, and the modiste disappeared to the back of the shop.

"I trust this isn't too tedious for you, my dear," Thea said.

"Not at all," Rowena replied. "It's was more fun than I'd expected." She hesitated, then gave Thea a nervous glance. "Did you mind very much?"

"Your asking for a petticoat? Not at all."

"No, not the petticoat. Did you mind my calling you Mama?"

Unable to speak, Thea shook her head and wiped the moisture from her eyes.

"I didn't mean to make you cry," Rowena said.

Thea took Rowena's hand. "Have you never heard of tears of happiness, Rowena? It warms my heart to think you've accepted me."

"You once said you didn't like me," Rowena said.

"If I recall, we both said that to each other," Thea replied. "But now, I love you as if you were my own daughter."

"What if you have more children? Will you care more for them than you do for me?"

"Of course not!" Thea said. "In any case, it's not likely to happen, so you needn't worry."

"I thought Papa might…"

"No," Thea said firmly. "But the three of us are a family, aren't we?"

Rowena sighed. "I suppose."

"Your father loves you, Rowena," Thea said. "We both do."

Rowena shook her head. "He doesn't. He just wants me to become a lady and dance at parties and balls to make him look good."

"I'm told parties and balls can be fun," Thea said.

"You're told? Haven't you danced at a London ball?"

"No," Thea said. "The few I attended, I went to chaperone my younger sister. Most of the time, I stayed behind to mind the children."

"And do you regret it?"

"To be honest, no," Thea replied. "Society balls are where single men hunt for a rich wife—or worse, a young woman to compromise—so they can boast about their prowess to their friends. As for the young women—they go in the vain hope that some titled man will sweep them away into a life of bliss."

"So, they're more fun for a *man*," Rowena said. "It seems like a ball is nothing more than a marketplace where the goods being traded are young women pressed into going by their parents."

"Do I take it you have no wish to attend such an event?"

"Papa won't give me a choice. It's the only thing he wants me to do—yet it's the last thing that will make me happy. I realized today what I want to do."

"Which is?"

"I want to study anatomy—perhaps medicine," Rowena said. "Aunt Attie told me, when she showed me her library, that women can be just as good as men when it comes to studying. But Papa doesn't understand. I've tried to tell him, but he thinks I'm better off married to some puffed-up lord. If I must marry, I want it to be for love. I don't want to be unhappy, not like…"

She broke off, coloring.

Thea squeezed her hand. "I understand," she said. "Let me speak to your Papa. I know he wants what's best for you—what will make you happiest."

"You'll speak to him?"

"Of course," Thea said. "But you must promise me something in return."

Rowena's eager smile disappeared. "Miss Ellis always said that when she wanted me to behave."

"I'm not Miss Ellis," Thea said. "All I ask is that you try to enjoy London while we're here. It's only for a month. And then, if your mind is made up, you and I shall speak to your papa—together."

"What if he refuses?"

"He won't, Rowena. Despite what you think of him, he's a kind man, and he loves you. You're all he has."

"He has *you*," Rowena said.

That might be true, but he didn't love her—not in the way Thea wanted to be loved.

But perhaps Rowena's love was all she needed. It was time she heeded her beloved brother's advice and drew her satisfaction from what she did have—a daughter who loved her enough to speak of her dreams and to ask her for help to fulfill them.

After all—wasn't that what a parent was supposed to do?

Chapter Thirty

A CLOCK STRUCK seven times in the distance. Griffin pulled out his pocket watch and checked it. Perfect timing. And it ought to be—it cost enough. He turned it over and ran his thumb over the inscription on the back.

John Arnold, London.

Such elegant craftsmanship! It looked fragile against his large, calloused hand. But he could appreciate it as much as any titled gentleman—probably more because he understood the merits of hard work.

It was one of the few indulgences he'd permitted himself in London—the other being the wardrobes for his wife and daughter. Madame Dupont's account hadn't been as eye-watering as he'd expected, but he hoped it had been money well spent.

He turned at the sound of a light footstep and let out a gasp.

A young woman stood at the turn of the staircase. Her hair—piled on her head in an intricate style, layered with curls, and studded with pearls—emphasized her height. Her gown, a pale shade of lilac, shimmered as she descended the stairs.

"Rowe…"

She approached him, an eager smile on her face.

"What do you think, Papa?"

"You look very well."

"Isn't it the prettiest gown? I wasn't sure about the color, but Mama Thea assured me it was perfect."

Mama Thea? Was Rowe, at last, warming to his wife?

"We'll make a debutante of you yet," he said.

Her smile disappeared.

Before he could ask her what was wrong, she let out a cry.

"Oh! You look wonderful!"

Standing on the stairs, a shy smile on her face, was his wife.

Her gown left little to the imagination. Pale blue silk folds outlined the shape of her legs and flare of her hips. He caressed her body with his gaze, following every contour—lines and forms which he could only imagine lay beneath her skirts. His gaze lingered at the top of her gown, where the swell of her breasts promised a paradise beneath the delicate lace trim.

And—if he were not mistaken—just below her neckline, he could discern two little peaks.

His mouth watered at the prospect of tasting them.

Madame Dupont's account most definitely *had* been money well spent.

What a sin it had been to hide such a body beneath those spinsterish gowns! He made a mental note to ask the butler to have each and every one of her old dresses destroyed.

As she moved toward him, he caught the unmistakable scent of woman—the honeyed spice of female desire.

Or was that his imagination? Whether it was real or not, its effect was almost paralyzing. His skin tightened and boiled with desire, and he curled his hands into fists to detract from the rush of heat which flooded his body and settled in his groin.

He held out his hand, fighting the urge to pull her into his arms and claim those lips. But before he could touch her, he heard voices outside.

Their guests had arrived.

>>>><<<<

GRIFFIN NEEDN'T HAVE worried about tonight's dinner. Though he struggled to understand the requirements of a host, his wife always seemed to know what to do, issuing quiet directions as the footmen served and cleared each dish and nodding encouragement to Griffin as he worked through each course. At one point, he struggled to identify the right cutlery, then he recalled her words from earlier in the day.

You start on the outside, Griffin, then work your way in.

As for the dessert course—he'd never tasted the like! How was it that the unappetizing-looking spiky objects from his hothouse could taste so exotic? Sharp, yet sweet. No wonder his wife had insisted on bringing one to London.

Now, he leaned back in a chair in the drawing room, his stomach straining against his breeches, while his wife circulated around the room with Rowe, tending to their guests.

"My sister scrubs up well, doesn't she?" a voice said.

Devon Hart took the seat next to Griffin. "You not having coffee?"

Griffin shook his head. "I couldn't fit anything else in."

"The trick to surviving an elaborate meal is to eat *half* of what's on your plate. I daresay you'll work off the meal soon enough if you indulge in a bout or two while you're in London."

Subtlety wasn't Hart's strong point.

"I've not forgotten my promise to teach you an uppercut," Griffin said. "That is, of course, if Lady Atalanta has no objection."

"My wife would thank you a thousand times over," Hart said. "If you batter my face, there's little chance of it lessening my looks—it'll probably be an improvement."

"Devon!" a voice admonished. The lady in question stood before them.

"Forgive my husband, Mr. Oake," she said. "Too often he speaks negatively of himself. I often wonder if it's his way of fishing for compliments."

"Your husband seems too intelligent to be susceptible to flattery," Griffin said. He nodded to the empty glass in her hand. "Would you like another brandy?"

"No, thank you." She took a seat. "I came over to ask my husband for assistance. Devon, darling—we're trying to persuade Dorothea to sing."

"I'm not sure I can help," Hart said.

"We both know she'll do anything *you* ask of her."

"Very well." Hart rose and crossed the floor to the pianoforte where Mrs. Pelham was picking through song sheets. Lady Hart stood beside the instrument, arm-in-arm with Dorothea, who looked decidedly uncomfortable.

Sir Dexter stood some distance away, a smile of amusement on his lips—he had the good sense to steer clear of an argument between women.

But Devon Hart had no such qualms. He took Dorothea's hand and whispered in her ear. She glanced toward Griffin, then shook her head, but he persisted.

Eventually, she nodded, and her companions moved away like a receding tide, leaving her standing beside the pianoforte, her body stiff with tension. She closed her eyes, and her chest rose and fell.

Mrs. Pelham began to play, and a soft melody filled the room. Lady Atalanta leaned toward Griffin.

"*Il desiderio del mio cuore*," she whispered.

"I beg your pardon?" he asked.

"*My Heart's Desire*. Few of my acquaintance can sing it successfully, given the vocal range, but it's perfect for Dorothea. I always find a contralto voice infinitely preferable to a soprano, don't you?"

"What the devil is…"

"Hush!" she whispered. "She's about to begin."

Dorothea opened her eyes, then began to sing. Her voice sounded strained at first, but after a few bars, she relaxed, and the tone grew in richness—a warm, sweet voice, which filled the room and soothed his heart.

Lord only knew what she was singing—Griffin couldn't even identify the language—but the emotion in her voice conveyed the meaning of the words.

She was singing about love—the deepest desires of a woman in love.

As the song continued, her eyes glistened, and he felt tears prick at his eyelids. He glanced to his left and saw Lady Atalanta dabbing her eyes with a handkerchief.

Once again, he was reminded of the raw passion which burned deep within her. And tonight, as she stood in the center of the drawing room, resplendent in her gown, singing the most beautiful love song he'd ever heard, his heart swelled until it almost burst.

Not to mention the heat which surged in his groin.

She finished the song on a long note, and their eyes met across the room. Then he placed his hand over his heart, and her lips curled into a soft smile.

For a moment, they simply stared at each other—twin souls connecting across a chasm. The room faded to gray, with his wife the bright splash of color, shining like a beacon in a storm.

A ripple of applause threaded through the room and broke the spell.

"Mama Thea, that was beautiful!" Rowe cried.

Major Hart approached her and squeezed her hand, and Griffin caught his whispered congratulation.

"Bravo."

Then Hart made a great show of checking his pocket watch.

"Atalanta, my love, I think it's time we left. It's the longest we've left Francine. Dorothea, do you mind?"

She shook her head. "Of course not. I'm only grateful that you came."

"I'm a little tired," Mrs. Pelham said.

"And we should retire also," Lady Hart said. "Dexter?"

Sir Dexter leaped to his feet, and Griffin suppressed a smile.

In less than ten minutes, Griffin stood in the front hall, alone with his wife.

Their guests had departed, and Rowe had retired after embracing her stepmother with a ferocity that warmed his heart.

"What a wonderful evening," he said. "Thank you, Thea. I wasn't expecting to enjoy it."

"A family supper is always preferable to a formal party," she said. "Now, if you'll excuse me, I'm very tired."

He caught her hand. "You have a beautiful singing voice," he said. "I had no idea."

She gave a shy smile. "Thank you. I sang all the time when I was growing up. Then..." she sighed, "...I had little reason to sing after we arrived in London. Delilah had lessons, but she took so little pleasure out of it that Dex gave up on her."

"Didn't *you* take lessons?"

She shook her head. "The opportunity never arose. Dex wanted to school Lilah in the ways of a lady. She was our best chance of elevating our status—and she did, in the end, when she married a duke. She's young and handsome. Whereas I..." She broke off and averted her gaze.

Griffin silently cursed Sir Dexter. The man had tossed Dorothea aside, thinking her worthless, merely because she was considered too old to attract a husband. No wonder she dressed and behaved like a spinster aunt—her brother had treated her like one for years.

What a damned waste! All that passion—all that love, suppressed by stays and a domineering brother. It was all the more tragic because

Sir Dexter had believed he was doing what was best for her.

Griffin lifted his wife's hand to his mouth and brushed his lips against her skin.

"I may not have a title," he said, "but I value you more than any duke would. And now I've had the immense pleasure of hearing you sing, I hope you'll do so again—just for me."

Her eyes widened with surprise. "You value me?"

"Very much," he said. "You have a heart as big as an ocean—you're beautiful and accomplished—and you've been undervalued your whole life."

He leaned toward her and captured her lips in a kiss.

"But not anymore."

Chapter Thirty-One

THEA RECLINED IN her bed, watching the flickering flame of the candle.

It had taken all her courage to sing such a personal love song tonight in front of her husband. But Devon's words of encouragement had given her belief in herself.

The ground won't swallow you whole, Thea, for singing in front of your husband. Given how he's been looking at you all evening, he'll be even more in love with you on hearing you sing than he is right now.

After the first verse, her nerves had disappeared, to let her love fly freely—her love for the song, for the words which conveyed the heart's desire.

And her love for her husband.

When had her regard for him turned into love?

He might be uncouth—and a mystery still surrounded his late wife—but on occasion, he strove to make her happy. He reminded her of a bird, eager to build a nest for his female, who procured all manner of trinkets in order to give her pleasure, standing back to await her approval. That afternoon she'd returned from an excursion to the park with Rowena to find her discarded silk shawl mended and folded neatly on her pillow. The tear was almost invisible—as were the tiny, delicate stitches.

Soft footsteps approached, then the door opened.

Griffin stood in the doorway, wearing nothing but his breeches.

Her breath caught in her throat, and she sat up, almost knocking the candle over.

"What's the matter?" she asked. "Is it Rowena?"

"No."

His eyes glittered in the candlelight, raw hunger in their expression.

"Griffin?"

He approached the bed, the movement of his huge frame resembling a panther stalking its prey. Then he grasped the bedsheet and pulled it back, his gaze fixed on her. His tongue flicked out and ran across his lips.

The bed shifted with his weight as he sat on it. He reached out and touched the neckline of her nightrail, tracing the edge with his finger before dipping it between her breasts. Her skin tingled with anticipation as he ran his fingertip across the swell of her flesh. Then he pulled the lace ties loose to reveal her breasts.

His mouth curled in a slow, lazy smile. But hunger blazed in his eyes.

A nugget of need swelled within her—but for what, she couldn't fathom.

Then he placed his hand on her breast, and her nipple hardened to a painful little point. He flicked it with his thumb, and a pulse of need ignited in her center.

"What are you doing?" she whispered.

"Something I've wanted to do from the moment I saw you in your brother's garden," he said, his voice hoarse. "Something I should have done weeks ago."

He dipped his head and captured her breast in his mouth. His hot, wet tongue swirled round her flesh, and a low growl rumbled in his chest as he began to suckle her—gently at first, then more insistent, as if he feasted on her.

She buried her hands in his hair, holding his head to her breast. He rumbled his approval, whispering gentle words of praise, then two strong hands clasped her shoulders and pushed her back until she lay before him. He lifted his head, and she was assaulted by a rush of cold and loss as he leaned over her, his mouth tantalizingly close. Was she dreaming? Or was this real, her dream come to life in the form of her husband, the man she had wanted for so long.

Unable to fight her need, she arched her back, offering her breast, chasing the pleasure. He reached down and drew up the skirt of her nightrail, exposing her legs.

"Do you want me, woman?"

Two large hands clasped her thighs, then nudged her legs apart. Wicked sensations pulsed in her body. Her husband was no gentle suitor, not a fine lord, but a savage. He was all man.

And he was all hers. And she belonged to him in every way.

"Tell me you want me," he growled, "for I'll not be gentle. All night I've waited for our guests to leave so I could bury myself inside you."

He fumbled with his breeches, and his manhood sprang free. Her heart gave a flutter—how could something so big fit inside her?

He gazed at her with hooded eyes, then eased on top of her. She yielded, drawing strength from his weight, and curled her hands round his arms, relishing the hardness of his muscles, the raw power simmering beneath the surface. Had she fallen in love with her beast, her husband?

Then she felt him, hot and hard against her flesh. A delicious ache formed deep within her body, and she shifted her legs, where an unfathomable moisture had begun to pool.

He let out a hoarse cry. "Oh, sweet Lord, you're ready!"

Then he thrust forward.

A sharp pain exploded inside her, and she bit her lip, tasting blood. Then he moved. The pain flared, then receded with each movement and, a distant sensation of pleasure began to build. A groan escaped her lips.

"That's it, my love," he murmured. "Come for me." He buried his head in her shoulder and increased the pace, his breathing coming out in gasps in time with each thrust, until he let out a sharp cry, then collapsed on top of her.

She tried to move, but he clung to her. By the time his breathing settled, the pain had lessened, but the pleasure remained out of reach.

Then he kissed her and withdrew. She winced at the sting, and his brow furrowed.

"Didn't I please you?"

The concern in his eyes tore at her heart. He reminded her of a young boy eager to please but afraid he'd failed in his attempt.

Then he glanced down, and the pleasure in his eyes turned to horror.

"What have I done!"

GRIFFIN STARED AT the blood on his wife's thighs.

Dear Lord, did that mean...?

"Forgive me," he said. "I shouldn't have done that."

Tears pricked at her eyes. "You regret what we did?"

"No," he said, "I mean...yes, I've hurt you. I had no idea, that..." he gestured toward her legs, "...that you were..."

"That I was what?"

"A maiden...untouched."

"This is our first time."

"Yes," he said, "but I thought..."

Her expression hardened. "You thought I'd lain with another. Is that why you've been unwilling to touch me before tonight?"

"I heard rumors," he said, "about a child out of wedlock."

"And you jumped to conclusions without bothering to ask?"

She was right, of course. Why hadn't he simply *asked* her?

"There was no child out of wedlock," she said. "My sister Lilah was with child when she married—not that it's any of your business—and my sister Daisy was seduced by a rake when she was no more than a child. Shall I continue, or have I quenched your thirst for gossip?"

His heart ached at the sadness in her eyes.

"At least I now see why you thought my brother had tricked you into marrying me," she said, "but I cannot understand why you agreed to it if you believed me a fallen woman."

"I thought you'd be more likely to marry someone like me, given you'd..." he broke off, cursing himself.

"You thought that as a ruined woman, I'd be desperate enough to accept your hand?" she asked. "I don't know whether to laugh at your low opinion of yourself or cry at your low opinion of me."

Bloody hell. He'd never been a wordsmith, but why could he never say the right thing?

"Forgive me," he said, "I didn't mean to shame you by inferring that you were desperate."

"I *was* desperate," she said. "I was the family spinster—who stood by and watched all my siblings find that which I craved. By the time Dex had made his fortune and brought us to London, my chance of finding love was already small. And as each year passed, it lessened."

"That can't be true," he said.

She laughed bitterly. "That only shows how little you understand society. But..." She turned her soulful gaze on him. "Do you know when I first felt a stirring of passion?"

"Tell me."

"When I first saw you fight—how you mastered and relished the raw power of your body—so completely at ease with yourself. It made me feel wild and free to see a man unrestrained by the customs of society, engaging in an activity which celebrated his physicality."

Her honest confession, spoken with such emotion, touched his heart.

"When you first saw *me*?" he asked.

"It made me feel sensations I couldn't have imagined."

"Physical sensations?"

She nodded.

"Can you describe them?"

"I-I don't know…"

"It would give me much pleasure to hear you speak of it," he said.

Her face flushed, and she lowered her gaze. "Inside my body, and between my…my…" She gestured toward her legs, and his manhood twitched in its eagerness to claim her sweetness once more.

"It felt like I had to touch myself…*there*…but I couldn't."

"Why not?"

"I was ashamed," she said. "Then, after the fight, I waited—hoping that if I could catch a glimpse of you, I'd feel that passion again. But I saw you with that woman."

"That was *you*?" he asked. "I knew someone was watching—standing apart from the crowd. Is that why you agreed to marry me?"

She nodded, and a tear slid down her cheek. "I knew I'd disgraced myself at my party—or at least, in Dexter's eyes. But it made me feel *alive*—and I'd rather be a fallen woman than an old maid."

"But you weren't a fallen woman," he said. "You had no need to marry, and you knew nothing about me. If I recall, I insulted you that night—you must have thought me an awful boor."

"You still don't understand," she said. "I knew marrying you was a risk—but with that risk came the prospect of feeling that passion again."

"No small risk for a woman to take."

"I know," she said, "but I was prepared to take it. I'd lived in the world for thirty years, and it was the first time I'd truly come alive." Another tear splashed onto her cheek, followed by another. "I had no wish to wait another thirty years."

He placed his hand on her cheek and brushed the tears aside, then he tipped her face up until their eyes met.

"You won't have to wait another thirty years." He leaned over and claimed her mouth, probing against the seam of her lips with his tongue. She gave a soft sigh and parted her lips, and he slipped his tongue in. He felt a familiar stirring in his groin, and he brushed his knuckle against her breasts. Her nipples beaded almost instantly.

"In fact," he whispered, "you'll not even have to wait thirty minutes."

Her eyes widened. "Don't you have to wait, I mean, Meggie told me that Dex..." she colored and looked away.

Sweet heaven, her innocence was almost his undoing!

He nuzzled her neck, then planted a stream of kisses along her skin until he reached her earlobe, which he grazed with his teeth. Her body shuddered, and he whispered in her ear. "I find I'm ready for you again," he said, "and this time, there will only be pleasure..." he dipped his tongue into her ear, and she gave a low cry, "...sweet, unbridled pleasure."

He reached for her nightrail and tugged at it.

"Griffin..."

"Hush, wife," he said. "I wish to look at you—to relish your body. I was overly hungry before and took my fill to quench my hunger. Now, I wish to savor you."

He lifted the garment over her head and discarded it. Then he placed a feather-light kiss on the swell of her breasts.

"Every inch of you..."

He peppered her skin with tiny, open-mouthed kisses, then flicked his tongue out. He circled her breast with his tongue, spiraling toward the center, where the little bud was already peaked for him.

A small mewl escaped her lips. The hands that clung to her nightrail were now fisted in the bedsheet as she arched her back, offering herself to him.

"Griffin…"

His name on her lips was almost his undoing. With his free hand, he caressed her skin, moving across the smoothness of her belly until he reached the thatch of curls at her center.

Then he slipped his finger inside her.

She threw back her head, and a long, slow growl rumbled in her throat as he drew his finger along her center. This time there was no doubt. She was ready.

Then he found what he was looking for—the delectable little nub. As soon as he touched it, she let out a cry, and her body shuddered.

"Are you my woman?"

"Yes." Her voice came out in a strained whisper. "Oh, yes!"

He circled her nub with his finger, and she shifted her thighs wider. Then he stopped moving, and she let out a cry of frustration and lifted her hips.

There was nothing so attractive as a female in a state of readiness. The raw, instinctive signals conveyed—with no thought or calculation—the most primal of needs.

The need to mate.

He drew in a deep breath, relishing the sweet, earthy scent of pure female need—a need which only he could satisfy.

Covering her once more with his body, he moved against her, the tip of his length rubbing slickly against her core, begging entrance.

Her body responded. Parting her legs wide, she lifted her hips to draw him into that sweet heat that was for him.

Only for him.

"Griffin…" the words came out in ragged gasps. "I need…" she drew in a shuddering breath. "I want…oh!" She let out a cry as he eased into her warmth, and her body began to draw him in. But he resisted, and she gave a whimper of frustration.

"Do you want me?"

"Yes!" she cried. "Oh, yes!"

Then he plunged into her, and she cried out again. He withdrew and thrust into her once more, and she lifted her hips, meeting each thrust. A wave of passion swelled within him, and he increased the pace, chasing the most intense, exhilarating pleasure he'd ever experienced. The pleasure morphed into a burning pain, and he slowed down for fear of hurting her.

"No! Don't stop, Griffin!" She fisted her hands in his hair and crushed her mouth against his and thrust her tongue inside, claiming him, as he claimed her body.

Then she lifted her legs and wrapped them around him, the action drawing him deeper inside. The world shattered around him, and myriads of light exploded in his mind. He roared out her name as his body disintegrated and his mind soared into the stars as he felt her womanhood pulse with pleasure.

As he returned to the solid earth, he clung to heruntil his breathing grew steady and his heartbeat slowed.

He closed his eyes and held her close, relishing the feel of her warm, soft body in his arms.

His Thea.

At last, he understood the difference between fucking and making love. Before, he'd experienced the physical release, which gave him a momentary satisfaction, but ultimately had left him hollow—craving something which was always missing.

And finally, he understood what he'd been missing.

A woman to love.

They lay together, basking in the afterglow of their lovemaking. When, he opened his eyes, he found her staring at him, her eyes filled with tears.

He caressed her forehead. "Is something wrong?"

She opened her mouth to reply, and a soft cry escaped her lips.

"Did I hurt you?"

"No," she whispered. "It was…" she sighed, "…truly wonderful."

"Then why are you sad?"

"I fear I've left it too late."

"It's never too late," he said. "We'll have many years to enjoy each other."

A tear spilled onto her cheek. "My dream..." her breath caught, and she sighed, "...was to have a child of my own," she said. "I even picked out their names—Marcus for a boy and Helena for a girl. I love Rowena as if she were my own—but I cannot help regretting the lost years. I may be too old to have children of my own."

"Never lose hope," he said. He drew the covers over them both. She nestled against his body and let out a sigh, and his heart soared at the feel of her in his arms.

"May I ask you something, Griffin?"

"Anything."

"Rowena has no wish to become a society lady. She's promised to enjoy the rest of our stay in London, but afterward—she wants to remain in the country and pursue her studies. Might you consider it?"

"What about you?" he asked. "Don't *you* want to live in London, where your friends and family are?"

She shook her head. "I love them, but London will always remind me of the constraints under which I was placed. In the country, I am free. I didn't think so at first, but now, it's my home."

"Then, if you wish it," he said, "we'll remain in the country."

"You don't mind?"

He kissed the top of her head. "No," he said. "Most of all in the world, I want my family—you and Rowe—to be happy."

"Thank you." She placed a light kiss on his chest, then curled her body into his. Soon after, the steady pace of her breathing indicated she'd fallen asleep.

However old his wife thought she might be—she was not too old to be loved.

And he loved her.

Chapter Thirty-Two

THE FAMILIAR SIGHT of the White Hart came into view from the carriage window. Every time Griffin returned to Sandiford, he couldn't help looking out for the inn—his pride and joy.

Dorothea sat opposite, Rowe sleeping peacefully beside her, even though thunder had been rumbling in the distance. She met his gaze, and her lips curled into the slow, satisfied smile of a woman well pleasured.

They'd made love every night in London since their first time, the pleasure increasing each time as she writhed beneath him, crying out his name—and, yesterday in the drawing room, he'd hitched up her skirts and taught her how to ride him. All that passion had lain dormant—now he'd unleashed it, he struggled to keep his hands off her.

Could life be any more perfect? He had a loving wife and a daughter—and he didn't care who'd sired Rowe—she was *his*. Rowe seemed happier than ever, with a loving stepmother and aunts and uncles who doted on her.

Louisa's memory would fade over time to be replaced by new memories. Finally, Griffin could lay her ghost to rest. And—more importantly—Rowe never need know the truth, for it would destroy her.

A lone figure emerged from the inn and hailed the carriage, which drew to a halt. Griffin pulled the window down.

"Ned—what's the matter?"

"I need to speak to you."

"Can't it wait?" Griffin asked. "We've just returned from London."

Ned glanced toward Thea. "Forgive me, Mrs. Oake. It shouldn't take long."

"That's all right," Thea said. "Take as long as you need, Griffin. We'll make sure supper's ready for you at home."

He leaned over and captured her mouth in a kiss.

"Until later," he whispered. He climbed out of the carriage and followed Ned into the inn.

"What's so important that I must abandon my wife?" he asked.

"Alex Ogilvie's returned."

Griffin's stomach clenched at the mention of his old friend's name. "Are you certain?"

"He was here yesterday. I said you were in London and sent him packing, but I doubt we've seen the last of him."

Griffin shook his head. "Ogilvie's too much of a coward to face me."

"He might want revenge."

"What for?" Griffin snorted. "I did nothing to *him*. You worry too much, Ned. Now—is there anything else you need, or may I return to my wife?"

Ned grinned. "I take it things have improved between you—I know the look of a man well-fed and a woman well bedded." He gestured toward the courtyard. "I presume you won't be attending the next fight if you're hanging onto your wife's apron strings."

"Don't be a fool," Griffin said. "My wife prefers a real man, not a milksop."

"That good, eh?" Ned laughed. "I knew there was a vixen beneath those prim little skirts."

"That's enough," Griffin growled.

Ned laughed and slapped him on the back. "You've got it bad, my friend," he said. "Go to her—if a good tupping improves your temper, then I salute your wife."

A low rumble echoed in the distance.

"There's a storm brewing," Ned said.

In more ways than one—if Alex Ogilvie was abroad.

Griffin set off on foot to Sandiford Manor, inhaling the clean, Sussex air. The walk would ease the ache in his legs after being cooped up in the carriage.

As he neared the manor, he heard Rowe's laughter, and he smiled to himself. Thea said something in her rich, warm tones, and the laughter resumed. A male voice joined in. That must be Will, or perhaps the new butler—Kerrigan was the name, if he recalled the agency's letter properly.

The laughter came from the dining room. Through the half-open door, Griffin saw Rowe chatting animatedly, waving her fork in the air. She leaped to her feet when she spotted Griffin.

"Papa! We have a visitor! I remember him from when I was younger—I can't think why I'd forgotten him before. Mama Thea says he can stay. Isn't that wonderful?"

Griffin entered the dining room.

His wife sat at one end of the table. At the opposite end—in Griffin's place—sat a man. Light blonde hair framed an angular face with full lips and pale blue eyes. He was as handsome as Griffin remembered.

He rose to his feet and offered his hand.

"Griff! My friend—you've no idea how wonderful it is to see you again."

He fixed his gaze on Griffin, a smile on his lips.

Griffin stared at the outstretched hand as if by sheer force of will he could make him disappear.

But he was here. And he was real.

"Aren't you going to greet your friend?" Dorothea asked.

Griffin took the hand, and lean, calloused fingers curled round his wrist, holding it in a firm grip. He increased the pressure, digging his nails into Griffin's skin, meeting his gaze as if in challenge.

Ned had been right to warn him.

"I can't say how delighted I am that your beautiful wife has invited me to stay."

Alex Ogilvie blinked slowly, then smiled.

Alex Ogilvie—the man who Griffin had once called friend.

The man had set Louisa on the path to destruction, leading to Griffin being accused of her murder.

⇶⇷

THEA GLANCED AT her husband, who glowered in the doorway.

"What are you doing here, Ogilvie?" he asked.

"I'm come to visit," Mr. Ogilvie said. "I've missed my friend—and my favorite girl, of course."

At first, Thea had been apprehensive when she'd seen the stranger waiting beside the main doors of Sandiford Manor. Still, Rowena recognized him and, with a cry of delight, had run into his out-stretched arms before eagerly introducing Thea to her *Uncle Alex*.

Mr. Ogilvie's charming manner and open praise of Griffin had instantly won her trust—not to mention how he'd lifted Rowena by the waist and twirled her round.

"Isn't it wonderful, Papa?" Rowena cried. "Uncle Alex has been telling me all about Mama."

Griffin glanced at her. "Is this true?"

"There's no harm in it, surely?" Thea said. "Rowena has a right to know about her mother. I've no objection—and neither should you."

"Some things are best left buried."

"Come, come, my friend!" Mr. Ogilvie said cheerfully. "Secrets always have a way of revealing themselves."

"In my experience," Griffin replied, "secrets are often revealed by those who wish to cause mischief."

"An innocent man has nothing to hide."

"I've yet to meet anyone who's truly innocent," Griffin said, "no matter how charming they appear to be."

"Griffin!" Thea cried.

He frowned at her, his expression darkening.

Mr. Ogilvie interceded. "*I'm* the one who's given offense. Forgive me, Griff. If I'm unwelcome, I can leave. You are master here."

"You'll do no such thing," Thea said. Griffin might be master of Sandiford Manor, but she was its mistress, and it piqued her to have to defer to him, particularly when Rowena glowed with such happiness. Surely Griffin wouldn't deny his daughter the pleasure?

"Perhaps I should let you discuss the matter with your wife," Mr. Ogilvie said. "I saw your manservant chopping wood in the yard—I'm sure he'd appreciate some assistance, while you'd appreciate a little privacy."

Before Thea could protest, he slipped out of the dining room.

"He seems pleasant enough," Thea said. "Rowe remembers him. Where's the harm in letting him stay for a day or two? We've a guest room already made up."

"So, his foot's already established under my door!" Griffin exclaimed. "Woman—you should have waited for my approval."

Woman?

"What's he done to make you dislike him?" she asked.

He glanced at Rowena, then shook his head. "Nothing of importance."

A loud rumble echoed overhead, and shortly after, rain spattered at the windowpanes.

The door opened, and Mr. Ogilvie returned, shaking water droplets off his collar.

"It's begun to rain," he said. "But I don't think the storm's coming toward us."

As if to contradict him, another rumble sounded, and Rowena let out a gasp. Mr. Ogilvie slid across to her and placed his arm around her shoulders.

"Poor little Rowe-ling. You always were terrified of storms, weren't you?"

Another rumble echoed overhead, and Rowena shivered in Mr. Ogilvie's arms.

"Your dear mother died during a storm," he continued. "Such a tragic loss for you. Doubly so—for you were there at the time."

"I was?"

"Don't you remember?"

"That's enough!" Griffin roared. "Can't you see it's upsetting her?"

"*You're* upsetting me, Papa!" Rowena cried.

"Perhaps your father's right, little Rowe," Mr. Ogilvie said. "If I left now, I can rent a room at the White Hart." He glanced out of the window. "I don't mind the rain."

"Don't go!" Rowena cried. "Mama Thea, he can stay, can't he?"

"Oh, spare me the nonsense!" Griffin exclaimed. "Ogilvie, you can stay the night. We'll discuss the matter in the morning without the women present."

The women?

Thea pushed her plate aside. "Rowena dear, shall we retire and leave *the men* to conclude their discussion?"

Rowena glanced at Griffin. "You won't turn him out, will you?"

Griffin sighed. "I promise."

"With your leave, I'll retire also," Mr. Ogilvie said.

Griffin shook his head, oh what he'd like to do to the man…

Ogilvie took Thea's hand and lifted it to his lips. "May I thank you for your hospitality ma'am," he said. "Such kindness is seldom to be found among friends—let alone strangers."

Ignoring her husband's scowl, Thea smiled back, then she led Rowena out of the dining room.

An hour later, she lay in her bed, listening to the sounds of the household retiring, the clatter of the pots in the kitchen, the distant footsteps of the servants—set against the backdrop of the receding storm. But the one pair of footsteps she waited for didn't come.

She had wondered whether she should wait for Griffin in his bed-chamber. In London, they'd abandoned tradition and slept together every night in his chamber, where the larger bed lent itself better to their enthusiastic and vigorous lovemaking.

But, at Sandiford, Griffin's room had been his realm for several years before she'd entered the household. She needed an invitation.

But the invitation never came.

Chapter Thirty-Three

GRIFFIN ENTERED THE breakfast room and froze.
Alex Ogilvie sat at the head of the table, spooning scrambled eggs into his mouth.

"Griff, my friend, how pleasant. I hadn't expected to see you so early." He gestured toward the buffet. "Do join me. I must congratulate you on the excellence of your cook. Or should I congratulate that intriguing wife of yours?"

Griffin folded his arms. "What do you want, Ogilvie?"

"What—no pleasantries for an old friend?"

"I think we both know that pleasantries are merely a foil to divert attention from the truth," Griffin said.

Ogilvie laughed. "You speak like a dandy! Has your wife been giving you lessons? She looks too much of a lady for your tastes.

"Just tell me what you want, *Alex*." Griffin almost spat out the last word.

"I find myself in need of funds."

"And you thought I'd give you a handout? You're more of a fool than I thought."

"I can work for it," Ogilvie said.

Griffin snorted. "You've no idea what honest work is."

"I could manage the White Hart—better than that numbskull Ned Watkins. I can't believe he's still there."

"Ned's been a faithful employee and friend," Griffin said, "which is more than I can say for you. At least he didn't seduce my wife."

"Louisa threw herself at me at every opportunity," Ogilvie said. "I wonder if her replacement will show a greater strength of will." He winked, then picked up his teacup and sipped it. "Mmm—hot and wet. Just how I like 'em."

"Why, you…"

"Good morning," a female voice said. Dorothea stood in the doorway.

Ogilvie rose to his feet, the slick, charming smile in place. "Mrs. Oake! I trust you slept well and weren't disturbed during the night." He cast a sidelong glance at Griffin. "The storm didn't come closer, did it?"

"No," she said. "It didn't."

"Ogilvie and I were discussing his departure," Griffin said. "He's leaving today."

"Am I?" Ogilvie's voice rose in challenge.

"I don't think you're suitable company for my wife and daughter."

"But he's an old friend of yours!" Dorothea exclaimed. "And Rowena's fond of him. She'll be disappointed to see him go."

"I dare say she'll recover," Griffin said. "But I won't have a criminal in my home. Did you know he spent four years in Horsham gaol? Do you want such a man in your home?"

Ogilvie's smile broadened, the smug expression on his face fueling Griffin's anger.

"Who knows what he might do?" Griffin continued. "Do you want to be murdered in your own bed?"

He aimed a smile of triumph at Ogilvie.

"I already know of Mr. Ogilvie's past," she said. "He informed me of that himself. He was imprisoned for debt—a circumstance of misfortune rather than a crime. And you accuse him of being a *murderer*?"

She shook her head. "You insult your friend—and you insult me by thinking me unwilling to give him a second chance. My brother, Devon, was persecuted by those who were too quick to judge—would you deny his friendship also?"

"Of course not," Griffin said.

"Mr. Ogilvie told me last night that he's anxious to repay his debts by working," she continued. "I see no reason why we shouldn't give him the opportunity."

She paused and glanced at Ogilvie. "Of course, if he cannot keep his word, then he's *not* welcome here, as I told him last night, didn't I, Mr. Ogilvie?"

Ogilvie's smile slipped a fraction, then he nodded.

Good—at least Dorothea's usual good sense hadn't completely abandoned her.

"Then I've no objection to giving him a chance." Griffin said, "But, rest assured, Ogilvie, I'll be watching you. I'll do anything to protect my loved ones."

Dorothea cast him a glance. Was she still angry?

He'd missed her last night—but he had no desire to give Ogilvie any opportunity to rile him further. The very notion of that man being in the house while Griffin shared intimacies with his wife—was not to be borne.

"Rest assured, Griff, my intentions are honorable," Ogilvie said. "I wanted to see my old friend again, and I heard about the fight at the White Hart. I thought I'd try my hand at it.

"*You?*"

"Why not? It's how I made my living—and the winnings would pay my debts."

"Assuming you win," Griffin said.

"I intend to." Ogilvie smiled, his eyes glittering with ambition.

"Then you must stay," Thea said. "We cannot deny you the chance to honor your debts."

The schoolmistress tone had returned—which meant she'd brook no denial.

"Very well," Griffin said. "You can stay until the fight."

Triumph gleamed in Ogilvie's gaze. But what harm could he do? Perhaps the old adage was true—it was better to keep one's enemies close at hand.

"I should speak with Mrs. Morris about the menus," Dorothea said. "Mr. Ogilvie, are there any particular meals that you favor?"

"I'm sure I'll relish whatever you offer me, Mrs. Oake."

Seemingly unaware of Ogilvie's hungry gaze, she nodded and exited the breakfast room.

Ogilvie sat and resumed eating, wearing a smile which could only be described as "punchable."

"Aren't you going to sit, Griff?"

Gritting his teeth, Griffin spooned eggs onto his plate and took the seat at the opposite end of the table.

"You seem fortunate in your choice of wife," Ogilvie said between mouthfuls, "though she's nothing like Louisa—at least, not in appearance."

Griffin refused to take the bait.

"Where did you find her?" Ogilvie continued. "I can't see you moving in the same circles."

"I met her in London. She's my banker's sister."

"Married you for your money, did she?"

"She's rich in her own right," Griffin said.

Not that you'll see a penny of it, if that's what you're after—he almost added.

"I congratulate you on your good fortune," Ogilvie replied. "A woman of her age is less likely to saddle you with a litter of brats, but her fortune will swell your coffers. You have all the advantages of a marriage and none of the disadvantages."

"You've no right to speak of her in that manner," Griffin said.

"She's not old, and she's a good mother to Rowe—she's even made provisions for Rowe's marriage settlement."

Ogilvie's eyes widened with interest. "Has she? You've really landed on your feet."

"Through hard work," Griffin said.

"Aided by good fortune," Ogilvie said. "You had a few lucky wins in the ring. It could have been me."

Griffin snorted. "You? Lazy, arrogant, never wanting to work or train, expecting success to fall onto your lap—you were unpopular with the crowd because you fought dirty. Whereas I…"

"Whereas *you* were loved in the ring, despite your true nature out of it."

"What the devil do you mean?" Griffin asked.

"You know full well," Ogilvie said. "I was there, remember, the night Louisa was killed? When Rowena found you over her dead, naked body, with your hands around her throat?"

Griffin's chest tightened at the memory…Louisa's broken body at the foot of the stairs, her soulless eyes staring up at him, the spark of accusation fading as the life left her.

And Rowe—little Rowe—her innocent face peering round the corner as she saw him drag her mother's corpse across the floor.

"Of course," Ogilvie continued, "you must be counting your blessings that she has no recollection of that night."

"How do you know she can't remember what happened?" Griffin asked.

"Because she doesn't hate you—and neither does your wife! What would they think if they knew the truth?" Ogilvie laughed. "I find it ironic that you've tried to paint *me* as a murderer in your wife's eyes."

"They won't believe a word you say," Griffin said, his voice tight.

"Are you prepared to take the risk?"

Griffin's hands itched to wrap round Ogilvie's neck. Then he heard a soft footfall, and Rowe appeared in the doorway.

Ogilvie pushed his plate aside. "These eggs aren't to my taste," he said. "I must ask your wife to instruct the cook to provide me with a little bacon each morning."

"Oh!" Rowe cried. "Has Papa given you leave to stay?"

Ogilvie turned his smile on Griffin. "Yes, dearest Rowe-ling," he said. "I rather think he has."

Chapter Thirty-Four

"COME ON, MAMA Thea!"

Thea pulled herself up onto the branch, then called up through the leaves.

"Are you sure it's safe?"

Rowena's face appeared above her. "I've climbed this tree hundreds of times," she said. "Where's your sense of adventure?"

"I left it with my stomach when that lower branch snapped," Thea said. "I've had enough of falling to the ground in gardens in an undignified heap."

Rowena laughed. "Uncle Dexter told me about the night Papa proposed to you," she said. "I think he said it to shock me into behaving properly."

"And did it?"

"Of course not! I think I shocked Uncle Dex when I said it seemed a better way of getting a husband than waiting to be asked to dance at some stuffy ball. Though I must admit, I do like my new gowns."

"Then we must ensure you have plenty of opportunities to wear them," Thea said. "Perhaps we could invite our London friends for a house party."

"And you could sing for us all again," Rowena said. "Papa was completely in love with you when he heard you sing in London."

He may have been, but since their return to Sandiford, he'd still not visited her bedchamber.

Perhaps it was due to the presence of their guest. Mr. Ogilvie was all charm, and Rowena adored him, but Thea found herself looking forward to the return of the relaxed family life they'd enjoyed in London. Griffin's reserve had returned, and Thea had become, once more, the neglected wife of a man who preferred to spend his waking hours in the White Hart.

When Mr. Ogilvie had earned his winnings and gone on his way, might the open-hearted man hidden behind her husband's gruff exterior return?

Was that why Griffin had forbidden her from attending tonight's fight? Because of Ogilvie?

She'd been tempted to argue against it.

In an act of rebellion, she'd suggested Rowena and she climb trees while the men beat each other into a pulp. She had forgotten the exhilaration to be found in climbing—something she'd enjoyed as a child before she'd been forced to succumb to the rules of London society.

It was a pity one had to grow up. Children enjoyed their indulgences with a relish borne of not understanding the world. Once Rowena's eyes had been fully opened to the world, her childhood would be over, irrevocably.

But for now—they could both enjoy the simple pleasure of climbing a tree, with no fear of admonishment.

As Thea placed her foot on the next branch, it snapped and gave way. She tumbled out of the tree onto the ground. The impact jolted her bones and forced the air from her lungs, but she closed her eyes with a smile. The warmth of the sun caressed her face, and she tipped her head up, relishing the soft pink glow through her eyelids.

She heard a rustle of leaves, followed by a thud as Rowena landed beside her.

"Are you all right?"

"Yes!" Thea laughed. "I'm fortunate not to have the type of gamine frame prized in London."

"What do you mean?" Rowena asked.

"I mean that my curves enable me to benefit from a soft landing."

"That they do," a male voice said, "and more besides."

Thea opened her eyes. Mr. Ogilvie leaned against the adjacent tree, a broad grin on his face. A large red mark adorned his cheek.

"Uncle Alex!" Rowena cried. "Have you been watching us?"

"Forgive me," he said. "I had no wish to disturb your joy—or mine, for that matter."

Thea brushed the dust from her skirts. He watched her, a glimmer of hunger in his eyes, then held out his hand.

She took it, and he helped her up. "Are you hurt?" he asked. "You took quite a tumble."

"Nothing compared to you," Thea said, gesturing to his face. "Who did that?"

"Your husband."

"Papa?" Rowena gasped, then Mr. Ogilvie laughed. "A lucky blow, little Rowe," he said. "We were merely sparring. I'll be more careful tonight."

"You're fighting my husband tonight?" Thea asked.

"No," he said. "I'm challenging Billy Bates. I've learned over the years that a successful man chooses which fights to face head-on and which to avoid."

"I hope you'll win," Thea said.

Ogilvie laughed. "So that I can be on my way? Are you as anxious as Griffin to see me gone?"

Rowena frowned at Thea, accusation in her eyes. "You want him to leave?"

"Of course not," Thea said. "But I'm aware how eager Mr. Ogilvie is to repay his debts." She turned to Ogilvie. "A sentiment which does you credit, sir."

He smiled, then nodded toward the house. "I should get going— the fight starts in a little over an hour. I came to tell you that your husband has changed his mind and wants you to attend."

"He does?"

"I also came for a talisman."

"A talisman?"

"A token," he said. "I wondered if you'd oblige me with a ribbon or handkerchief—to bring me good fortune in the fight."

"Shouldn't I give one to my husband instead?" Thea asked.

"*I'll* give you one, Alex!" Rowena cried. She pulled a ribbon from her hair and handed it to him. "You'll be my champion—like Sir Lancelot and Lady Guinevere."

He tied the ribbon around his wrist.

"Can I come, too?" Rowena asked.

"I'm sorry, Rowe," Ogilvie said. "It's no place for you."

Rowena pouted. "I'm not a child!"

Ogilvie took her hand. "Your father would never forgive me if I brought you with us. A fight can be a dangerous event, and I wouldn't want to be worrying about your safety when I'm knocking Billy Bates to the ground. No unmarried woman should be seen at a fight—unless she's of a certain sort."

"But…"

"Why don't you see if your cook needs help with supper?" Ogilvie suggested, interrupting Rowena's protest. "We'll be hungry after the fight." He lifted the ribbon to his lips. "You'll be with me in my heart tonight."

Rowena sighed. "Oh, very well."

"Run along, then," he said.

Rowena smiled, then ran back toward the house.

Mr. Ogilvie offered his arm. Thea took it, then they followed at a more leisurely pace.

"You certainly have a way with Rowena," Thea said. "She'll do anything for you."

"She's an exceptional young woman. I'm quite in love with her."

For a moment, hunger glimmered in his eyes, and a shiver ran across Thea's skin.

"She's still a child, Mr. Ogilvie," she said.

"Griffin doesn't seem to think so. Didn't he want her to have a London season before you put a stop to it?"

"Rowena didn't want a season," Thea said, "and I agreed with her."

"You're wise," he said. "She's a pretty girl, and London is a cesspit of libertines. Better she find a husband nearer to home—one that suits her better than some titled dandy."

"She's barely fourteen," Thea said. "Courtship's out of the question."

"Courtship!" he laughed. "Where a man dances around a woman, making a fool of himself to persuade her to marry him? I prefer the old ways of securing a mate."

"I take it you're referring to animals in the jungle who fight their rivals to establish ownership of the females?" Thea laughed. "London society may be degenerate, but it has, at least marginally, risen above the realm of the beast."

"But you must admit that most women take pleasure in witnessing male prowess—such as what you'll see in the White Hart tonight?"

Thea blushed at the memory of Griffin's naked torso—and the desire which swirled deep within her each time she imagined him parading around the ring, dominating both the arena and his opponent—his sheer, male potency…

"Mrs. Oake?"

He fixed his gaze on her, a quizzical expression in his eyes.

"Forgive me," she said. "I became a little distracted."

"You'll need your wits about you tonight," he said. "A woman as beautiful as you—I swear you'll start a riot."

As they reached the main house, she withdrew her hand. "Mr. Ogilvie," she said, "you're quite mistaken if you think a woman like me is likely to cause a riot."

>>><<<

THEA STEPPED THROUGH the threshold of the White Hart, accompanied by Mr. Ogilvie.

The night was in full swing—the air filled with a cacophony of drunken male voices and the excited squeals of a woman. A wicked thrill coursed through Thea's body at the thought of seeing her husband dominating the arena.

This time, she could enjoy watching him—openly, not hidden among the shadows—knowing he was hers. *She'd* be the one he'd take to bed after winning a fight—not some bar-room doxy.

A woman squealed in delight, and another roar rose.

"Tilly will part those fat thighs before you've even dropped your breeches, Billy!"

"She's a fine cunny, that one!"

Thea recoiled at the profanity, then drew her shawl round her shoulders. One or two men leered at her, their expressions clouded by ale.

"Are you sure my husband wanted me here, Mr. Ogilvie?" she hissed. "Perhaps I should wait in the courtyard until the fighting starts."

"It always gets a little rowdy before the fights start," he said, "though it's a bit livelier than normal tonight."

A hand grasped Thea's arm, and she found herself pulled toward a thickset man with a ruddy face and sour ale on his breath.

"Whoa—take a look at this tasty piece!"

"Get your hands off me!" she cried.

"Bloody hell—listen to the tart!" another man cried. He shoved the first man aside. "Let me take care of you," he said. "I like 'em posh, and I'll pay you a good deal more than Johnny. He never dips his hands into his pockets unless he's fisting himself."

He yanked her closer and pursed his lips, and she recognized the man Griffin had fought in London.

"Give Billy a kiss for luck, wench, and I'll give ye a good time once I'm done in the ring."

"What the fuck are you doing!" a new voice roared.

The room fell silent. Through the haze of smoke and sweat, Thea saw her husband's face, dark with fury.

He grasped her assailant by the shoulders and threw him aside.

"Steady on, Oake!" The man laughed. "I saw her first."

"Lay another finger on her, Billy Bates, and I'll cut it off and feed it to the pigs!" Griffin growled.

"Don't be so tight," the man laughed. "You've a wife waiting at home, so your cock will be well served tonight. Surely you wouldn't deny me a few minutes with this tart before I beat your balls in the ring?"

"That woman *is* my wife," Griffin said.

A sharp intake of breath rippled through the crowd.

Griffin turned his angry gaze on Thea. "I did *not* give you permission to come tonight, woman."

Thea's fear turned to indignation. "Permission?" she cried. "Since when must I ask your leave to do anything?"

"Since you vowed to obey me," he said, glancing at the crowd before resuming his green gaze on her. Then, he grasped her wrist. "Come with me—you can wait in the parlor until the fight's over."

Did he think her some doxy to be ordered about?

"I will not!" she cried.

"Do you want me to take my hand to you, wife?"

"Steady on, Griff," Ogilvie intervened. "That's no way to talk to a lady."

"What the bloody hell were you thinking, bringing *her* here?" Griffin demanded.

Laughter broke out among the crowd, and Thea's cheeks burned with humiliation.

"I can defend myself, Mr. Ogilvie," she said. "As for you, Griffin, you've no right to speak to me so!"

The laughter continued, punctuated by crude remarks and gestures.

"Has the Mighty Oak been felled by a wench?"

"You're no man, Oake," Billy Bates said, "if you can't keep your woman in check." He reached for Thea's hand. "Come with me, lass. You can order me about as much as you wish—I like a wench to take control."

Griffin shoved him aside. "Don't touch her. She's *mine.*"

"Then stake your claim!"

"With pleasure," Griffin said. "In here. Now."

"Don't be so foolish!" Thea cried. "You can't fight over me like a pair of dogs!"

Griffin pulled her close, then hissed in her ear. "The rules of society don't apply here, Dorothea. The challenge has been made, and I must honor it, or they'll tear me apart. Can you now see why I told you not to come?"

He released her. "Clear the room!" he cried.

The crowd parted like a receding tide, leaving a space in the center of the room.

"Ned!" Griffin roared.

Ned Watkins appeared at the far door. His eyes widened when he saw Thea. "Bloody hell—Mrs. Oake!" he cried. "Griffin, I thought you said she wasn't to come."

"I did." Griffin pulled off his jacket and unlaced his shirt. The material tore as he ripped it off his torso and tossed it aside, his expression grim, mouth set in a firm line. Thea shivered at the fury in his eyes—

he looked intent on committing murder.

His opponent raised his fists. Griffin remained still for a moment, then he balled his hands and waited.

"First man to the floor loses."

"Fine by me," his opponent said. He paced the floor, then he rushed toward Griffin. With one swift, smooth movement, Griffin drew back his arm, then thrust forward in a single, solid punch. His fist connected with the man's jaw, and his opponent reeled back, then crashed to the floor, motionless.

Ned ran forward and kneeled over the still form.

"He's out cold."

Murmurs of disappointment threaded through the crowd.

"Bloody hell, Griffin, what the hell have you done?" Ned cried. "Most of these men came to see Billy fight!"

"I had no choice," Griffin said quietly, his gaze leveled at Thea.

"I know—but—bloody hell!"

Griffin's body shook with suppressed anger. His nostrils flared, and his eyes shimmered with lust. Then, he stepped forward, grasped Thea's wrist, and marched across the room.

She almost stumbled to keep pace with him. "Griffin…"

Ignoring her plea, he strode up a flight of stairs and along the passage until he reached a door, which he kicked open.

"Griff…"

He pulled her inside the chamber and silenced her with his mouth, crashing his lips against hers like a man starved. Was this the bloodlust she'd heard of—when a male animal fought a rival for his mate?

Rough hands pulled her against his body, which was hard and ready. Her own body tightened with anticipation. A thrill coursed through her—swelled by the hunger she'd endured ever since they'd returned from London—a hunger which had gone unsatisfied.

Until now.

He fisted her skirt in his hands, then plunged his tongue into her mouth—a victorious beast marking ownership of the female he'd won. Her whole body shook with the thrill of his hands against her skin, and she squirmed against him and parted her legs.

Then he thrust forward and speared her in a swift, hard motion, slamming her back against the wall.

"Oh, yes!" she cried. Grasping his arms, she lifted her legs and wrapped them around his waist, drawing him deeper inside, until a fire sparked inside her, glowing brighter as he continued to pound into her, until it burst, and her body shattered around him. She screamed out his name as wave after wave of exquisite, pleasurable torture ripped through her—so intense, so ecstatic—that she thought she'd die of it.

She threw back her head and howled as a myriad of stars exploded above her. Then he roared out her name as his body joined hers in pleasure. She placed her head on his shoulder and sighed, listening to the sound of their hearts, beating in unison—twin hearts and twin souls.

It had been a fortnight since they'd made love. Whether it was the wait or the manner by which he'd taken her against the wall—the pleasure had been immeasurable.

There was no denying that her husband was a beast.

And she loved it.

"That was wonderful," she whispered.

He stiffened, then pulled free. She lowered her legs, and a wave of cold rippled through her body, together with a sense of loss.

"Husband?"

He said nothing and stared at her. But rather than pleasure, she only saw one emotion in his eyes.

Regret.

WHAT THE DEVIL had he done?

Griffin's wife—the delicate lady he'd married—stood before him, face flushed, hair tangled—as if she was some roadside whore he'd fucked in the bushes.

The beast within him, which had been growling for the past weeks in its eagerness for release, had devoured her, taking his pleasure with no thought of her sensibilities.

What had possessed her to come here tonight after he'd expressly forbidden it? Didn't she know that a roomful of drunken, lustful men wouldn't have been able to resist her?

"Forgive me," he said. "I should never have done that."

"It's all right," she said. "I..." she hesitated and blinked. "...I enjoyed it."

She reached toward him, and he stepped back, shaking his head.

"It was wrong, Dorothea."

She withdrew her hand, a flicker of hurt in her eyes. "Didn't you want me?"

"Not like that," he sighed. "You're my wife—not my whore."

She flinched. "Are you saying you'd rather pleasure a whore?"

"Good Lord, no!"

"Then what?" she cried. "Am I not permitted to surrender to passion?"

"Passion leads to weakness, Dorothea. I've seen it too often—when a woman succumbs to the needs of the flesh."

"Do you have any notion how ridiculous you sound?"

"My first wife..." he began, but she interrupted him.

"Oh, so *now* you choose to speak of your first wife—when you're condemning my sex!" The hurt in her expression turned to fury. "Do you compare us and find me wanting?"

"No, of course not," he said. "I..."

She held up her hand. "Pray, do not elaborate," she said. "It's plain to see that you don't want me here. If you'd like the services of a whore, feel free to take your pick from the doxies in the bar. All you need do is drag her by the hair into your cave."

She picked up her shawl and approached the door.

"At least let me find someone to escort you home," he said.

"I can look after myself, thank you," she replied. "I'll not throw myself at the first man I encounter on the way, lest you feel the need to beat him to a pulp."

"I was protecting you!" he protested.

"I can shift for myself," she said, "or perhaps you're astonished that someone of my age and plain looks can attract the attention of any man?"

She glared at him, but there was no mistaking the hurt in her voice. Did she still see herself as undesirable?

"Dorothea…"

"Spare me," she interrupted. "You forget, husband, that my experience in life has taught me to recognize when I'm unwelcome."

She pulled open the door and strode out. He buttoned his breeches, then followed. As she reached the bottom of the stairs, she almost collided with Alex Ogilvie.

Curse the man! Was there no getting rid of him?

The barroom door opened, and Ned appeared. "The fight's about to start," he said, "but Billy's still out cold."

"Bugger," Griffin muttered.

"You're telling me. The crowd's none too happy. They were looking forward to a good fight."

"Well, they got one for free," Griffin said. "I wasn't going to let Billy get away with manhandling my wife." He gestured toward her. "Show her out, Ned. Take her through the back, so she doesn't have to endure the mob."

"I can take care…" she began, but Ned interrupted her.

"Ma'am, I wouldn't want you to come to harm." He bowed and held out his arm. She stared at it, then she smiled and took it.

Why didn't she smile at *him* like that?

After they disappeared, Griffin rounded on Ogilvie.

"What the bloody hell were you doing bringing her here?"

"She wanted to come," Ogilvie said. "It's not her fault—or mine—that you treated her like a whore."

Griffin opened his mouth to respond then closed it. How could he defend himself when Ogilvie spoke the truth?"

"Shall I go after her?" Ogilvie asked. "You'll be occupied with managing the fight, and she looked upset."

The last thing Griffin needed was that man causing more trouble. "*I'll* go after her," he replied. "She's *my* wife."

"You thought that about Louisa," Ogilvie said. "Then she spread her legs for every man in the place. I presume that display of male prowess just now was your way of staking your claim on your wife. It didn't work with Louisa—your neglect drove her into other men's beds—and it won't work for this one, either."

Griffin's hands itched with the need to obliterate Ogilvie's smug grin. But he wanted to be rid of the man—and pummeling him into a pulp would have the opposite effect. Ogilvie was clever enough to elicit sympathy. He had to be beaten at his own game.

"Go and join the fighting, Ogilvie," Griffin said. "The sooner you can repay your debts, the sooner you'll be on your way."

"Eager to be rid of me?"

"Just make sure you win."

Griffin pushed past Ogilvie's grinning form and followed in his wife's wake. He encountered Ned outside the back door.

"You didn't escort her home?"

"She threatened to cut my balls off if I accompanied her," Ned said. "She's a feisty one, but she shouldn't be taking out her anger on *me*."

Ned was right. He didn't deserve to bear the brunt of Dorothea's anger—Griffin did.

"She'll not be angry at you for long, Ned," Griffin said. "She's a good-hearted woman and a fair one."

"Then you should go to her," Ned said. "I'll take care of everything here. Now Billy's out of the competition, there's no need for you to stay—unless you fancy a shot at Ogilvie."

"There's nothing I'd like more than to smash that bastard's face in," Griffin said. "But it's not passion, or anger, that wins a fight—it's a level head. And whenever I'm in that man's presence, I'm anything but level-headed."

"Then let Johnny Tighe beat the life out of him for you."

Griffin had seen Tighe fight once before, and he'd acquitted himself well. But though he relished the thought of Tighe beating Ogilvie, he needed Ogilvie to win enough prize money tonight to be on his way.

But first, he needed to make peace with his wife.

Again.

⇶⇷

HE FOUND HER in the drawing room on the two-seater sofa, a copy of her sister's book in hand. She glanced up, then resumed her attention on the book.

"Supper's at nine," she said. "I didn't expect to see you home early."

The matter-of-fact tone she used irritated him more than the histrionics Louisa had always displayed when she didn't get her own way.

Or was it perhaps that he hadn't cared one jot about Louisa's feelings, given that she'd cared nothing for him? Whereas his Thea was the kind of woman whose love was worth earning.

"May I sit with you?" he asked.

"Of course."

He closed the door, then approached the sofa and sat beside her. She continued to read, but her breathing had quickened, almost

272

imperceptibly.

He reached out and took her hand, and she looked up, assaulting him with her clear blue gaze.

"Forgive me," he said. "I-I can never find the words to articulate how I feel...please believe me when I say I had no intention of hurting you."

She sighed, then set the book aside. "I do believe you. We were both..." she swallowed, and a faint color bloomed on her cheeks, "...caught up in the moment. But I fail to see why it's something to be ashamed of."

"We're from different backgrounds," he said. "I am what I am, and you're a lady. I don't want you thinking that I view you as a..." He gestured in front of him, unwilling to voice the word.

"A passionate woman?" she prompted.

Now it was his turn to blush. A smile curled in the corners of her mouth.

"Our backgrounds are not dissimilar," she said. "You forget, I grew up in poverty."

"I can never be your equal, Thea," he said. "You're my superior in understanding and character."

"You do yourself a disservice," she said, "except in one quarter."

"Which is?"

"The matter of your late wife. Has it never occurred to you that I'd rather *not* be compared to her? I am not her and never will be. And yet, you refer to her to justify your anger or frustration, such as earlier today. Rowena should be able to speak freely of her mother—and *I* deserve your honesty."

"Some secrets are best kept hidden," he said.

"Not in my experience. The truth always has a way of revealing itself, often when we're least prepared for it."

She folded her arms and fixed her direct gaze on him, and he felt himself withering under her scrutiny. If ever the militia wanted to employ an expert at extracting secrets from the enemy, the perfect candidate sat before him.

Then, uncertainty—and vulnerability—glimmered in her eyes.

"Tell me honestly, Griffin," she said, "do you see me as a harlot for enjoying the...*relations*...we shared just now?"

"No."

"Then you view me as a burden...undesirable?"

Oh Lord—why was it that women not only spoke in riddles, but they sought to entrap a man by asking questions such that a denial landed him in just as much trouble as an affirmation.

He shook his head. "Am I to be condemned whatever I say in response? Is there nothing I can say to prove that I love you?"

Her eyes widened, and she drew in a sharp breath, and he squeezed her hand.

"Can you be in any doubt of my love?" he asked softly.

"Then tell me the truth."

"Sometimes the truth breaks hearts," he replied, lifting her hand to his lips. "I have no wish to break your heart—or Rowe's. The truth—it might destroy her."

She continued to gaze at him, her silence doing more to pierce his conscience than any words of condemnation.

"I've kept the truth inside me for ten years," he said. "When Mr. Ogilvie has gone, and the balance of harmony is restored in our home—when I am among those I love and trust—I'll explain. I trust you with my life, my darling Thea—and I also trust you with Rowe's peace of mind. I will have need of you when the time comes. Will *you* trust me enough to wait until then?"

Her expression softened, and she reached up and placed her palm on his face.

"Yes," she whispered, her breath a warm caress, "I trust you."

He leaned forward and captured her lips, then brushed his knuckles along the neckline of her gown. The color of her eyes deepened, and her body shuddered. He lowered his hand and cupped her breast.

How the devil had he got so lucky to be able to call her his?

"Perhaps we might retire to my chamber before supper," he whispered, "to enjoy a little appetizer."

His blood warmed at her coy smile. "Wouldn't that be ever so wicked?"

"What is pleasure if we cannot indulge in a little wickedness?" he asked. "But I promise to be gentle. I wouldn't have my wife think me a caveman."

"I find I relish having a caveman for a husband."

He caught his breath as he almost spent in his trousers at the devilish glint in her eye.

He grasped her hand, then in a swift movement, lifted her into his arms.

"Griffin! What are you doing?"

"What I should have done the very first day I brought you here," he said. "I'm carrying my wife to my bed."

"Mmm!"

Her murmur of encouragement was all he needed.

Chapter Thirty-Five

"**S**O, YOU BEAT Johnny Tighe?"

Thea's husband pushed his dessert plate to one side, his slice of pineapple untouched.

Mr. Ogilvie nodded and drained his wineglass. "I won myself ten guineas, which I'll collect at the White Hart tomorrow," he said. "What do you think of that, little Rowe-ling?"

"I think it's wonderful," Rowena said, smiling across the table.

So did Thea, if it meant he'd be moving on.

At least Rowena was smiling now. As soon as Mr. Ogilvie had returned from the fight, he'd disappeared into the garden with her, and since then, Rowena's mood had darkened, and she'd spent most of the meal frowning, answering Thea's questions with monosyllabic responses.

Thea glanced at her gown. The lace tuck had a small tear near the neckline—evidence of her husband's enthusiasm for their earlier lovemaking. Her cheeks warmed at the memory of her cries when he'd brought her to pleasure. Not even her fear that their guest would interrupt them had dampened her desire. In fact, she'd found a particular thrill in the risk of being caught.

And to think—she'd lived thirty years in the world not knowing such exquisite pleasure existed!

"Tighe's a good fighter," Griffin said. "How did you best him?"

"He'd had a few too many ales."

"Which you encouraged him to drink, I suppose," Griffin said, "and probably supplied yourself, to increase your chances."

Ogilvie shrugged. "It's not my fault if he's too fond of his ale to remain upright."

"And you hit him when he was down? Hardly the mark of a champion—or a gentleman."

"Gentleman—hah!" Ogilvie snorted. "You're hardly one yourself—considering how you treated Louisa. How soon after you married her did you tire of her?"

"That's enough," Griffin growled. "As soon as you've collected your winnings, I want you gone."

"Papa—no!" Rowena cried.

Ogilvie laughed. "Eager to be rid of me? Is it because I'm a reminder of a past you'd rather forget?"

"Mr. Ogilvie," Thea said, "perhaps we should continue this conversation another time."

"No, *Dorothea*," Rowena said, glaring at her, "I want to hear how Papa treated my mother. Wouldn't you like to know what will happen when he tires of *you*?"

"Forgive me, Mrs. Oake," Ogilvie said, "but the truth deserves to be told, no matter how painful it might be."

His sentiments echoed hers, but his tone carried a certain glee that set her teeth on edge.

Her husband gripped the edge of the table, his knuckles white, a dark glitter in his eyes which caused her stomach to twist in apprehension. When he spoke, his voice was quiet and cold.

"I know what you're about, Ogilvie, and it stops. Now."

"*I'm* not the one with something to hide."

"We're neither of us saints," Griffin said, his voice rising. "I'll *not* have you turn my daughter against me!"

Rowena leaped to her feet, pushing her plate aside. Her fork fell to the floor with a clatter.

"You're doing that all by yourself!" she cried. "Alex has done nothing wrong!"

"*Alex*, indeed!" Griffin scoffed. "Since when have you lost all notion of propriety?"

Rowena snorted. "You wouldn't know what propriety was if it bit you on the arse!"

"Rowena!" Thea cried. "I won't have you using such language at the dinner table."

"Shall I swear in the drawing room instead?"

"You shouldn't swear at all."

"Why should you care? You're not my mother…" Rowena pointed toward Griffin, "…and from what Alex says, *he's* not my father!"

Griffin stared at Rowena, open-mouthed. Thea waited for his denial.

But it never came.

"Griffin?" she asked. "Is that true?"

"Be quiet, woman," he said. "I'll not discuss it here."

"Forgive me, Mrs. Oake," Ogilvie said. "I've no wish to upset you."

"I think we've gone beyond that, Mr. Ogilvie," Thea said. "I'm anxious to know what you've said to make Rowena believe my husband is not her father."

"He's not my father!" Rowena cried. "He's a—a swiving whoreson!"

Griffin leapt to his feet. "That's enough!" he cried. "I ought to beat you black and blue, girl!"

"No!" Thea cried. "You can't settle this with your fists—she's a child!"

"I'm not a child—I'm a woman!" Rowena cried. "And you're an old hag!"

She burst into tears and ran toward the door. Ogilvie rose to his feet.

"No, Mr. Ogilvie," Thea said firmly. "You've done enough. Leave Rowena to me."

"I don't want you!" Rowena cried. "I want my real mother," she pointed to Griffin, "but she's dead because of *him*." She exited the dining room, slamming the door behind her.

"What have you said to her, Mr. Ogilvie?" Thea demanded.

"Nothing that wasn't her right to know."

Thea shook her head. "My husband was right—we had a harmonious home until you arrived. It's time you left."

"Leave him to me," Griffin said. "You deal with Rowena. Ogilvie and I must settle our differences like real men."

Ogilvie loosened his necktie. "It would be my pleasure to best you once and for all."

"No!" Thea cried. "The rules of the cave do not apply here. I'll not have this kind of behavior in my home."

Ogilvie let out a laugh. "She's got the measure of you, all right!" he cried. "That's what a certain type of woman always does to a man— turns him into a wet rag. That disgusting display of hauling her upstairs for a good fuck at the White Hart didn't fool anyone."

Griffin fisted his hands at his sides. "Woman, leave the room this instant unless you wish to be forcibly removed."

Thea's gut twisted with anger. How dare he treat her so dismissively!

"Very well," she said. "I'll go—but don't think you'll be welcome in my chamber tonight."

As Thea left in search of Rowena, all she could hear was Ogilvie's laughter.

GRIFFIN WATCHED HIS wife disappear, his blood boiling with rage.

"Your second wife despises you as much as your first," Ogilvie said. "I'd call that justice."

"What the devil's wrong with you?" Griffin demanded. "You strive to turn my daughter—and now my wife—against me. Why?"

"Because you had what I wanted," Ogilvie said. "From the very beginning, they all raved over the Mighty Oak. If I'd had half your luck, I could have done so much more!"

Griffin snorted. "You never fought fair."

"Fair?" Ogilvie spat. "Louise only married you for your money. Had life been fair to me, I would have been the one she'd wanted."

"She did want you, in the end," Griffin said. "She'd have run away with you if you'd so much as snapped your fingers. But you rejected her."

"You think I'd want your leavings?" Ogilvie sneered. "She was tainted—and pregnant. I had no wish to become saddled with a brat when the father could have been anyone. Didn't you wonder why little Rowe-ling was born within seven months of your marriage?" He placed his hands on his hips and gave Griffin a smile of triumph as if relishing the thought of breaking news which Griffin had known for years.

"You think I didn't know that she'd already lain with you when I married her?" Griffin asked. "I know when a woman's been touched by a man."

His thoughts turned to Dorothea—and her innocence when he'd taken her for the first time.

"Rowe's father could be anyone," Ogilvie said. "Half the men at the inn had their turn."

"*I'm* her father," Griffin said, "in every sense that matters. Blood means nothing. You didn't want her. You only wanted Louisa for the satisfaction of securing the heart of the woman I'd married. Once you'd achieved that, you lost interest."

"And when did you lose interest?" Ogilvie asked.

"When I first caught the two of you in my bedchamber!"

"Why didn't you throw her out?"

"Because of the child," Griffin said. "I loved Rowe even though I knew she wasn't mine. I wasn't going to let Louisa take her away from me. And though I'd stopped loving her, Louisa was my responsibility—no matter what she'd done."

"You got rid of her in the end, though, didn't you?" Ogilvie sneered. "Does little Rowe-ling know her father was suspected of murdering her mother?"

The spring snapped. With a roar, Griffin grabbed Ogilvie by the lapels and slammed him against the wall.

"Careful," Ogilvie said. "What would your wife think?"

"You leave—this instant," Griffin said through gritted teeth. "If I see you again, I'll break every bone in your body and to hell with the consequences."

Ogilvie's eyes gleamed. "How much is it worth?"

At last—Ogilvie revealed his true colors. But Griffin didn't care—he would pay anything to rid himself of the man.

"Fifty pounds," Griffin said.

"One thousand."

Griffin barked out a laugh. "Don't be a fool."

"It's nothing compared to your fortune," Ogilvie said, "or should I say—compared to little Rowe-ling's. I hear she has twenty thousand, courtesy of your wife's marriage settlement."

Could the man sink any lower?

"I'll give you two hundred now," Griffin said. "Take it or suffer the consequences."

Ogilvie's smile wavered, then he nodded.

Griffin loosened his hold, and Ogilvie made a show of brushing his collar.

"You've torn my jacket."

"I'll throw in an extra shilling to have it mended if it means I can rid myself of you."

Ogilvie smiled, then held out his hand.

"Done."

Griffin took the proffered hand and squeezed it. Ogilvie reciprocated, and they locked gazes, each man increasing the pressure until Ogilvie released his hold and wiped his hand on his jacket.

"I'll wait in the hall."

TEN MINUTES LATER, Griffin strode across the hallway with a bag filled with notes and coins—almost all the cash in the house—but worth every penny.

Ogilvie took the bag. "Thank you."

"Aren't you going to count it?"

"I trust you."

Griffin snorted. "You'll never understand what trust is."

"For what it's worth, I always trusted you," Ogilvie said.

"Then why did you betray *my* trust?"

"I envied you. Perhaps you're right—I only wanted Louisa because she was yours."

He held the bag out to Griffin. "I can't accept this," he said. "I have my winnings—and I promised that I'd go if I won the fight. Let me honor that promise."

"No, take it," Griffin said, "for the sake of the friendship we once shared. But I never wish to see you again."

"You won't." Ogilvie pocketed the money and approached the doors, where he stopped and turned.

"Please pass my apologies to your wife."

Then he exited the house and, without a backward glance, strode down the path and out of sight.

The change of heart that Ogilvie had shown at the end might be the first step toward redemption—but it had come too late. Griffin felt only relief that finally, he'd rid himself of his former friend for good.

Now came the greater task.

Apologizing to his wife.

Her chamber door was closed, but a sliver of light shone through the crack at the bottom. He knocked on the door, then pushed it open.

His wife sat in bed, the book of poetry in her hand. She closed the book, then assaulted him with her clear gaze.

Her expression—which he'd once likened to that of a disappointed schoolmistress—he now saw for what it was.

The pain of a wronged wife.

"Has he gone?" she asked.

He nodded. "Yes. And Rowe?"

"She's retired," she said. "She was angry and upset, but I sent Rosie to tend to her, and she's settled. When I checked in on her, she was fast asleep."

So quickly? Perhaps his fortunes were taking a turn for the better—and not before time.

"Are you going to tell me what's going on?" she asked.

He opened his mouth to respond, and she held up her hand.

"Think before you speak, Griffin," she said, "because I'm tired."

"So am I." He unlaced his shirt.

"No," she said, "I'm tired of your lies."

He approached the bed and offered his hand. She stared at it, and he kneeled before her.

"Will you take my hand?" he whispered, "and accept my apology?"

She slipped her little hand into his.

"Forgive me, Thea," he said. "You've borne your life here—with me—with such fortitude. I couldn't have asked for a better partner, and it only pains my heart, knowing that there's nothing I can do to deserve you."

She stroked his hand with her thumb, and his body stirred at the light caress.

"There's one thing you can do for me," she said.

"Anything."

"Tell me the truth. I know you're unwilling to speak of—Louisa..." she colored and looked away, then she lifted her gaze and looked directly at him, her eyes glowing in the candlelight, "...but you owe me the truth."

"I know," he said. "I should have trusted you, but I was afraid."

"Of what?"

"There's no going back," he said. "What's said can never be unsaid. And I fear the truth will hurt you. As for Rowe—it'll break her heart."

His eyes stung with unshed tears.

"Griffin?"

The pain and disappointment in Dorothea's eyes had gone—replaced by compassion.

And love.

He dipped his head and kissed her knuckles.

"Will you be there for me?" he asked, "when I tell her? I want to tell you both together—the two people I love most in the world."

He waited, and his heart skittered. He'd asked her so many times to trust him, and he'd let her down at every turn. Had he hurt her once too often?

Then she lowered her head and brushed her lips against his hand.

"May I stay here tonight?" he asked, daring to hope. "I need you to hold me." He caught his breath, waiting—expecting to be rejected.

Then she opened her arms and drew him into an embrace.

"My love..."

His body sighed, and he buried his head in her chest, listening to the soft, steady rhythm of her heartbeat.

WHEN GRIFFIN OPENED his eyes, at first, he didn't recognize his surroundings. Then he remembered last night.

Beside him, his wife lay sleeping.

In the morning light, her chamber looked warm and welcoming— a haven from the world outside.

She shifted in her sleep and nestled against his body.

If only he could lie in bed with her all day! They could breakfast in bed, make love all morning to work up an appetite for luncheon—then try something a little more energetic, perhaps using the hearthrug, or even the armchairs to explore a variety of delectable positions...

...and then, in the evening, they could indulge in a wicked adventure with Mrs. Morris's chocolate sauce.

His manhood stirred to life at the thought of smearing sweet sauce over her wife's delectable form, then licking every inch of her. Unable to stop himself, he thrust against her, relishing the surge in his blood as he rubbed his length against her back.

"Griffin?" she murmured.

"It's time to break our fast," he rasped. "I'm hungry."

"Griffin!" she rolled over to face him, then placed a kiss on his lips.

"You're insatiable," she said, "and I love it. But pleasure must wait. Rowena will be awake."

The fog of lust dissipated—replaced by the realization of what was to come.

Rowena.

Today was the day he'd break his daughter's heart.

He climbed out of bed and picked up his clothes. As he was buttoning his breeches, hurried footsteps approached, and the door burst open.

"Mrs. Oake, madam, I—oh!"

Rosie stood in the doorway, eyes wide with shock. She bobbed a curtsey.

"Well?" he demanded. "What is it, girl?"

"Something terrible has happened, begging your pardon, sir," the maidservant said, her voice thick with tears.

Thea climbed out of the bed. "What's happened, Rosie dear?"

"It's Miss Rowena!" the maid cried. "I took in her morning tea, but she's not in her chamber!"

"That's nothing to worry about—she often goes for a walk before breakfast." Thea gestured toward the window. "It's a beautiful day—I fancy a walk myself."

"No—you don't understand, ma'am," the maid sobbed. "Her belongings are gone. Her valise is missing—her gowns from London and her books!"

A ball of nausea curled inside Griffin's stomach.

Rowena had run away.

And he knew damn well who she'd gone with.

Chapter Thirty-Six

THEA EMBRACED ROSIE, who continued to cry.

"It's my fault! When I was helping mistress Rowena undress, she said she was unhappy—and she wished Mr. Oake wasn't her father! I should have told you."

"You're not to blame," Thea said, caressing the girl's hair. "In the heat of the moment, all young people say things they don't mean."

"You don't understand! I—I told her that she should find a way to be happy! What if she left because of me?"

Griffin swore.

Rosie flinched. "Are you going to beat me?"

"Of course not," Thea said. "Others are to blame—those who made her unhappy in the first place and those who sought to turn her against the people who love her. Now—why don't you go and ask Mrs. Morris to make you some sweet tea?"

"Tea?" Griffin cried. "My daughter's missing, and all you can think about is tea?"

"Rosie needs to calm down," Thea said. "And *we* need to apply reason to the problem by first determining how they left."

"I want to hunt down that bastard and kill him! How can you speak of reason?"

"Because that's how we'll find them," she replied. "If they left on foot, they could have gone in any direction but will be traveling slowly. If they left on horseback, they're likely to have stuck to the roads."

"We have no way of knowing in which direction they've gone."

"Did Mr. Ogilvie speak of where he was going when he left last night?" Thea asked.

"Do you really think he'd be that foolish?"

"Overconfidence leads to folly," Thea said. "And Mr. Ogilvie is nothing but overconfident, particularly when boasting about his prowess in the arena."

"That's it!" Griffin cried. "His winnings—he'd have to collect them from the White Hart."

"Then we'll start there," she said.

"He'd be long gone by now."

She rolled her eyes. Why were men such knuckleheads? "The easiest route to finding our quarry is to follow his exact path," she said. "Like a trail of breadcrumbs."

Griffin pulled his jacket on. "I'll check the stables first, then the White Hart. Wait here until I return."

"I'll do no such thing. I'm coming with you."

"It might be dangerous."

"Rowena's my daughter, too," she replied. "I'd never forgive myself if I didn't do everything I could to find her."

His expression softened, and for a moment, she thought she saw moisture in his eyes. Then he addressed Rosie.

"Find Will and tell him to ready the carriage. Help him if necessary."

The maid sniffed and nodded, and he patted her shoulder, his eyes narrowing with guilt as she flinched.

"Then take your tea," he said, "with plenty of sugar and some of Mrs. Morris's shortbread. You mustn't blame yourself. If anyone's at fault—it's me."

The maid bobbed into a curtsey and fled the chamber.

"Dear Lord!" Griffin cried. "Is this my punishment for concealing the truth?"

"You weren't to know this would happen," Thea said. "You told me last night that you'd done it to protect her."

"But I didn't protect her," he said. "Oh, Thea—what if I never see her again?"

"Hush, husband." She drew him into her arms. "Let us not worry while there's every chance we'll find her."

Rather than indulge in her own pain, Thea needed to be strong for her husband. But though she yearned to reassure him—the fear remained in the back of her mind.

That Rowena might never be found.

***

"NO, GRIFFIN—HE'S NOT here."

Breathless from running, Thea leaned against the bar in the White Hart while her husband quizzed Mr. Watkins.

"Are you sure, Ned? It's important."

"He's gone, all right," the barman said, "along with one of the horses. He arrived late last night to collect his winnings from the fight, then he took a room. The bastard left before I was up—without paying. Some people never change." He set down the glass he'd been polishing. "I thought you wanted rid of the man."

"I did," Griffin said, "but not with my daughter!"

"Rowena's gone with him? Bloody hell!" He glanced at Thea. "Begging your pardon, ma'am, for cursing. How much does Rowena know?"

"Not everything," Griffin said. He shook his head. "What if Ogilvie tells her? It'll destroy her!"

"We must find them before he does," Ned said.

"But where the devil do we look?" Griffin asked, his voice rising.

Thea took his hand, and he drew in a breath as if calmed by her touch. "Remember the breadcrumbs," she said. "Where was he before he came here—Horsham Gaol?"

"Surely he'd not take Rowe there!"

"If he wishes to conceal himself, he's more likely to go somewhere he knows," Thea said.

"What about the Royal Oak?" Ned suggested. "Tom Barnes told me he'd seen him there some months ago."

"Is it far?" Thea asked.

"It's in Dencombe—the next village but one," Griffin said. "We'll need the carriage—it's ten miles away. Ned, will you come?"

"The carriage should be ready by now," Thea said.

"*You're* not coming, Dorothea."

Thea glared at her husband. "She's my daughter as much as she's yours."

His eyes narrowed in pain, and regret flooded through her as she realized what she'd just said.

"Forgive me, Griffin," she said. "I only meant that I love her as much as you."

He drew her to him and kissed the top of her head. "There's nothing to forgive, my love. This is *my* fault—and it's for me to deal with. I don't want you in danger."

"What of the danger Rowena's facing?"

"I can take care of Alex Ogilvie," Griffin said. "I'll knock him into the next century and drag that child back home, trussed up like a hog if I have to."

"Then you need me more than ever," Thea said. "Haven't you learned by now that it takes more than brute strength to achieve your heart's desire?"

"You'll not take no for an answer, will you?"

"No," she said. "I, too, will fight for those I love. The only difference between us is the weapons we use."

"Then I shall relent," he said, "for I've come to learn that my wife is a better warrior than I'll ever be."

Chapter Thirty-Seven

THE CARRIAGE DREW to a halt at the edge of Dencombe, and Griffin lowered the window. The Royal Oak was at the opposite end of the street, its sign swaying in the breeze—a tree topped by a crown.

He pushed open the door and climbed out.

"Wait here," he said to the driver. "We don't want Ogilvie spotting the carriage."

Ned followed, helping Thea out, and Griffin spotted a familiar object sticking out of the pocket of his breeches—the polished wooden handle of a pistol.

The village was already coming to life. A farmer whistled a merry tune as he strode along the street, a Smithfield collie trotting beside him. Further along the street, a boy emerged from a building, carrying a basket, and almost collided with Ned.

"Steady on, lad!" Ned cried.

The boy touched his cap. "Begging your pardon, sir. I'm in such a hurry, I wasn't looking where I'm going."

Griffin's stomach growled at the aroma of freshly baked bread—a sharp reminder that breakfast was long overdue.

"Where are you going?" he asked.

"Morning deliveries, sir."

"At the inn?"

"The Oak?" The boy shook his head. "No—I was there earlier. This lot's for the big house."

"But you've been to the Royal Oak this morning," Griffin said, towering over the boy.

"I don't want no trouble, sir."

Dorothea hissed in Griffin's ear. "You're frightening him. The poor child's half your height, if that."

She nudged him aside and smiled at the boy.

"You're not in any trouble," she said. "Do you know if there are any rooms vacant at the inn?"

Why the devil was she asking that?

"I don't know—they had two new arrivals just after dawn."

"An unusual time for guests to arrive," she said.

The boy nodded. "That's what *I* said. A man and a woman on horseback—I reckon they'd eloped, though Mr. Miller said they couldn't have."

"Why not?"

"The man's old enough to be her father!"

Griffin drew in a sharp breath, then a slim hand touched his wrist. He glanced at his wife, and she frowned and shook her head.

"Thank you, young man," she said, reaching inside her reticule and pulling out a coin. "Here's a shilling for your trouble."

"Thank you, ma'am!" The boy bowed, then resumed his path along the road.

Griffin let out the breath he'd been holding.

He'd found Ogilvie. All he needed now was to get Rowe back.

IN THE YEARS since Griffin had last visited the Royal Oak, it had changed ownership several times, and, by the look of it, fallen from grace. Paint peeled off the doors, and several windowpanes were cracked. What had once been a thriving inn and a magnificent Tudor building now looked desolate and unloved.

He pushed through the main door and called out.

"Hello there!"

A sandy-haired man in his forties emerged, brandishing a cloth. He stepped back when he saw Griffin, then he glanced at Ned, and his frown turned into a smile.

"Ned!" he cried. "What brings you round these parts—and at this hour?"

"I'm here with my employer, Sam," Ned said. "Mr. Oake and his wife."

"The Mighty Oak—I thought I recognized you." He glanced at Thea and bowed his head. "Begging your pardon, ma'am—Sam Miller, at your service."

Griffin fisted his hands, ready to knock the man aside. Then a soft hand touched his, and delicate fingers curled round his fist—as if she sensed his rage.

"Mr. Miller," she said in her soft voice. "I understand you welcomed two new guests this morning. We have reason to believe one of them is our daughter."

"Mr. and Mrs. Ogilvie?"

Dorothea gasped. "I beg your pardon?"

"Aye—newlyweds. Or so the gentleman said."

Griffin's body shook as fury boiled deep inside his gut.

"He's no gentleman," he said. "Where are they?"

"Room six, on the top floor. But he asked that they not be..."

"I don't care what he asked!" Griffin sprang forward and shoved the man aside, then climbed the staircase, taking the steps two at a time until he reached a low-ceilinged passageway.

"Ogilvie!" he roared. "Where are you—you whoreson!" He came to a door with the number six scratched into the wood and rammed it with the full force of his body.

The door flew open, and he fell forward into the chamber. A familiar high-pitched scream rang out.

"Papa!"

Rowe stood at the far end of the room, her face streaked with tears, face flushed, hair tangled. Beside her stood Ogilvie, a smile of triumph on his face.

"So you found us," he said. "More quickly than I expected." He took Rowe's hand and lifted it to his lips. She frowned and snatched it away.

"Get your fucking hands off my daughter!" Griffin roared. "Rowe. Come here."

Rowe shook her head.

"I remember what happened," she said. "The night my mother died. I *saw* you."

"You don't know what you saw," Griffin said.

Rowe pointed to Thea, who stood in the doorway next to Ned. "Does *she* know you killed her?"

Thea drew in a sharp breath, and her hand flew to her mouth.

"She doesn't, does she?" Rowe cried. "You've lied to her as well."

"Then it's time for the truth," he said, "and Ogilvie hasn't told you the truth."

"Don't listen to him," Ogilvie said. "He'll say anything to discredit me."

"Ned!" Griffin growled. "I think it's time we silenced this bastard."

Ned drew the pistol out of his pocket.

"So, you'd have your lackey shoot me?" Ogilvie sneered. "What would your precious daughter think? She already hates you."

"*You've* made damned sure of that," Griffin said. "But Rowe's welfare is more important than her opinion of me—which is why I never told her the truth. And you took advantage of that, didn't you? Just like with her mother—you poisoned Louisa against me, spinning your lies to lure her into your bed. And then what? After she spread her legs, you cast her aside. Is that what you intended to do with Rowe?"

"No," Ogilvie said. "Little Rowe-ling is a much better prospect."

Rowe moved away from Ogilvie, her face growing pale. "What do you mean—prospect?" she asked.

"He wants your fortune, Rowena," Thea said. "Isn't that right, Mr. Ogilvie? Did you intend to marry Rowena? Or merely to ruin her reputation, then persuade my husband to buy your silence?"

Rowe's eyes widened, and she glanced at Ogilvie.

"What did he promise you, Rowena, dear?" Thea asked. Rowe seemed to grow calmer at Thea's soft voice. Thea moved toward her and held out her hand. Rowe's lip wobbled, and a tear splashed onto her cheek.

"I'm sorry, Mama Thea," she said. "I don't know who to believe."

"Neither do I," Thea said. "Sometimes, we must take a leap of faith and follow our heart—and not be influenced by those who promise us the world. The more they promise, the less they can be trusted."

"Don't listen to her!" Ogilvie cried. "She's your father's plaything—and she'll do anything he tells her to."

Griffin almost laughed at Ogilvie's words. Thea might be his wife, but she was no more likely to obey him than the clouds in the sky.

And Rowena knew it. She stared at Ogilvie, the confusion in her expression turning into suspicion. At length, her gaze landed on Griffin.

"Tell me the truth, Papa," she said, gesturing toward Thea. "Tell us both."

The moment had come. After today, Rowe might lose her peace of mind. But his daughter—and his wife—deserved the truth.

"Very well," Griffin said. Ogilvie opened his mouth to protest, but Ned cocked the pistol and aimed it at his chest, and he closed it again.

Griffin swallowed his fear at the hurt Rowe would inevitably suffer and began.

"Your mother was already pregnant when I married her…"

"You took advantage of her?" she interrupted.

He shook his head. "She'd lain with a number of men before we married—Ogilvie included. I loved her so much, it didn't matter. When she told me she was pregnant, I couldn't believe how happy I was. But then..."

He hesitated, the raw pain of the memory overcoming him, and blinked back the sting of tears.

"Griffin?" Thea's face swam into view, the concern in her expression touching his heart.

"She fell down the stairs..." He drew in a deep breath. "...I thought it was an accident. I—I called the doctor, and you cannot imagine my relief when he said the child hadn't been harmed. But when Louisa regained consciousness, and I told her the good news, she started to hit me—she screamed at me, saying..."

He closed his eyes, but the image of Louisa's face, distorted with hatred, swam before him, and he opened them again. Rowe's face had grown ashen.

"What did she say, Papa?"

"She'd wanted to rid herself of the child—the man she loved had spurned her because he didn't want to be saddled with a brat. So, she tried to lose the baby—for him—even though there was every chance he was the father."

Rowe glanced at Ogilvie, and the pain in her expression tore at Griffin's heart. But now he'd started, there was no going back.

"After that," he continued, "I did everything I could to keep her safe. I made her promise not to harm herself or the child. She agreed on condition that I care for the child and let her do what she liked—and with whom—once it was born."

Thea shook her head. "You wanted her to be unfaithful?"

"I was prepared to do anything to protect the child," he said. "By then, I realized Louisa had never loved me. When the child came..." His voice caught. "Oh, Rowe! You were the most beautiful thing in the world! You gave me something to live for—someone to love and take care of."

"And my mother?" Rowe asked.

"I hoped she might grow to love you—but she didn't. She was as good as her word and hardly touched you. Night after night, she'd come home late—drunk—stinking of the men she'd been with."

Rowe's eyes glistened with moisture and tears rolled down her cheeks. "What about the picnics she took me on? The bedtime stories?"

"I'm sorry, Rowe," he said. "I wanted you to believe you had a mother who loved you. So, after she died, I pictured the pretty girl I'd fallen in love with and told you about my dreams—a happy marriage with a loving wife and a child we adored. You were too young to be burdened with the truth."

She closed her eyes and bent her head, her body shaking.

"Rowe..." Griffin reached out to her, and she shrank back, hostility in her eyes.

"Did you kill her?"

"No," he said. "The night she died, I caught her in the White Hart, in bed with *him*." He gestured toward Ogilvie.

"It was quite by chance, Rowe—you and I were caught in a thunderstorm during a walk, and we sheltered at the inn. Ned told me your mother was there, and he took care of you while I went in search of her to bring her home. Then, I found them—in bed, both stinking of ale. I—I couldn't take any more, so I said he was welcome to her. But he was leaving for London and didn't want her. She was pregnant again, and though she crawled at his feet, he refused to take her with him."

Griffin shook his head to dispel the memory, but it was burned into his mind—the image of Louisa's broken body, illuminated in the flash of lightning as she fell to her death.

"Perhaps it was the ale or her obsession with him..." He glanced at

Rowe's face. "She—she must have thought she could persuade him a second time."

"What did she do?" Thea asked.

"She threw herself down the stairs—to rid herself of the child she carried. I—I tried to stop her, but she was too quick. When I reached the bottom of the stairs, she was already dead—her neck broken."

"Dear Lord!" Thea cried. Beside her, Rowe remained silent, her eyes wide with shock.

"She was unclothed. I couldn't bear the thought of her body being manhandled. So I took my shirt off and put it on her to give her more dignity in death than she'd ever had in life. Then, I looked up and saw you, Rowe—your little face, lit up by the lightning. Forgive me—my poor child! I never meant for you to see it. Ned led you away, while I took care of your mother, and neither of us spoke about that night since. I hoped you'd forget or think it just a bad dream. But it was there, always, in the back of your mind. Every thunderstorm since that night, I've lived in fear of you remembering."

"Oh, Griffin!" Thea cried.

Rowe wiped her face. "It can't be true," she said. "My mother loved me—you said so!"

The raw pain in her voice sliced through his heart. No child wanted to be told that their mother hated them so much, she wanted to rid herself of them.

"Your papa speaks the truth," Ned said. "I was there. And so was he." He waved the pistol at Ogilvie, who stood, arms folded, watching, a smile on his lips.

"Why do you smile, you bastard!" Griffin demanded. "You take pleasure out of my daughter's distress?"

"That's just it, Oake," came the reply. "She's not *your* daughter."

"She is, in every sense that matters," Griffin said. "Her mother didn't want her—and neither did *you!* Don't tell me you want to play the doting father now."

"You really are a simpleton, aren't you?" Ogilvie sneered. "You think telling her the truth changes anything? What will the gossips say about her running off, unchaperoned, with a man twice her age? What will that do to her prospects?"

"I'll not consent to you marrying her," Griffin said. "I'd rather shoot you dead and swing from a gibbet."

Ogilvie laughed. "Submit myself to the leg-shackles and a life of being hen-pecked, just like you have with your prim little schoolmistress? Of course not! But little Rowe-ling has a tidy fortune—twenty thousand, I'm told. I'm not a greedy man. What say you to a nice round ten?"

Rowe burst into tears, and Thea pulled her into an embrace, glaring at Ogilvie. "How dare you!" she cried. "Was this your plan? To turn Rowena against us and seduce her into running off with you so you could blackmail my husband? Don't you care for her at all?"

"Dear me, you can't control that woman of yours, can you, Oake?" Ogilvie said. "I always thought you were less than a man. Perhaps that's why Louisa turned to others—your cock wasn't up to the task."

Griffin fought the urge to smash his fist into Ogilvie's face.

"Why don't we settle this matter, once and for all," he said. "Right now. Outside. Last man standing wins."

"What's in it for me?" Ogilvie asked.

"If you beat me, you can have your ten thousand."

"And if you win?"

"Then you leave—and if you return, I'll have you arrested for abduction and blackmail."

"Very well," Ogilvie said. "One last fight. I've waited ten years to best you—and this time, I'll be the victor."

Chapter Thirty-Eight

A S SOON AS the men left the chamber, Thea held Rowena at arm's length. The broken expression in her husband's eyes tore at her heart—but she first needed to ensure Rowena was unhurt.

The girl continued to cry, but aside from her distress, she didn't seem to be physically harmed.

"Rowena, dear, can you tell me what happened?"

Rowena stiffened. "Are you angry?"

"No," Thea said. "But there's something I must ask—your papa and I need to know."

Thea's heart shuddered at the stricken look on Rowena's face.

"W-will Papa beat me?"

"Has he ever given you cause to think he'd hit you?"

Rowena paused, then shook her head. "N-no, but he's so angry! I said such terrible things last night."

"We often say terrible things when there's no other way to express how much we're hurting," Thea said. "Your Papa's anger comes from fear. He was dreadfully worried about you—as was I."

Thea squeezed Rowena's hand. "Tell me the truth, Rowena, my darling. Did Mr. Ogilvie—touch you?"

Rowena shook her head. "He brought me here, and when I said I wanted to go home, he shouted, saying I was a selfish whore like my mother. I'm so sorry! I wanted to believe my mother loved me. Uncle

Alex had said such wonderful things about her—but after we left, he changed. Why didn't I see it before?"

Thea kissed the top of Rowena's head. "I was taken in by Mr. Ogilvie as well."

"I'm sorry I said what I did—I don't really hate you."

"It's forgotten."

"And Papa!" Rowena cried. "I don't want him getting hurt thinking I hate him!"

"Then we'll go and show him that we love him."

Rowena nodded, and they exited the chamber together.

By the time they reached the courtyard, Griffin and Ogilvie were already circling each other, stripped to the waist, fists raised.

A handful of onlookers stood around the edge of the courtyard, including Ned and Mr. Miller. At the far end, beside the water pump, stood three others, whispering among themselves, and Thea could swear she heard the clink of coins changing hands.

Griffin glanced up and frowned.

"Good luck," Thea mouthed. She held her hand over her heart, and he mirrored the gesture.

Ogilvie rushed toward Griffin and delivered a blow to his stomach. Griffin stumbled back but kept his balance.

"That was underhand, Ogilvie—but you've always fought dirty."

"I fight smart, not dirty," Ogilvie replied. "You always aspired to be a gentleman—thinking yourself above the rest of us...but you're just the same. A savage."

"Savage—ha!" Griffin laughed. "Fine words for a man who stoops to abducting young women to secure your fortune, rather than fighting fair. I did all I could to help you—I gave you money, yet you gambled it away because you never wanted to work. I wasn't lucky, Ogilvie. I worked hard—I didn't languish around, expecting good luck to rain upon my head."

"What girlish nonsense!" Ogilvie scoffed. "Has that harridan you married turned the Mighty Oak into a sapling?"

Griffin moved toward Ogilvie, who backed away and tripped, landing on the ground. One of the onlookers cheered.

"Get him!"

But he lowered his fists and waited for Ogilvie to stand.

"What's Papa doing?" Rowena asked.

Thea smiled, a rush of pride coursing through her. "He's fighting fair," she said. "He always has."

"I love him," Rowena said. "I want him to know it."

"As do I."

As soon as Ogilvie was on his feet again, he rushed toward Griffin, who sidestepped him and threw a punch that connected with Ogilvie's jaw. Ogilvie swung his arm, but Griffin darted away.

He was magnificent.

And he was hers.

Ogilvie snarled, then swung at Griffin, who dodged the blow and, in a fluid motion, swung his own fist upward until it connected with Ogilvie's jaw with a sharp crack. Ogilvie crumpled to the ground and lay still.

The onlookers cheered again, and more coins changed hands as Griffin raised his arms in salute. Then he approached Thea and Rowena and opened his arms.

"My family—my beautiful wife and daughter."

"Papa—I'm sorry…" Rowena said, her voice thick with tears.

"It's forgotten, my Rowe," he said. She rushed toward him, and the two embraced.

Thea blinked, moisture stinging her eyes. But they were tears of joy as father and daughter clung to each other.

"I'm sorry I didn't tell you the truth about your mother," he whispered, dipping his head to kiss her hair. "I wanted you to be happy, believing that you were loved. And you *are* loved."

He looked up and his gaze met Thea's, and he smiled. "You both are."

Behind him, Thea caught a blur of movement. Ogilvie was on his feet and running toward Griffin, brandishing a stick.

"No!"

Ogilvie lifted his arm, and Thea flew at him. With a rush of air, the stick came toward her, and before she could move, pain exploded in her head, and she plunged into oblivion.

⤗⤜

GRIFFIN WATCHED IN horror as his wife fell to the ground. Ogilvie stood before her, stick in hand, eyes wide with horror.

"Mama!" Rowena cried.

"You bastard!" Griffin roared.

"The blow was meant for you," Ogilvie said. "It's not my fault if your wife's foolish enough to get in the way."

With a bellow of rage, Griffin rushed forward, dealing blow after blow. Pain exploded in his knuckles as he felt his skin tear with each punch. Ogilvie reeled back, his face bloodied, and Griffin felt a satisfying crack as his fist crashed into Ogilvie's nose. He landed another punch, and Ogilvie fell to the ground.

A hand caught his arm. "Stop!" Ned cried.

"Let me go, Ned," Griffin said. "I'm going to kill the bastard!"

"Don't give him the satisfaction," Ned said. "Be the better man. I'll deal with Ogilvie. You take care of your wife. She's more important."

Thea lay on the ground, unmoving. Rowe kneeled beside her, sobbing. "Mama!"

Ned pulled the pistol out of his pocket and aimed it at Ogilvie.

"Leave," he said. "Now. If you return, I'll make damned sure the whole world knows that you murdered the first Mrs. Oake and tried to murder the second."

"I'll tell them you're a liar," Ogilvie said.

"Who'll believe you?" Ned asked. He gestured round the court-yard. "We have witnesses to your assault on Mrs. Oake, and Sam here will testify that you abducted Miss Rowena, won't you, Sam?"

"Aye, that's right," the barman said. "I've no time for a man who hits a woman."

Ogilvie glanced around the courtyard, looking for a friendly face. But there were none. He struggled to his feet, dusting himself down, then limped toward the building.

"Go with him, Ned," Griffin said. "Make sure he leaves."

"Aye." Brandishing the pistol, Ned followed Ogilvie back into the inn.

Griffin collapsed to his knees beside his wife.

"Thea? My love?"

"She's breathing," Rowena said. "But she won't wake up—please make her wake up!"

"We need a doctor!" Griffin cried. "Now!"

"Doctor Pearson's in the next village," the barman said.

"Then stop talking and fetch him!"

He cradled Dorothea's body in his arms. Why wasn't she waking up?

He may have found his daughter—but had it been at the cost of his wife?

Chapter Thirty-Nine

GRIFFIN SAT IN the corridor, outside one of the guest chambers. Behind the door, he heard the doctor's voice, but though he strained to listen, he couldn't hear his wife. After Sam had disappeared in search of the doctor, and Ned had marched Ogilvie off the premises, Griffin had carried her into the chamber and placed her on the bed. Her face was deathly pale, and a large bump was forming on the side of her head, a bruise darkening on the surrounding skin.

By the time the doctor arrived and shooed him out of the chamber, she still hadn't stirred. What if she didn't wake up? He'd seen enough fights to witness grown men being felled by a blow to the head and never waking up—or poor Jimmy Pierce last year, who'd seemed to recover after being knocked to the ground at the Queen's Head, but had woken up a different man—frightened of his own shadow, and unable to fight again. He could have earned a fortune on the circuit—but a single blow had destroyed his life.

What if Thea—his beautiful wife—had also been destroyed?

A slim hand slipped into his and squeezed it.

"Try not to worry, Papa."

Rowe's soft words, spoken with love, unlocked the armor surrounding his heart, and the tears which he'd kept at bay began to fall. Why was it that a man could withstand all manner of horrors and adversity—yet a few gentle words of kindness could shatter his defenses?

"Oh, Rowe…"

She dipped her head and kissed his knuckles, and he winced as she brushed her lips over the broken skin.

"What will I do without her?" he whispered.

"Mama will recover."

"Mama?"

"Yes," Rowe said. "She's the best mother in the world, and I love her." She lifted her face and fixed him with her clear, brown gaze.

"And I love *you*, Papa."

He pulled her to him—the child he'd always loved as his own, finally, loving him back as her father.

The door opened, and the doctor emerged, wiping his hands on a cloth.

Griffin stood, his heart thudding, and Rowe tightened her grip on his hand.

"Your wife's conscious."

"Oh, thank heaven!" Griffin moved toward the door, but the doctor blocked his path.

"Before you see her, I must speak with you, Mr. Oake."

"Is something the matter?" Griffin asked.

"Her condition is such that she mustn't be moved until I'm satisfied it's safe to do so." The doctor frowned, giving Griffin a look that reminded him of one of Thea's—that of a disappointed adult admonishing a wayward child.

"I haven't divulged her condition," the doctor continued. "She's already distressed, and in such cases, it's usual to defer to the husband."

In such cases? What the devil was wrong with her?

"No…" Griffin shook his head. "Not my Thea! What have I done to you, my darling?"

The doctor huffed through his nose. "Not the reaction I'd expected."

"Will she be the same again?" Griffin asked. "Or is the damage permanent?"

"The damage?" The doctor rolled his eyes. "Your life will certainly change from now on, Mr. Oake, but not in the way you expect."

Rowena gave a cry of delight.

"Ha!" the doctor said. "I see your daughter possesses greater wit than you."

"Then my wife's not maimed?"

The doctor's gaze softened as he recognized the pain in Griffin's voice. Then he placed a hand on his shoulder. "No, Mr. Oake," he said. "Your wife is with child."

⟫⟫⟪⟪

VOICES ECHOED IN Thea's head, exacerbating the ache which throbbed behind her eyes. After poking and prodding her for what felt like hours, the doctor had covered her with a bedsheet and reassured her that she'd recover. He lacked the gentle, tender care of her sister-in-law Atalanta, but his crisp efficiency cut through her distress, and by the time he finished examining her, she found a semblance of calm at his words, delivered in a business-like tone.

Each time she tried to move, fiery agony ripped through her mind. But the doctor refused to give her any opiates—or anything at all, save a few sips of water.

The door opened, and the doctor appeared, flanked on either side by Griffin and Rowena.

Griffin turned to the doctor. "Leave us. This is a family matter."

The doctor tutted. "Say nothing to distress your wife," he said. "She needs complete rest. I won't have her over-excited."

A low growl reverberated in Griffin's throat. "Do you want me to throw you out of the window?"

Thea smiled to herself. Her husband would never be a fine gentleman. He was a savage—a wild animal. But he was hers, and his primitive approach to protecting her made her feel safe and loved, as she'd never felt before.

The doctor dispatched, Griffin shut the door and approached the bed. Rowena sat on the other side and took Thea's hand.

"Ogilvie's gone," Griffin said. "He'll not be bothering us again."

A bruise was already darkening on his cheekbone.

"Did he hurt you?" she asked, wincing as the pain in her head throbbed.

"Nothing I don't deserve," he said. "I only care about the hurt *you've* suffered."

Rowena caressed Thea's hand, her light fingertips as soft as silk.

"How are you feeling, Mama?"

Mama...

The girl's eyes shone with love, and tears stung Thea's eyes at the endearment.

"My head hurts," she whispered. "The doctor won't give me anything for it."

Griffin lifted her hand to his lips, his warm breath caressing her skin. "He's being careful, my love."

"I want to go home," she said.

"You can, but only when Doctor Pearson says it's safe to move you."

She smiled. "I thought my big brute of a husband didn't take kindly to being given orders."

"In this case, I'm prepared to obey every instruction, however irksome." He exchanged a glance with Rowena, then smiled. "There's someone else to consider, now."

Why was he smiling when her head hurt so much?

"Are you going to tell her, Papa?" Rowena asked.

"Tell me what?" Thea whispered.

Griffin placed her hand over his heart.

"You're going to be a mother."

A spark of hope flared then died.

"You mean Rowena?"

He laughed softly. "Rowena is indeed your daughter," he said. "No—you're going to be a mother—*again*."

She glanced at Rowena, who nodded and smiled, tears in her eyes.

"Isn't it wonderful, Mama? I'm to have a brother—or a sister!"

"So, I'm..." She caught her breath, hardly daring to speak the words.

"Yes, my love," he said. "You're pregnant."

He leaned over and brushed his lips against her forehead.

"I never thought I could be so happy," he said. "What is wealth, or being the Mighty Oak, compared to a loving family? And now, with my beloved wife and daughter—and another on the way, I can truly say I'm the luckiest man alive. And though I regret the circumstances which forced us together—I will never regret you coming into my life."

She tipped her face up, offering her lips for a kiss.

"Nor I, you."

Epilogue

T HEA'S BODY TIGHTENED with pain—so much pain.

Voices tore through her head—Atalanta's crisp tones, Meggie's words of praise...

And Griffin—his voice was always in the background—deep, soft, and filled with love—which she clung to, like a lighthouse in a storm.

The pain had been coming in waves—building then fading, but always returning until she could bear it no more. Finally, she threw back her head and screamed as a burst of agony tore through her. Then it subsided, and she lay back.

The voices receded.

A cry rose up—a high-pitched, pitiful wail, which called to her body at a visceral level, igniting a deep-seated need. A second cry joined the first.

Then a third—a voice she knew and loved.

"Griffin..."

She blinked away the tears of pain, and the blurred shape before her sharpened into the familiar form of her husband. He stood at the foot of the bed, Rowena beside him—each holding a bundle.

Rowena's face glowed with joy and love. Ever since the altercation at the Royal Oak, she'd done everything possible to show both Thea and Griffin that she loved them. And though her wild streak would never be properly tamed, she was growing into a lovely young woman—bright, kind, and strong.

A credit to any parent.

Griffin's face was streaked with tears, but they were tears of happiness. The joy in his face illuminated the whole room—the joy of a loving husband and doting father.

He cradled the bundle in his arms as if it were the most precious thing in the world.

"You have a daughter."

He leaned forward, and she caught a glimpse of a tiny pink face, eyes tightly closed—with long, dark lashes, a button nose, and a perfect little rosebud of a mouth.

"She's beautiful," she breathed.

He leaned over and kissed her forehead. "Just like her mother."

"And you have a son," Rowena said. The bundle wriggled in her arms, and a fat pink fist appeared. Shortly after, a cry of protest rang out.

"He's as troublesome as his father." Griffin laughed.

"Twins?" Thea croaked.

Griffin nodded. "Which explains why you were so..." He broke off, coloring.

"So...what, husband?" Thea asked sharply. "Huge?"

He shook his head.

"Whale-like, perhaps? Elephantine?"

His eyes widened in alarm.

Thea winked at Rowena, who winked back.

"Gargantuan?" Rowena suggested. "Colossal?"

A bubble of laughter rose inside Thea at Griffin's stricken expression.

Meggie and Atalanta stood side by side, watching the scene unfold. With her best icy glare, Atalanta placed her hands on her hips.

"Do you mean to insult my sister, Mr. Oake?"

"Especially when her condition is the result of your actions," Meggie added.

"I was a willing participant, Meggie, believe me," Thea said. Griffin frowned and cocked his head to one side.

"Are you teasing me?"

The bubble burst, and a ripple of laughter filled the room. Griffin's face went as red as fire, and Meggie nudged Atalanta. "Come on, Attie, I think we should leave this little family to get to know their new additions."

The two ladies exited the chamber, leaving Thea alone with her husband and children.

"My children…"

She held out her arms, and Griffin placed her newborn daughter into the crook of her right arm as Rowena placed her son in her left.

"Have you thought of any names?" Rowena asked.

"Give her time to say hello to them, Rowe, my love," Griffin said. "Besides, I'd like to suggest names with your mama's approval."

He smiled eagerly at Thea, a plea in his expression.

He took her hand.

"Marcus and Helena."

She caught her breath. "You remembered?"

"Aye, my love," he said. "I remember the story of woman who, in the eyes of the world in which she lived, was past her prime—a woman who believed herself unwanted and that she'd never achieve the thing she wanted most in the world. A family of her own."

He dipped his head and captured her lips in a kiss. "She harbored a dream of children of her own, and she even gave them names. But when she was forced into marrying a gruff stranger with no manners, she believed her dream had died."

He drew back the blanket with his fingertip to reveal the face of his daughter and stroked her cheek. The baby pursed her lips, then gave a contented sigh.

"Little did I realize that my dreams would become entwined with yours," he said.

"And you have taught me, also," she said.

"Me?"

"Yes," she whispered, lowering her head and kissing each baby on the forehead. "You taught me that no matter what—you should never give up on your dreams."

About the Author

Emily Royal grew up in Sussex, England, and has devoured romantic novels for as long as she can remember. A mathematician at heart, Emily has worked in financial services for over twenty years. She indulged in her love of writing after she moved to Scotland, where she lives with her husband, teenage daughters and menagerie of rescue pets including Twinkle, an attention-seeking boa constrictor.

She has a passion for both reading and writing romance with a weakness for Regency rakes, Highland heroes, and Medieval knights. Persuasion is one of her all-time favorite novels which she reads several times each year and she is fortunate enough to live within sight of a Medieval palace.

When not writing, Emily enjoys playing the piano, hiking, and painting landscapes, particularly the Highlands. One of her ambitions is to paint, as well as climb, every mountain in Scotland.

Follow Emily Royal:
Website: www.emroyal.com
Facebook: facebook.com/eroyalauthor
Twitter: twitter.com/eroyalauthor
Newsletter signup: mailchi.mp/e5806720bfe0/emilyroyalauthor
Goodreads: goodreads.com/author/show/14834886.Emily_Royal

Made in the USA
Middletown, DE
15 October 2021